CRAIG MARTELLE

STARSHIP LOST

PRIMACY

aethonbooks.com

PRIMACY
©2023 CRAIG MARTELLE

This book is protected under the copyright laws of the United States of America. No part of this publication may be reproduced, stored in a retrieval system, or transmitted, in any form or by any means, without the prior permission in writing of the publisher, nor be otherwise circulated in any form of binding or cover other than that in which it is published and without a similar condition including this condition being imposed on the subsequent purchaser. Any reproduction or unauthorized use of the material or artwork contained herein is prohibited without the express written permission of the authors.

Aethon Books supports the right to free expression and the value of copyright. The purpose of copyright is to encourage writers and artists to produce the creative works that enrich our culture.

The scanning, uploading, and distribution of this book without permission is a theft of the author's intellectual property. If you would like to use material from the book (other than for review purposes), please contact editor@aethonbooks.com. Thank you for your support of the author's rights.

Aethon Books
www.aethonbooks.com

Print and eBook formatting by Steve Beaulieu. Artwork provided by Vivid Covers.

Published by Aethon Books LLC.

Aethon Books is not responsible for websites (or their content) that are not owned by the publisher.

This book is a work of fiction. Names, characters, places, and incidents are the product of the author's imagination or are used fictitiously. Any resemblance to actual events, locales, or persons, living or dead is coincidental.

All rights reserved.

ALSO IN STARSHIP LOST

Starship Lost

The Return

Primacy

Confrontation

Fallacy

Engagement

SOCIAL MEDIA

Craig Martelle Social
Website & Newsletter:
https://www.craigmartelle.com

Facebook:
https://www.facebook.com/ AuthorCraigMartelle/

Always to my wife, who loves me even though I work every day writing stories.

Starship Lost team includes:

BETA / EDITOR BOOK

Beta Readers and Proofreaders - with my deepest gratitude!
James Caplan
Kelly O'Donnell
John Ashmore
Rita Whinfield

Get ***The Human Experiment*** for free when you join my newsletter. There's a zoo, but the humans are the ones being studied.
https://craigmartelle.com

PREVIOUSLY FROM STARSHIP LOST TWO (CHAPTER 28)

The stars care not for the machinations of man.

The ship settled lower into the atmosphere, going slowly to keep from accelerating around the planet and being caught by the troopship.

"Now! Take us down." Captain Jaq Hunter stabbed a finger at the main screen.

The ship nosed over and accelerated, impacting an atmospheric layer with a great ka-thump. The nose forced its way up despite Mary's best efforts. The engines argued with the forces arrayed against them, but in the end, the ion drives won.

By force of will, the ship dove below the outermost reaches of the atmosphere and settled high in the Sairvor sky, so high that it was invisible to an observer on the ground and too low to be a blip on the Malibor's space-based radars.

The narrow-beam communication signal from *Starstrider*

was barely strong enough to penetrate, so they developed a brevity code that repeated ten times.

It would have to be good enough.

Running with full power was an added bonus, one Jaq never took lightly. A single gunship was no match for *Chrysalis*.

Jaq had a plan.

If the Malibor cooperated, it would be a good plan. If they didn't, there'd be one less gunship in the Malibor order of battle.

They received a burst transmission that arrived in pieces with ten iterations. Slade reconstructed the data. "Gunship is on course. No change. Troopship is static and not radiating."

The main screen showed the updated positions. The intercept data was solid. "Prepare to take us out. Comms, give me that gunship."

The communications officer gave her the thumbs-up.

"Malibor gunship. This is *Chrysalis*, flagship of the Borwyn fleet. You will stand to and prepare to be boarded."

"We will not," came the immediate reply. "Who is this? Buster, is that you, making a joke? It's not funny. I don't know how you changed your voice, but that's a good one."

"Why didn't the troopship contact them?" Commander Crip Castle wondered.

Jaq shook her head, surprised that the gunship was in the dark.

"Buster is on his way elsewhere," Jaq replied. "This is Captain Hunter, and you *will* stand to. When we appear, if you fire at us, you will be destroyed without hesitation. I'd prefer to talk with you first."

"Of course you would. The Malibor don't take kindly to upstarts playing games with fleet ships and personnel. You threatened us. Now show yourself!"

Jaq nodded at Mary and Ferd. "Put us right in their face. Taurus, all weapons trained. Fire a warning burst encircling the ship to show them what we have at our command."

"Imminent death," Taurus replied. "Initial targets established. Will revise once we clear the interference."

The ship surged to three gees and slammed into the upper atmosphere, jerking the crew in their seats. The steep angle shortened the duration of the transition but did nothing to lessen the violence.

The ship followed the nose through and accelerated quickly once it was in space. The gunship was barely twenty thousand kilometers away.

The E-mags barked in unison, sending hundreds of obdurium projectiles past the gunship. *Chrysalis* twisted to keep the nose pointed at the Malibor vessel until it was inverted. Mary used the engines to slow the ship quickly, running up to five gees to shorten the distance traveled.

The gunship continued into a high orbit, and *Chrysalis* came at it from behind.

"They didn't fire," Crip noted unnecessarily.

Jaq watched the screen. Bow thrusters were at maximum to slow the ship without having to invert once more.

Taurus kept the batteries trained on the enemy, which was dwarfed by the cruiser closing on its tail.

"Now that I have your attention," Jaq started, "I want to know why you're here."

"Is that it?" a voice replied.

"Please answer my curiosity. We have a bet, you see."

"I don't think so. I'll not share anything with the enemy. I'm no traitor."

"It's easy to be tough when you're over there. Don't mind us linking to your airlock and coming aboard, then."

"Can't allow that either."

"Yet another Malibor dying for their cause. So be it. Do you know what happened to the armada you sent to Sairvor? Two cruisers, six gunships, a cargo hauler, and a troopship."

"We don't see any vessels besides the troopship."

"If your sensors were better, you'd see plenty of debris. They stood for their cause too. Good for them!" Jaq taunted. Crip wasn't sure if she was overconfident or if she'd become a victim of their success.

Silence answered her. "Fire one more warning burst."

Taurus complied with a cheer. The rounds blasted past, less than a hundred meters beyond the gunship's hull, drawing a solid circle around it.

The gunship slowly rotated to face *Chrysalis*.

"What are you doing?" Jaq asked the Malibor. "You have two seconds to turn around, or we will destroy you. Taurus, fire the kill shot on three, two..."

"Stand by," the Malibor said. The gunship stopped its rotation but didn't return its nose to its original heading. It flew through space a hundred and sixty degrees out of sync with its direction of travel.

"Power down your systems. We're coming aboard."

"We don't have the combat team," Crip said.

"We have you. Take four."

Crip popped out of his seat. "Come on, Tram. You know how to shoot."

The two headed out.

Mary adjusted the heading to match the gunship's orientation. Ferd used the thrusters to match the ship's speed. *Chrysalis* eased toward it as they traveled at twenty-five thousand kilometers per hour.

"Gil, be ready to fire. We're inside the E-mags' weapons envelopes."

"Weapons are energized," the defensive weapons officer confirmed.

Chrysalis bumped the gunship, and it started to spin.

"Not me!" Mary cried. "They're maneuvering."

"Fire!"

Chain guns rattled fire into the gunship.

Thrusters rotated the cruiser to bring the Malibor vessel into the best angle for maximum E-mag engagement. Taurus didn't wait for the command. She triggered one battery, and the gunship was nearly vaporized in front of them.

Jaq made a fist and shook it at the screen.

Taurus accessed the intercom and called Crip and Tram back to the command deck.

Jaq fumed for another ten seconds. After that, she was over it enough to move forward. "Take us to Farslor. Get there ahead of *Bessie Mae*, please."

Mary put the course in, and Ferd kicked the ion drives to all ahead full.

She relaxed into her seat. Crip and Tram hurried in while the ship accelerated through one gee. They ran to their seats and jumped in before the acceleration became oppressive.

"We tried," Crip said. "It didn't have a high probability of success."

"We abandoned a dead troopship," Jaq lamented. "This one has been a complete debacle."

Crip leaned sideways, fighting the three gees. "You ask too much of yourself. They aren't going to surrender. They're Malibor, who think themselves invincible. We took the cargo ship, which was the most important. None of the others mattered."

"They all matter," Jaq argued. "Winning hearts and minds will deliver victory in this war."

"I think it'll be when we kill enough of their ships that they have no choice but to surrender. We're going to defeat the Malibor by beating them in battle. They don't understand anything else. And this is me, the play-nice guy. They demand we fight them, so we do. Next time, let's not get so close that they can hurt us."

"If it was only that easy," Jaq replied. "I wanted that ship. We need to grow our fleet. One ship is vulnerable, but two become a force much greater than their individual parts."

Crip snorted. "Having multiple ships didn't do the Malibor any favors."

"They're used to fighting each other," Jaq replied. "Let's get those missiles, restock our electrical components, and try Phase Two once again, a high-speed pass of Septimus. Let's see what kind of damage we can cause."

"When you say high-speed, are you thinking what I'm thinking?"

"What are you thinking?" Jaq asked.

"Two million kph. Nothing but a streak of light whizzing past the unwashed mass of Malibor bodies."

"Maybe we'll get going that fast, but then we'll make a circuit of the star if we can get centripetal force working in our favor."

"I'm not sure that's how it works, but we'll fight to keep from flying off into deep space."

Jaq continued to scowl at the main screen.

"That's one less gunship, and we took no damage," Crip said. "Seven and eighteen. They cannot stand before us. With a successful fast pass of Malpace, we might end the war, although we won't find out for sure until after we've circled the system and made our way back."

"If we remain within the orbital plane, we can shape an optimal angle from Septimus toward Armanor. We'll slow down with a slingshot around the star added to the judicious use of economical braking."

Tram interrupted, "Hear me out. How about if we use a slow approach and hit them with long shots until we can strafe them mercilessly? We can end this, but what do you say we walk in there and show them the boss is back?"

Jaq wasn't sure what she wanted to do, but she had her heart set on a high-speed pass. Show the Borwyn flag to Septimus without risking the ship.

"What do you think about landing on Septimus?" Crip asked. "We can take a lander down if we make a slower pass."

"You guys are killing me. We only have so many people and one ship. I need to think about this. We have time before we need to decide, and maybe the New Septimus-produced missiles will be ready before then. They'll be better than repurposed Malibor junk."

Jaq closed her eyes and focused on breathing while the gel of her seat squeezed her tightly.

The battle was joined, and so far, victory had been theirs.

CHAPTER 1

We have a chance in this war. Not because of a fast ship or better weapons, but because of the good people behind them.

Chrysalis maintained steady acceleration toward Farslor until they hit the halfway point, and then they decelerated for nearly the exact same amount of time. This approach kept them consistently at one-point-two gees of apparent gravity. They could exist like real people.

Captain Jaq Hunter had jogged the corridors until her legs ached, and she repeated it until her body threatened to throw her brain out an airlock.

She had finally rested, sleeping for thirteen hours straight. When she woke up, she plopped down behind her desk and reviewed recent system readiness reports.

The energy gauge showed a steady seventy-four percent, the same as it had been when she went to sleep. Bec and Teo were working miracles with the engines. Jaq vowed to give them a week to take the engines offline for preventive maintenance and to protect them from future failure once they arrived at the Expeditionary Resupply Station—the hulk previously known as *Butterfly*.

"The Malibor on Septimus!" She shook her head. "That grates on my soul."

She returned to reading the reports and noting who she wanted to visit to thank for their hard work repairing recent battle damage.

The ship was born from battle damage, though it took fifty years and a new generation. Now she had a mix of oldsters, called originals, and the new, those born after *Chrysalis* had fled to Armanor's outer planets. The originals came from New Septimus, a moon orbiting Sairvor, the twin planet of Septimus in the same orbit but on the opposite side of the system's star.

Even though the new generation crew had spent the majority of their lives in zero-gee, they slept better with the tug on their bodies that gravity provided. Humanity was never meant to survive without gee forces.

Those from New Septimus struggled. They had grown accustomed to point-seven gees. Increasing the force by nearly fifty percent took a great deal of their energy.

The food supplies they'd loaded from the captured Malibor cargo vessel were providing the extra calories their bodies needed.

The Malibor food was uniquely gratifying, providing a feast with each variant opened. The crew was burning through them at an alarming rate, but it gave Chef the opportunity to rebuild the Borwyn's own supplies bagged from the hydroponics bays and algae farm.

Jaq relaxed in the sanctity of her quarters. The crew was operating at half strength without any current threat, which meant more than twelve hours off out of each twenty-four. It was a welcome reprieve after the first month of operations against the Malibor.

Too much had happened. The battles fought were lessons to help her fight the next one and the one after that.

According to Tram Stamper, the order of battle for the Malibor stood at seven cruisers and eighteen gunships remaining. With the loss of five cruisers and thirteen gunships, the Malibor had been punched in the mouth and had to be reeling. She counted on that to give the cruiser *Chrysalis* the edge as the Borwyn continued their campaign to retake Septimus.

"We will defeat them," she said aloud. She had her doubts but kept them to herself. Her public affirmations were to maintain the crew's confidence.

A gentle tapping on the door signaled the arrival of the one she'd summoned.

"Come in." She stood to greet her visitor.

Tram stepped through. He closed the door behind him, shook hands with the captain, and took a seat on the small bench opposite the captain's desk. "You called?"

"Battle planning and battle staff. We need to up our targeting game, too."

"I thought we already had a plan for a high-speed pass of Septimus. We'll angle away from Farslor toward the inner system, and then begin accelerating until we reach a million kilometers per hour. Battle staff? I didn't know that was a question. With Gil Dizmar on the defensive systems and

Taurus Lindman on the offensive weapons, we have a good team. We're doing what we can on targeting. It's a difficult problem."

Jaq leaned back and smiled. This meeting wasn't about being contentious. "I know our plan for the next phase of our operation to return to Septimus. That's not what I'm talking about with battle planning. During the battle. Managing the systems. I think we need both a targeting officer and firing officer for offensive weapons. Two positions where we now have one."

"Integrate the sensor data with the targeting computer. That doesn't need a dedicated person."

"I suggest it does since we will have very little time to make adjustments. We missed our targets on the high-speed pass of the Malibor armada. We can't miss our targets when we get a chance. The odds are not in our favor, because we remain grossly outnumbered. We don't need to fight ourselves. One shot. One kill."

"Or flood space with projectiles. Big space, little bullet. We improve our odds with more projectiles." Tram held his hands out in his celebration of a successful countermove.

"Or something like that. But what part of space needs to be flooded with projectiles?"

"The part with Malibor ships?" Tram ventured.

"Targeting and firing are two different skills. And firing includes maintenance. You showed what you were capable of when you went outside and fixed the cannons."

"I had a lot of help," Tram countered. "Am I getting demoted?"

"What? No. You're gaining a person for your section.

You're getting promoted out of the fun stuff." She saluted with a bag of water. "Welcome to the club."

Tram's countenance twisted, visible emotions moving through surprise to confusion to anger to sadness. "Your club sucks."

Jaq laughed. "You understand, then. Find me a whiz kid to integrate the sensors and targeting that takes into account our direction and speed. Taurus is good, but this is different. Maybe get Bec to think about it or one of those from New Septimus. They brought all their smartest people."

"What about Teo?" Tram asked with a tinge of apprehensive hope.

"Let's talk about Teo. I don't care how the crew pairs off, but I do care if it's detrimental to good order and discipline. Your pursuit of her is one way."

"Jaq! How can you say that? What makes you think I'm pursuing her?"

"This conversation will continue endlessly if we can't accept facts as they exist," Jaq replied.

Tram hung his head. "Life is hard, Jaq."

"And it's harder when you're alone. I understand. When we liberate Septimus, you can search, you can find, and you can court. Until then, you cannot let it detract from your job. You are one of the top five people on this ship. I need you, Tram, but I need you focused on putting rounds on target. Anything else and we don't survive. You can see how the associative principle comes into play here."

"If we don't survive, then there's no one to love."

"No rounds on target. No joy. Exactly."

Tram grumbled. "I knew she wasn't interested, but I didn't want to give up hope. She's something special."

"That is perceptive and right on target. Are we ready to talk about who can fill the integration spot?"

"Ask an original," Tram suggested.

"I'll ask Teo," Jaq offered. "Geniuses have a tendency to gravitate toward each other. Us normal people are on the outside looking in."

Tram stood. "Rounds on target. Nothing else matters."

"Not getting hit, while delivering well-targeted munitions," Jaq added.

Tram shook his head while smiling. He waved as he left the captain's quarters and returned to the bridge. She followed him out but turned toward the central shaft, where she summoned the elevator. Under gravity, they couldn't fly freely up and down the shaft. Jaq regarded the inconvenience for a few moments before laughing at herself.

She had grown used to getting her way. Add that to being impatient, and a simple event like waiting for the elevator stressed her in ways that it shouldn't. She leaned against the bulkhead and tried to relax.

After thirty-one heartbeats, she had counted, the doors opened to reveal a nearly full car. She squeezed inside.

"You know how many can fit inside the ship's lift?" she asked.

No one answered.

"One more."

No one laughed.

"Hard crowd. Are you getting enough to eat?"

"More Malibor rations! Those people should be enormous if they always eat like that," someone replied. The others cheered.

"They get their food from Septimus, our home. That's just one more incentive to drive us to retake our home."

The mood sobered because they understood only too well the point Jaq was trying to make.

The elevator stopped at each deck. Crewmembers got off, more got on, until it reached the second-lowest level where Engineering was located. Jaq strolled stiffly. Her muscles were still healing from the abuse she'd levied upon them. She clenched her teeth in grim satisfaction.

The hatch to Engineering stood open. She didn't have to wonder if Bec and Teo were in. The volume of their argument announced their presence throughout the ship.

They paused to stare at Jaq.

She attacked the target of opportunity. "You two argue like an old married couple."

The pair recoiled, but the argument didn't renew.

"I don't even care what you're arguing about. If it's part of your process, fine, but at least stop while I'm here." She gave each of them her best look. "I only came to tell you that we are at Farslor and will soon reach *Butterfly*. I want to give you a week of downtime to do as much preventive maintenance as you can on the engines. Will that be enough?"

"Eight days," Bec blurted.

Teo made a face at him. "We should be able to do it six."

"That's why I planned for seven. Bec, why are you asking for eight?"

He shrugged. "Me being me."

"How about you level with me so I don't have to give you ridiculous orders?"

"I told you!" Teo shouted in his face.

"Why do I have mean women in my life?" Bec threw his hands up and stormed away.

"You're the only one I'm mean to!" Teo yelled after him. "And my brothers."

Jaq waved and walked away. She called over her shoulder, "Prep for refurb. You have seven days starting in about twelve hours."

She ran into Danny Johns patrolling the lower decks with a pulse rifle in hand. She pointed at it.

"Setting an expectation that we're a warship and are at war," the original replied, smacking the weapon's handguard.

"We've lost a lot of people. Everyone knows we're at war because we've watched friends and family die at the hands of the Malibor. This has been a very hard month, but the truth is, it was worse when we lost twenty of our parents in the same space. They succumbed around the same time. It made us colder, more driven, but it also stabbed a pain that wasn't going to go away until we came back to complete their life's work. Fight the Malibor. Free our planet and our fellow Borwyn. Free ourselves to live on our ancestral home."

"We pray to Septiman for that, too, but He helps those who help themselves, Captain," Danny Johns replied. He slung the weapon. "I'll return it to the armory, but I'm anxious for action. I'm ready to take it to the Malibor."

"I have no doubt. Talking about delivering rounds on target, would you know anyone who joined us from New Septimus who is a genius with astrophysics? We need to integrate sensor data with our targeting computers when the ship is traveling at high speed, like two million KPH."

"What I hear you saying is that you want a generalist?" Danny joked. Jaq threw her hands up and started to walk away. "Relax. Donal is the one you want. Donal Fleming. I don't know how he spells it because he's got an accent. He's from one of those islands in the Partan Sea."

"Donal, huh?" Jaq crossed her arms. "You're not messing with me, are you?"

"Not anymore, no. Find Donal and talk to him. I bet he'd love to work on those problems. He's really geeky."

"I'm not sure that's a bad thing. Have you seen where we live?"

Danny Johns laughed. "I'm a farmer turned soldier turned back into a farmer and now back to a soldier. My life has been wildly thrilling intermixed by long periods of cleaning dirt from under my fingernails using a blade of grass that I've grown. Anything different from that is geeky."

Jaq nodded and thought for a moment. A comm panel was nearby. She tapped for the intercom and spoke clearly. "Donal from New Septimus. Please report to the bridge. Donal to the bridge."

She closed the connection and walked away.

Danny appreciated the efficiency.

The elevator took a while to arrive. Danny Johns tipped his chin as he passed on his way down to the lander deck.

By the time Jaq got to the bridge, Donal was there talking with Tram.

"What do you think?" Jaq asked.

"Think about what?" Tram shrugged.

"Your new targeting officer also known as a systems integration officer. Once the two programs are talking and resolving the relational astrodynamics, we can throw streams of railgun projectiles to a target of our choosing. This is how we'll win the war."

"I can do that," Donal said with a touch of swagger.

Tram jerked a thumb over his shoulder. "Dolly and Taurus will both feed you data. Your job is to make sense of it and help us direct our railguns so we're not guessing." He nodded to Taurus. "No disrespect intended. We need someone who can specialize in this. Rounds on target. That's the captain's guidance."

Taurus tapped on her terminal. "I missed seven out of eight targets. All of them were sitting out in the open and flying without maneuvering. There was no excuse. I would have fired me."

"Too bad. You're still on the job. Teach Donal how you target and most importantly, the programs running to support it. You'll still be the trigger puller, Taurus."

"Like I was purpose-built for it," she replied, bringing up the systems she used to give her new teammate a look.

Donal smirked.. "I'm the math guy."

Taurus and Dolly shared a glance. "So is she." Taurus pointed at the diminutive thirteen-year-old.

"Then this shouldn't take too long—three, maybe four years."

The captain clarified, "You have a week for initial adjustments, and then you'll need everything fine-tuned and operational another a week after that. Two weeks until deployment."

Donal laughed heartily. He doubled over, tears streaming from his eyes. The bridge crew watched in confusion.

When he was able to talk, he told the captain, "I know. When have we ever had the time we need to do something to perfection?" He slapped his thigh. "I promise you that I'll give you my best and if it can be done, it will be done. One of eight on non-evasive maneuvering targets isn't a distinction we wish to maintain. No disrespect to you, Taurus, and no, you shouldn't be fired. We need to bring the technology up to speed. You built the engines before you built the targeting systems because the engines bring life. First and foremost, we, the Borwyn, want to live."

"Exactly that, Donal. Now get to work. You have three years of things to do in the next two weeks, sooner if you can manage, but definitely not later." She gave him a thumbs-up.

Donal leaned close to Taurus. "Is she always like this?"

"She is very supportive of short deadlines for impossible tasks. Have you talked with Bec?"

"The engineer? I was told to avoid him as if my life depended on it."

Taurus tried not to laugh, and Jaq bit her lip. She had been listening but returned to her seat for no good reason. She kicked Crip's leg as she passed.

He refused to make eye contact.

"That's not bad advice," Taurus said.

CHAPTER 2

History never favors the oppressor.

Chief Slade Ping pointed. "You'll have to take that workstation toward the back. It's an old sensor position that isn't used anymore."

Donal shrugged and helped himself to the computer. It took a while to power up. Dolly waved to get his attention. "Maybe you can look at what I do and the information I receive first?"

"And I'll show you my systems." Taurus left her programs on the screen. She didn't turn anything else on. She had to figure out what her job would entail. Taurus leaned back in her seat. Tram saw the look on her face and immediately jumped to his feet.

"Let me buy you lunch," he told her, nodding toward the corridor.

She followed him out, her shoulders slumped. Crip wanted to go to her, now that they were a couple, but it wasn't his place to interfere. He'd find out later, after a painfully long wait, what they talked about.

In the corridor, Tram stretched his back and leaned against the bulkhead. "I need to work out more to strengthen this mush that's supposed to be muscle."

Taurus responded to his quip with a crooked smile. She didn't say anything.

"Don't sweat the new talent. We need technical integration to make sure we hit what we aim at, but if we leave it up to the mathletes, we'll be shooting at the highest-probability targets instead of the right targets. With eight ships coming toward us, what were the best primary and secondary targets? How much fire should we have allocated to each? That's the tactical part that you understand, and it's your job to deliver a sound plan to me and the captain."

Taurus asked, "Is this a pep talk?"

"It's whatever you need it to be so you keep your head in the game. You are the trigger puller and that means you fire our weapons when the best targets present themselves, and then you destroy them in the order that minimizes our risk. That means you need to memorize what every single one of their ships carries as armaments and how they can be used against us, then develop a strategy to take them down. Now that you've been there, you know that you might have only seconds to decide."

Taurus nodded. "I'll spend all of my shift preparing for ten seconds of excitement."

"As will I. Offensive and defensive weapons. Missiles. Angle off the bow. Best orientation to deliver an optimal number of batteries. All of it. Every time we practice is an opportunity for the enemy to do the same to us. But you know what our secret to success is?"

"We have better engines?"

"We have better damage control teams." He clapped her on the shoulder and then stretched once more. "I'm so weak."

She pushed him mid-stretch, and he nearly fell over. "You should be embarrassed. Ask Max to work you out. I'll cover for you during your shift."

"Thanks for that. I'd rather stab myself in the neck with pins."

Taurus laughed and waved as she returned to the bridge. Crip made eye contact long enough for her to wink at him.

He grinned with the promise of time off that would be worthwhile.

Tram nodded and drifted toward the bridge.

"We're a full day in front of *Bessie Mae*," Crip said. "Maybe we can snag one of those weapons platforms to take with us to the Expeditionary Resupply Station."

"I thought we were calling it *Cornucopia*?" Jaq asked. She stared at the main screen that showed a tactical view of Farslor with the two weapons platforms and one aging gunship that they knew were orbiting it. She pursed her lips. "What do you say we grab the gunship instead?"

"If we only have a day, the gunship is probably out. It'll take longer to secure since it won't fit in our cargo bay," Crip replied.

"Throw the grapples on it and drag it to the ERS."

"How do we keep it from hitting us?"

Jaq gestured toward the flight control team, Lieutenants

Ferdinand Alpinist and Mary Minshaw. "Can you drag a gunship using the grapples and make sure it doesn't hit us?"

Ferd and Mary glanced back and forth between Crip and Jaq.

"We can try," Ferd replied.

"See? Let's grab that gunship and see if we can make it our own." Jaq hatcheted her hand toward the screen. "Take us around the planet to slow us down until we can ease next to that derelict."

"You're not selling me on the quality of our future acquisition," Crip said.

"Then figure out how to attach it to Chrysalis so we don't have to use the grapples. Prepare an engineering team to board it."

Crip nodded. He touched his screen but stopped and looked up to find Jaq watching him. "You knew all along we shouldn't use the grapples."

"Of course I don't want to use the grapples. Have a Malibor ship ram into us? We get enough of that from them without doing it to ourselves. Our damage control teams finally got to take a break."

"Concur." Crip smirked and opened the ship-wide broadcast. "All hands, Commander Castle here. We're going to use Farslor to slow down before coming to a stop. We're planning on acquiring a mothballed Malibor gunship. I'll need to meet with Tram, Teo, Benjy, and..." He hesitated. "...other people who are on the cargo ship we're calling *Cornucopia* following us to the ERS. We'll make do. Our challenge is how to secure the gunship to our hull for travel to the resupply station. If anyone has any ideas, you'll find us in the lander corridor on the lowest deck. Prepare yourselves for zero-gee. Crip out."

"You called a meeting with people who aren't on the ship?" Jaq chuckled softly.

"I started talking before I was finished with the thinking part," Crip admitted. "I'll be on the lander deck."

Crip hurried out.

Jaq leaned back in her seat but only for a moment. She preferred to spend time in the captain's chair only when she had to. She preferred walking around when they had gravity or swimming free when they didn't. Her muscles gave her grief, but the pain was lightening with more movement of the less-strenuous variety.

"I'll be on the mess deck," she told the command crew. "You have the conn, Tram."

Tram moved from his seat to the middle of the bridge. Everyone was doing something but him. The challenge was to spend one's time in the best way possible to deliver in the moment and for the future. If he was going to properly fill in for Jaq or Crip, he needed to spend more time learning what they knew. He continued to the navigation and thrust control stations.

"Can you explain what the limits are to what you do?"

———

Sergeant Max Tremayne wandered through the cargo ship, nodding at people on the rare occasion when he passed one. He was looking for Deena, who was looking through crates of electronic equipment for a parts list that she'd received from *Chrysalis*.

"I'm never going to find what Bec wants," Deena complained.

"And Teo and the damage control teams wanted stuff, too. I think it's their ultimate wish list of parts. We'll see what Alby was able to recover off *Butterfly*."

"I don't know Alby." She tossed a small box back into a crate. "You call a warship *Butterfly*. At least the Malibor called it a name that didn't belie what it was—*Hornet*."

"*We* didn't call it anything. Our ancestors named these cruisers. I'm not sure what we'd name a new ship."

"*Cornucopia*?" Deena said, referencing the new name for the cargo hauler.

"It's uplifting and descriptive of the joy this ship brings us." He grinned. "What were we talking about?"

"Finding Bec's junk."

Max stared into the distance. "That descriptive phraseology alone is enough to make me cry real tears and beg you to stop looking. Let Bec find his own junk, with both hands if he's so inclined. Let's hunt down Brad and grill him about something innocuous." Max took her hand, and she rolled in to hug him.

"What would I do without you?"

"Where are you going?" She pushed away from him.

"Nowhere. Why would you think I was going somewhere?"

She studied him to determine if he was leading her on.

He leaned in close and opened his eyes wide. "Look all the way into my brain, if you need to. I don't care how much you act insecure as if I'm going to leave you, I'm not. You're stuck with me, woman."

"Man!" she shot back before relaxing into his arms.

"The universe is hard enough. We don't need to tackle it alone, Deena. I'm happy that we met. I'm happy that we're Borwyn and treat you like a real person, regardless that you're part Malibor. We'd love it if the Malibor would talk with us, because the longer this war lasts, the more people are going to die."

"If only I had any influence. I would command the Malpace and make it so." Deena twirled her finger in the air and struck a pose while pointing toward a nebulous point in the distance. At Max's lack of understanding, she explained, "It's a statue in Freedom Square."

Max's face dropped. "In the capital city of Pridal?"

Deena shook her head. "Sorry. It's not called that anymore. If there were original Borwyn names, they've been completely erased from history. The capital city is called Malipride."

"Of course it is." Max tried to smile. "I'm sorry. I've spent my entire life thinking one thing while the reality is completely different."

Deena laughed lightly in musical tones that melted Max's heart. "It is the same for me. The Borwyn were evil and would eat your children."

Max felt the relief that came with a burden shared. "We eat our food from bags, and it comes from the hydroponics bay. The children go to school on a completely different deck."

"I love you, Max. Never lose your sense of humor. One day, this war will be over."

"And that's when we can start to live," he finished her thought.

"Did you find those parts yet?" a voice bellowed from between the pallets. Brad strolled down the walkway. "I've been looking for you two."

"We were looking for you first! I have a question," Max replied.

Brad stopped before them and waited. "Well?"

"How many scout ships do you have available?" Max asked.

"How many did you see on the parking pads at New Septimus?"

"Four."

Brad raised an eyebrow. "What did you really want to know?"

"You think we can win this fight?"

"I wouldn't be here if I didn't. You give all the Borwyn more than a fighting chance. Jaq, *Chrysalis*, and warriors like you and Crip." He gestured toward Deena. "You even won a Malibor to your side. Do you understand that implication?"

Max and Deena's eyes met. Neither had the answer Brad was leading them to.

"You've shown that our two races are compatible. There is nothing preventing our intermingling and strengthening each other," Brad explained.

"There's only one race, though. That's been known for a hundred years. We're all human."

"And you reinforce that point by shoving it right in their ugly Malibor faces."

Max started rolling up his sleeves. "I'm going to fight you right now."

Brad laughed. "Calm down, lover boy. You took the bait. Remember what you said? Same. We're all the same inside."

"No wonder Teo is so tough," Max replied. "How can we fight them better?"

"Do what Jaq tells us. Seems simple to me." He jerked a thumb over his shoulder. "*Chrysalis* is dropping into Farslor's orbit. They sent us a message telling us to continue to the ERS."

"Did they say when they'd join us?" Max wondered. "This isn't the honeymoon cruise. We're sleeping in a nook between crates."

"I'm sleeping on the floor at the back of the bridge. I don't think Buster ever sleeps."

"He got us here." Deena shrugged. "Malibor might be raised to hate the Borwyn, but most of us don't have a death wish like the fanatics who were in charge of *Hornet*."

"My people have pulse rifles and have shown that they'll use them. We haven't caught the crew having secret meetings or strange boxes showing up on critical systems. We'll have to take extra care once we're close to *Butterfly*. No surprises when it comes to our people and Bec's junk."

"What about Bec's junk?" Brad asked.

"We've determined that he couldn't find it even if he used two hands."

Brad used his old man look, something he fought hard to suppress. "What are we talking about?"

"The ridiculous list of desired electronics, circuit boards, capacitors, and who knows if this is the right stuff without an electronics lab with all the right test equipment." Deena gave the finger to the crate she had been working inside.

"Then why did you look at all? Sounds like it was a waste of time."

"Jaq!" Max started to laugh and kept laughing. "That's exactly what it was. Gave us something to do that we had no hope of finishing before reaching *Butterfly*."

"Keep you two lovebirds out of trouble," Brad added. "You weren't supposed to be here."

"I know," Deena said. "I'm sure Chef managed without me, just as I'm certain that it'll cost me when I get back."

"We'll figure something out," Max said. "What else do you have, Brad?"

"That's it. Hammer is right behind us and will follow us in."

"Why doesn't he marry up with the airlock and ride along with us. No sense burning your fuel. And Jaq didn't kick him off *this* ship," Max replied.

"That's a good idea, and we've slowed enough that we aren't going to kill my son during the maneuver." Brad made it real for Max and Deena.

"Let's see how we can do this with the least risk." Max clapped Brad on the shoulder and walked hand-in-hand with Deena down the narrow aisle between the endless pallets. Brad followed them.

Buster was half-asleep, firmly embedded in the captain's chair. One of Max's team stood guard at the entrance to the bridge, watching both in and out. A net had been put across the corridor with jangles attached so anyone trying to get past would make a noise.

Or anyone trying to escape would be slowed down. It was something the soldiers came up with. If it made the combat team feel more secure, Max was good with it.

The crew were still their prisoners, but they were civilians and not Malibor military. It created the conditions for a fragile truce. Max and Brad reinforced the expectation that they wouldn't be able to fly cargo for the Malibor forces until after the war was over. The crew of *Chrysalis* had given it two months. *Bessie Mae's* crew had given in. They didn't have a strong negotiating position, which they recognized and took what gave them the most freedom. Flying to Farslor and the secret Borwyn station beyond the planet gave them information that could not be shared with the Malibor. This ensured they would remain captive, no matter how much personal freedom they enjoyed aboard the cargo ship.

At least they were eating well and getting access to showers more often. The little things that the Malibor did not give them made all the difference. Humanity was more than a paycheck and a new contract.

Buster roused with the noise of Brad, Max, and Deena's arrival.

"You guys," he snapped. "Not you. You're a babe and always welcome on my bridge."

Deena looked down her nose at the unrepentant space hauler.

"We want to bring the scout ship to the airlock and then fly the rest of the way to *Butterfly* with it attached. What do you think?"

"I think you're stupid, along with being an ugly Borwyn."

"We'll be traveling at nominal KPH. The risk is minimal. We need to save fuel on the scout ship."

"Then attach it to the ship-hauling brackets on the underside."

Max and Brad looked at each other. "Show me." Brad leaned over the captain's shoulder.

He brought up a loading diagram of the cargo ship. On the section deemed the underside was an impact deflector and heavy clamps, complete with an airlock attachment.

"We'll use that then. I'm not sure the airlock will marry up with the one on our ship, which is oriented to the side and not on the underbelly since ours are for landing in a gravity environment."

"La-ti-da." Buster waved dismissively. "You can figure it out or burn your fuel instead of ours. Who's going to reimburse us for that, by the way?"

"We'll pay you in good Borwyn scrip."

"They haven't used that garbage since I've been alive. We use it to paper the cages of pet birds."

"Then your pet birds shall be the wealthiest of them all once Septimus is returned to our control."

"You think you can change the entire economic system of a planet like Septimus?" Buster asked.

"Probably not. We're just a bunch of space pirates, after all."

Buster harrumphed and loosened the locks on the external attachment. "Have your ship belly up to the bar. I've activated a short-range beacon that your people can ride to the spot. There's a big X. Get it? X marks the spot."

Brad activated his handheld comm device. "Hammer, this is *Cornucopia*. We want you to attach to the outside of the cargo ship. There's a beacon pinging to guide you in."

"I hear it, Dad. It almost blasted me out of the cockpit."

Brad tapped Buster on the shoulder. "Turn off the beacon. It's not as low power as I'd like." He turned to Max. "Get your guy Larson to disable that thing."

Max nodded and activated his team radio.

Larson wasn't far away. He decided to talk to him in person rather than interrupt whatever he was doing.

Deena trailed along. Without conducting the endless search for parts that didn't match, she was free to do whatever she wanted.

When they arrived, Larson stared at their handholding. "I wish I could have brought my girlfriend with me."

Max let go. "I'm sorry. Deena wasn't supposed to be here but got stuck with the emergency pull-off when the Malibor troopship tried to ram us. We make do, Larson. Sometimes we get a good deal, but most of the time not." Max turned to Deena. "This guy hooked us up with movies in the lander when we were killing time while the oxygen generator charged."

"Movies? I thought your landers were a long way from anything modern."

"They are utilitarian, to say the least."

"But some of us are willing to make them less so." Larson beamed. "And now I know what to do, it'll be easy to modify the other three. We're down to four, aren't we?"

"The Malibor blew one up around Farslor, and the other is with *Butterfly*. So technically, we have five."

Larson nodded. "Did you want something?"

Max replied, "I did. There's a beacon to direct a ship to a docking mechanism on the underside of the ship. Hammer said it was powerful despite Buster's contention that it was a weak signal. I want it disabled, just in case. There's an airlock down there too for the attached ship to use. Hammer will have to spacesuit his way in since the hatch doesn't line up with the scout."

"Brad will make sure he gets inside. The captain will stop being mad at him soon enough, but we won't. He made us look bad."

"We're going to have to get past that. We all want to carry our pulse rifles. They give us a feeling of power, mastery over our environment. I don't blame him at all. What do you say we educate him on what it means to be a soldier? He is a strapping lad."

Larson pursed his lips while he thought about it. "We could use some extra muscle. I like Danny Johns, but he's old." He scowled at the deck. "Train him to understand why his actions were so screwed up. We don't need a child on the team, but we can use a man-mountain trained warrior. That's why you're in charge, Max. You're thinking well ahead of the rest of us."

"We lost two and now we have two, maybe three. I'll see if Anvil will join us."

"What will Anvil do?" Brad called from down the corridor.

"Hammer and Anvil on the combat team. We could use them, and they will be able to handle the pulse rifles, safely and efficiently, without having to take them."

"Hammer will never live that down. I promise you that," Brad declared. "But I'll lose my flight crew."

"You can handle a scout solo, I suspect," Max replied.

"I can. As Hammer just demonstrated, too. They're made for one person. Three is a little cramped."

"Then why did you have your boys with you?"

Brad laughed and pointed as if Max had walked into an ambush. "Can you imagine the havoc those two would wreak if I left them alone?" He continued to laugh until he remembered what they'd been talking about. "But they'll be good on the combat team. You'll whip them into shape."

"Nice backpedal. We'll give them a trial run, but we've been training as a team for years." Max tapped his finger to his nose.

"But you've lost two already, and Crip is getting more involved with the ship and your growing fleet."

"It'll be a trial run. They have a lot to learn if they're going to help us board a hostile ship or conduct ground operations. We'll ask them to get their commitment. It also means they'll join our damage control teams. Fixing the ship comes before all things."

"As it should," Brad agreed. "Thanks for considering my boys and giving them a chance at something they are optimally suited for."

"And Teo, too. Your family is doing great things for us."

"And yours is doing great things for all Borwyn."

Deena smiled at the three men. "They're easy to love, but we all have things to do."

"Larson, cut that beacon's line. Brad, bring your boy into the docking clamps once we cut acceleration, and he'll have to spacesuit to the airlock. Once he's inside, we'll refire the engines."

Brad and Larson hurried to their respective tasks, leaving Max and Deena on their own.

Max said, "It's almost like I'm in charge."

"To the galley and let's see what we can treat the crew to for dinner." Deena took his hand and led him away.

"*Almost* in charge..." Max muttered.

CHAPTER 3

There is no instance of a nation benefiting from prolonged warfare.

Alby cheered long and loud. "*Chrysalis* will be here in less than two days," he announced to Godbolt. She jumped on the comm and broadcast it to all hands, also declaring a feast for the evening's meal.

"They also said a cargo ship is coming with more rations and spare parts."

"Did they say they were going to become pirates?" Godbolt wondered aloud.

Alby nodded with a smile. "Crip talked about that. Seizing ships and growing the fleet. They started with a loaded freighter. How long will it be before the Malibor lose their minds about it?"

Godbolt replied, "They probably already are, but they have to be flailing since there's no way they could know where we took it, is there?"

"I'm sure they dismantled the transponders and tracking devices on the ship. They must have taken it at Farslor and then sent it here. A whole cargo ship filled with up-to-date spare parts, equipment, and food. It could be the greatest gift we've ever received."

"Then I look forward to climbing aboard and doing an inventory with our team."

"I bet they've already done that. Maybe they have parts that will upgrade the Malibor missiles. Those things are junk. I give it fifty-fifty that they even leave the tube."

Godbolt gave Alby a thumbs-up and left the bridge.

Alby returned to digging into the computer system. All the Malibor military knowledge was there, but it was buried in convoluted organization. He had a hard time getting a complete picture in a way that would give the Borwyn an edge. What were the Malibor strengths and weaknesses?

There were reams of operations reports from each ship. They showed problems, but they were couched in the dissembling phraseology that buried the extent of the issue. It left Alby reading between the lines. Every single ship.

After reading the reports, Alby was surprised any ship was able to leave space dock, but *Chrysalis* had already faced a great number of Malibor ships. Maybe the reports highlighted the crew being miracle workers. Operational ships were disguised as broken so when they were ordered to space, they could head out. Alby could come to no other conclusion.

"You people are screwed up in the head," he told the computer. "Who organizes their stuff like this?"

He continued to grouse under his breath while attempting to navigate his way through the myriad of screens.

Alby abandoned his efforts for the day. He'd given it his best for two to three hours and then gave up in frustration. He didn't feel he was any closer to knowing more about the Malibor than when he first boarded a month earlier.

His team's list of accomplishments was growing by the day. Six functional missiles, enough fissile material to operate four separate power plants for a year each, and spare parts for electrical systems on *Chrysalis*. Bec had complained for years about cobbling fixes and repairing failure after failure. They had crates packed with parts pulled from the non-functional sections of the ship. The debris floated in space, still attached but blasted apart.

Butterfly would never be spaceworthy again, nothing beyond the section they'd been able to seal and channel power and life support to. That didn't mean it would fly, only that those within would be able to live.

It was good enough. Alby and his engineering team had made it a home, but he was ready to return to *Chrysalis* and get back to fighting the Malibor more directly.

He floated above the consoles, the zero-gee as comfortable as it had been the first day they arrived on board. There was no way to impart spin and create the impression of gravity, no way to accelerate. He'd grown accustomed to perpetual zero-gee, but he liked the periods of gravity on board *Chrysalis*.

"Capacitor for your thoughts?" Godbolt asked.

"I didn't see you return."

"Stealth mode, and you were occupied."

"Thinking about going back home. I've had enough of being the engineering guy. Bec can have it."

"Bec wouldn't come over here. This is a bit austere for his royal majesty."

Alby laughed. "There's nothing that needs his attention. He's better on *Chrysalis* nursing that ion drive of his. Someone else can spot us. At dinner tonight, we'll see who wants to stay. We have some nutcases who like it here."

"The food, Alby. If *Chrysalis* has the same cuisine, they might be happy to go home."

"Do we know that for sure? If not, then we won't mention it. They may figure it out when the cargo ship arrives, but they might like the autonomy. Like I said, we'll ask. No sense wasting time speculating."

Godbolt gave him a thumbs-up and did a backflip out the hatch, leaving Alby alone once more. He opened the confusing Malibor file system again, hoping for a shining light of inspiration.

———

Crip looked at Tram through the New Septimus Borwyn helmet squeezed onto his head. "When did this become me and not you?" Tram wondered aloud.

"When you seemed too happy not doing anything on the bridge."

"I was learning your job!" Tram countered. "See what I get for trying to improve myself."

"I have it on good authority that Alby is coming home from *Butterfly*. By restoring this ship to operational condition, you'll cement your place in history as the go-to guy."

Tram sighed. "I'm not sure I want to be the go-to guy, but

I do need some time away to reevaluate my life." He lowered his voice. "I'm the biggest failure when it comes to women."

Crip looked around to make sure no one was listening. "Don't you know who you're talking to? I had the failure record before Taurus took mercy on me. Your time will come, Tram, and whatever you do, don't ever ask me for relationship advice again. Now, make us proud. Get that gunship hooked up to us. You have six hours."

"Because these suits have eight hours of air. Got it." Tram lowered his visor and turned on his air. He entered the cargo bay where the weapons platform used to be. The dents and scratches proved that it hadn't been an optimal fit. The team of six would launch out the cargo bay door using their mobility packs with pneumatic thrusters. They had two external thrusters with them to help move the ship if they couldn't restore power.

Having worked on the weapons platform, they knew what the power source looked like. With the initial recovered fissile material from *Butterfly*, they'd fabricated a unit that would plug into the engine if it was similar to the weapons platform's—or close enough that they could modify it.

Kelvis had done the work and was coming along, even though he didn't want to. He considered himself an inside talent and not a spacesuit type.

"We're are war, Kelvis," Tram told him. "Everyone has to do what they do best. It helps us all. We get this gunship powered up, we bring extra firepower to the battle. This thing will give us an edge. We win fights when we have the edge. If we lose the fight, we die."

"I get it!" Kelvis shot back. "I just don't like working with a spacesuit on. This requires a delicate touch."

Tram tapped on top of the nuclear engineer's helmet. "You have all the time in the world to make this happen. As long as it's six hours or less."

"What if I need more? I'm supposed to bring a spaceship to life that uses a system I've never seen before."

Tram replied, "What I hear you saying is six hours will be plenty of time." He pointed toward the cargo bay doors that were sliding aside to show space beyond. The gunship was close, barely a hundred meters away.

"At least we don't have far to go. Clip on the tether and just ride. Don't slingshot yourself into deep space." Tram didn't let Kelvis do anything. Tram hooked him up and then forced the tether's slack into his gloved hands. "Hang on."

By managing the slack, he would reduce the slingshot effect and not bounce over Tram's head. The recent extravehicular activity to repair the electromagnetic guns had given Tram a great deal of confidence in using the mobility pack. He released his boots and gestured for Kelvis to do the same. When the engineer floated free, Tram tapped the control and headed for the gunship. Two other pairs followed them out. Three mobility packs for a six-person team.

Tram led the way to the ship's port-side airlock. He tried to use the screen, but it had zero power. He released the manual lever and cranked it until the hatch popped. It was a small space that would only fit one person at a time. He pushed Kelvis inside and then released the tether.

Kelvis pulled the outer hatch shut, cranked the manual level inside to seal it, and then used the hand crank on the inside to open the interior hatch. He crawled through into the zero atmosphere and closed the hatch, sealing it manually from inside the ship.

Tram was displeased with how long the process took. "Leave both hatches open. We don't have pressure in here." He undid the hatch and cracked it open.

When the two tried to undog the outside hatch, they found the crank wouldn't move. A mechanical safety. Unless they found an override, they couldn't have both hatches open at the same time.

"One at a time, people," Tram broadcast and resealed the inner hatch.

Once inside, he found Kelvis in the aft section, looking for the power plant. He left him to it and focused his efforts amidships, where the bridge was located. The forward section contained storage and weapons, and in between were multi-crew quarters and a small mess deck.

Tram guessed that the gunship might have a crew of eight. He'd always thought of them as far more substantial with a crew of twenty or thirty, while a cruiser had two hundred or more. Tram had to recalibrate his expectations. If there were eight on the crew, that meant the ship could operate by four, maybe even two. The ship had been stripped of all personal touches and foodstuffs. The shelves and cabinets were empty except for one and that contained cleaning supplies in pristine condition, like they were staged for a crew to touch up the ship should they return.

Although a sealed ship with zero atmosphere gathered no dust or dirt. They couldn't smell the air since environmental controls weren't functioning.

Tram left the austere bridge and returned to the forward weapons compartment. The forward railgun banks were stacked in tandem, two on the port side and two on starboard. Tram couldn't find defensive weapons, only the four railguns.

The third and fourth engineers made it on board and headed aft to help Kelvis bring the power online.

He was upside-down, elbow-deep into the system under a panel.

"You'll have the power online in ten minutes or so?" Tram prodded.

Kelvis replied, "I think you should return to *Chrysalis*. I'll let you know when the power is online."

Tram laughed. "Now you get how the game is played. Understand that we have complete confidence in you. You'll get it."

Tram gestured for the two to remain. He spoke over the general channel. "We only need four. You last two can return to *Chrysalis*. This ship is little bigger than Brad's scout ship."

"Crip here. According to our instruments, it's much bigger than Brad's scout ship, about three times the size."

"Standby. You two, examine the outside of the ship before returning to *Chrysalis*. Is there something we're missing that makes this ship bigger on the outside than it is on the inside?"

"Roger," the two replied. "Beginning the survey of the outside of the gunship."

Tram activated his boots and clumped around the mid-level of the gunship. The ship held no personality, no allure for someone to commit to serving aboard it. Tram stood at the captain's position envisioning what command would be like.

The dark screen arced around the sides of the space, through one hundred and eighty degrees, ostensibly to show the tactically generated view of the flanks and forward space.

The weapons position with targeting controls was to the captain's right and the flight controls to the left. If the captain flew the ship, he'd have to change positions to fire the railguns. One person could do it, but it would be inefficient. There were two other positions on the small bridge, but they looked to be supplementary rather than for full-time use. Only the three main seats were built for high gees, not gel but hard packs to support a body during the rigors of acceleration.

"Lots of armor," the external survey reported, "along with deflector panels, possibly to reduce its radar cross-section. It looks big on the outside, but that's this extra stuff. Survey is complete with plenty of imagery. Returning to *Chrysalis*."

"Thanks for the extra eyeballs. Drop the suits off for cleaning and refilling the air tanks."

Tram wasn't sure if he needed to give the extra instructions, but it was better to be certain. Once at the ERS, they'd be performing a great deal of external operations. Every suit they had would be put to use. And if they had a gunship to bring up to speed, they'd be putting in long hours.

Despite its age and lack of creature comforts, the gunship could take a great deal of pressure off *Chrysalis*. A second threat. A diversion. Much better than a Malibor missile.

Tram was lost in his own thoughts when the lights flickered. They remained low for a minute before slowly increasing in intensity. The computer system came to life, as Tram expected. If they left cleaning gear, then they'd have left the ship with minimum operational capability. That took the computer.

Tram unlocked his boots and flew through the ship to where Kelvis was. "Excellent work!"

"It's the same power system as the weapons platform. We've had a month to figure it out. It would have been embarrassing if I couldn't plug in the new module and power it up."

"In that case, what took so long?" Tram asked.

Kelvis rolled his eyes while making a face. "I didn't want to blow the system, so brought it up with minimal power. We should be able to bring environmental controls online, then incrementally, one system at a time."

"Does this thing have any transponders that might activate?"

Kelvis shrugged. "That's a good question. We won't bring communications online, but we will need to power up the navigation system. That's where a beacon or signal might be hidden."

"I'll dig into it," one of the other engineers said and disappeared into the ship.

Tram checked the time. They'd only been on board for two hours. He called *Chrysalis*. "Captain Hunter, Tram here with an update."

Crip answered, "Jaq is off the bridge. What can I do you out of?"

"Nice. Gunship power is online. Now all we have to do is bring up the systems, one by one. We are looking at the nav system to isolate any beacons or transponders that may activate once it's energized. I'd say not to power it up, but if we're going to fly this thing, then we need those systems, even for something as simple as hitching a ride on *Chrysalis*."

"Well done, Tram! Do you know if the railguns are operational?"

"I don't. I'd like to wait on the weapons systems. Ammo storage is empty, so we'll need a stock of obdurium projectiles before we can even test these things."

"We have work to do, but you think we can have ourselves a fully operational gunship. That's what I like to hear."

"I'm pretty sure I didn't say that," Tram replied. "Let's agree that I'm cautiously optimistic."

"How long until you're ready to fly that ship out of here?"

"Fly the ship? Crip, you and I have significantly different ideas about what cautiously optimistic means, but we'll do our best. Do you have any other unrealistic expectations, like an artificial timeline based on inbound enemy aircraft? We have two hours to bring the ship online and engage a relentless Malibor armada."

"We don't see an armada," Crip replied. "Why do we only have two hours? Where are they?"

"Crip, you're losing it. We'll get back to you when we've made progress."

"I'm still not seeing a Malibor armada."

Tram signed off before the madness of a stream of consciousness conversation could go any further. He smiled to himself. This project was going well. Jaq and Crip had been right. The strategy of adding a second offensive punch to their attacks would give them the edge.

The order of battle suggested *Chrysalis* only had four or

five battles remaining before establishing primacy, dominance so profound that the Malibor would have to surrender or flee the field of battle.

Would each battle become deadlier?

Tram doubted it. The last ships into the fight would be the last ships able to fight. The next couple battles would be the most significant.

Tram headed to the weapons area forward to measure the loading size for the projectiles to make sure they didn't put in something too big that wouldn't accelerate quickly enough. He determined the specs of the projectiles and forwarded them to the fabrication laboratory on board *Chrysalis*.

With his mission nearly complete, he backstroked through the gunship, feeling better than he had in a long time.

Fight the good fight.

"Kelvis, are you done yet?" he asked as he casually swam into the engineering section.

CHAPTER 4

He who is prudent and lies in wait for an enemy who is not will be victorious.

The ships rolled in, three of them. *Butterfly* was helpless if the inbound ships were anything other than Borwyn, but they were not.

Chrysalis, *Cornucopia*, and a gunship that called itself *Matador* announced their arrival. Tram Stamper spoke for the gunship.

The ships eased up next to the hulk and settled in using thrusters for station keeping. There was no airlock to marry up to, so they aligned in ways that were easiest for crew using spacesuits and mobility packs to move back and forth between the ships.

The gunship sought the port roller airlock and settled into place.

Crip waited at the airlock inside *Chrysalis*. First through was Tram, grinning and pumping a fist until he spun out of control. Crip caught him. "Good job, Tram. We have ourselves a gunship."

"Thank Alby for snagging that weapons platform and then Kelvis for being the power guy. And thank you for sending me and then giving me credit."

The two shook hands. "Something like that." Crip waited for the rest of Tram's team to leave the gunship, but Kelvis didn't appear.

After a hearty thank you, they sent the other two engineers back to their work sections.

Tram led Crip into the aging Malibor ship to give him a quick tour.

"I see what you mean about how small this thing is. I wouldn't want to serve on it, definitely not for any mission longer than a couple days."

"That's the challenge, Crip. We're going to need someone to crew this beast. The computers aren't advanced enough to allow remote operation, and you know we don't have anything we can spare on board *Chrysalis*."

"What about *Butterfly*?"

"How much time can you give me?" Tram asked.

"The captain isn't keen on losing our advantage. Right now, we've cleared Farslor and Sairvor of Malibor fleet assets. The more time we take, the more time they have to rejuvenate their fleet. What if they were the ones who brought this gunship back to life? That's our challenge. A ship brought out of mothballs can shoot us just as readily as one of their ships of the line. Which Malibor projectile is the magic one, the one that explodes our ion drive? That takes the ship with it, and we're done. The Borwyn from New

Septimus have no way to prosecute a war without a ship like *Chrysalis*."

"Which brings me back to my point. We need a crew for the gunship." Tram knew there was only one answer but didn't want to admit it. He kicked his way aft until he found Kelvis with a panel torn apart.

They'd only been docked for five minutes and last time Tram had looked, everything was intact.

"What are you doing?" he asked.

Kelvis looked up. "Their power distribution system is trash. I heard we have real Malibor spares, modern stuff, unlike the fifty-year-old junk in here." He held out his hand as if Tram would instantly deliver the part.

"We haven't linked up with *Cornucopia* yet." Tram retreated. "I'd say that if you provided a list of parts, we'd get them for you, but we have no idea how to describe the right replacements. You'll have to get them yourself. Put your suit back on and cross-deck to the cargo ship."

They'd gotten environmental controls online as the first system after power had been restored. The air had been stale, but the oxygen tanks were intact and contained a sufficient supply to get the small Borwyn team to the ERS without having to wear their spacesuits the entire trip.

"That's the last thing I want to do," Kelvis admitted. "But you're right. No one knows these systems better than me. I have to be the one who goes."

He left everything as it was and started putting his spacesuit on.

"I appreciate you taking ownership," Tram said.

"Does that mean I'm screwed? You don't have to answer

that because I know. I'm stuck on this tub for the rest of the war, aren't I?"

"We'll have the agro folks bring plants," Crip offered. "And good Malibor food. Your own pillow, too."

Kelvis snorted. "I'll take it, but he has to come, too. I'm not one to suffer in silence." Kelvis pointed at Tram.

"I think I won't have a choice either, Kelvis. We need a pilot-navigator and a weapons officer for a crew of four. I wouldn't want to subject anyone else to this bucket. There's enough space for a small team to work comfortably."

"No slobs," Kelvis said. He finished putting on his spacesuit. Tram helped him seal his helmet. "I like order and cleanliness."

"Do you know how to operate the mobility pack?" Tram asked.

"No." Kelvis grinned. "Guess you're coming, too, boss man."

Tram's face fell.

Crip laughed. "Your orders are to bring this ship up to speed and flesh out your crew. Prepare to launch in a week's time when *Chrysalis* makes our high-speed run to Septimus."

"You planned this all along," Tram said.

"I guessed well, shall we say." Crip clapped Tram on the shoulder. "I'll leave you to it."

Tram looked to Kelvis for sympathy but only saw the engineer laughing.

"*Bessie Mae* is stable. Thrusters are on automatic," Buster announced. "With that, we are your prisoners once more as there is no ship to fly."

Max and Brad frowned. "You've done right by us," Max replied.

Brad blew out a long breath. The Malibor had been his enemy since he was driven away from Septimus. Finding them tolerable was unexpected, and he even liked the crotchety, skeletal cargo ship captain. He turned to Hammer, who only shrugged.

"Let's see what we can do. Rally your people and let's talk about the future." Brad twirled his finger in the air as a sign to get to work.

Max had his team report along with Deena. They waited on the bridge for the remaining crew.

Brad walked the short corridors of the freighter with his son. The long walkways were in the cargo areas. He stayed away from those because they were endless. The cargo ship had been filled to bursting. The Borwyn tried to survey the load, but it was simply too much for the small team attempting it. The stock and pallets were in a bit of disarray from the efforts, despite getting latched to the deck. Nothing was floating free, but some of the aisles were hard to squeeze through because of obstructions.

When Brad and Hammer returned to the bridge, he found all of Max's team, plus Deena, Buster, and six others from the Malibor crew.

"Who are we missing?" Brad asked.

Buster didn't even have to look up. "It's Cryl Talan."

"Is he in his rack or something?" Brad asked.

Buster shrugged. The others looked away.

"Max, send someone to check crew berthing and the common areas. I hope he's not an overzealous patriot who thinks he's doing a duty to the Malibor by trying to hurt any of our people or take your ship out of the sky. If he blows up *Cornucopia*, or *Bessie Mae* as you call her, then you'll go down with your ship."

"Leave it to the Borwyn to make threats when they don't get their way," Buster droned.

"Max..." Brad turned to the combat team leader, but Max was already gone with five of his team and Deena. That left Brad and Hammer plus two soldiers facing the seven Malibor civilians. Seven were more than enough if they wanted to foment further discontent. Brad pointed at the deck. "Move over there and lock your boots down."

The Malibor must have understood the gravity of their situation. They didn't argue. They didn't even grumble. They took their position in front of the main screen, where there was no equipment, and activated their magnetic boots. They flowed like plants in hydroponics as environmental control cycled the air through the space. The soldiers held their weapons at the ready while Brad glared.

He was having a hard time biting his tongue, just until it became impossible.

"We treated you decently. We could have put you in cold storage the second we found your kill-switch, Captain, but we didn't. Your freedom was contingent on your cooperation, but now, you'll be nothing more than prisoners of war. We didn't ask you to fight your people. We'll do that, but we'll fight the warriors, not the civilians. Your parole ended the second you decided to become combatants."

"We're not combatants," Buster countered. "We're simply the crew who didn't take matters into their own hands. Why are you punishing us for any perceived transgression of our fellow?"

"If he were here, we wouldn't be having this conversation or this problem, so there you are. Buster, get on the horn and tell your man to give himself up."

"You're punishing the ones who actually followed your orders. It doesn't make me want to do anything you say. You've removed the incentive to cooperate." Buster sucked on a tooth, arms were crossed, and stared with tired eyes at his captor.

Brad looked at the overhead and wanted to scream.

"Of course, you are correct, but understand that we cannot let you go until your man is found. Would you like something to drink?"

"That sounds good," Buster agreed.

"Too bad. None of us are going anywhere." Brad glowered at the captain.

Buster laughed. "That's a good one. I thought we had something, you and me, a connection that transcended our births. But no. You're an evil Borwyn, and everything we've ever been led to believe is true."

"Come on, you jags. We'll invade the galley and eat and drink to our hearts' content." Brad waved for them to follow. The soldiers encouraged the group from behind. They all walked instead of taking advantage of zero-gee.

Brad crouched on one of the benches while the small

group filled the rest of the seats. The two soldiers remained near the entrance. That left Hammer to perform the duty. Brad chuckled softly, more to himself than anyone else. Here he was, watching his son serve the Malibor after trying to extract his kilogram of flesh. It would be up to Max to end the threat from a rogue Malibor.

"Check the airlocks," Max ordered, sending Danzig and Barrington fore and aft. The two used the advantage of zero-gee to move quickly while Max remained near the bridge. His other people raced up and down the corridors and passageways. It wouldn't take long while seeming like it took forever.

Max moved to the door to the galley, where he found Hammer serving the Malibor crew. The prisoners were complaining about each thing he gave them, from water to full meals. Max watched in mild amusement until Hammer gave up and threw the bags at them. "Maybe you're better off as prisoners. I tried, but no, you want to stick it to the Borwyn."

Brad gestured to the two soldiers. "Put them in the forward ballast compartment."

"Hey! That's downright inhuman." Buster shook his fist.

Brad lunged toward him and grabbed his coverall. "You're responsible for it all. That's how it is, Captain. I listened and tried to play nice, but you wanted to have a laugh. You shouldn't have pushed me. You shouldn't have allowed one of your people to go rogue. Now you'll all suffer, regardless of your idea that we're punishing the group for the misdeeds of one. You're all complicit." He jerked a thumb over his shoulder.

One crewman tried to stand up to the soldier. When the soldier pushed, the Malibor grabbed for the pulse rifle, earning himself a butt stroke across the face. The crew finally stopped making noise. Their collateral was exhausted. They glared at their captors. Brad returned their looks.

They shuffled out of the small galley. Buster stopped next to Brad.

"You've made enemies here today."

"And if we don't catch your man before he does something stupid, we'll accept our place as your enemy, and you *will* regret it."

Once they were gone, Max and Brad shared a moment of sadness.

Brad said, "I wanted to do it Jaq's way and treat them like decent people. I hate locking them up, but they gave me no choice."

"They gave *us* no choice. You and I need to join the search. We need as many looking as we can get. Worse than this guy running around is that we gave them a lot of latitude during the trip here. They could have sabotaged the ship in a hundred different ways."

Brad shook his head. "I don't see them all being in on it. This crew doesn't want to give their lives for the Malibor cause. I think we made progress on that front."

"I'll go aft, you go forward?" Max suggested.

Brad pushed down the corridor where the crew still shuffled their way toward the forward ballast compartment. He stayed behind them until Hammer and the two soldiers moved beyond a transverse walkway through the cargo containers. Brad took the new walkway and checked high and low, looking for gaps where someone could hide, but found nothing. He'd been through the cargo bay a hundred times since they left Sairvor. It was packed, and that made inventory difficult.

What they needed was an assist of the electronic variety. Brad contacted Max on the combat team's channel. "We need *Chrysalis* to scan the ship and look for people."

"Already requested that," Max said, "about twenty seconds ago when I looked at how much junk we'd have to sort through."

"Brilliant minds think alike," Brad replied.

Max chuckled. "I'd like to think that a soldier's penchant for being as lazy as possible carried the day. Work smarter, not harder, something I never used to say until getting stuck on this tub."

"At least the food is good. Eat 'til you're tired. Sleep 'til you're hungry."

"Brad, you make me feel all warm inside."

"If you two are finished, we have your data," Jaq interrupted.

"I was on the team channel!" Brad blurted.

"Obviously not. Do you want to know where all the people are or not?"

"Here's what I have. We have seven Malibor crew in the forward ballast. Three standing guard. Brad forward. Deena and I are aft. A soldier at the forward airlock and another at the aft airlock. That leaves three searching the crew spaces before expanding to the cargo holds."

"And that's what we see. Aren't you supposed to have eight Malibor?"

Max answered, "That's the issue. We seem to have lost a Malibor by the name of Cryl Talan."

"He's not on *Cornucopia*," Jaq reiterated.

"What about outside the ship?" Max asked.

"There are all kinds of people outside the ships because of the work being done on *Butterfly*. We've already sent a dozen people over there."

"Rally everyone at the mess deck. Free the Malibor and bring them," Max ordered.

He was one of the first to arrive, with Deena right behind him. The others trickled in one at a time until the two soldiers brought the Malibor.

Max addressed the group. "Cryl has managed to elude us. He is no longer on the ship. The question I have is did he sabotage *Bessie Mae*? And what does he intend to do to *Butterfly* or *Chrysalis*?"

CHAPTER 5

Opportunities multiply as they are seized.

Jaq crossed her arms and braced her legs, as if ready to handle the buffeting of the worst space storm, even though the ship was at rest, holding steady four hundred meters from the aft section of *Butterfly*.

She ground her teeth in frustration. A Malibor was free somewhere between all the ships.

"Give me broadcast to all ships surrounding the ERS and all personnel currently engaged in extravehicular activities." She looked to the communications officer, who was someone different than she expected. "You're from New Septimus."

"Call me Amie, Amie Jacobs." She tapped her buttons and nodded to the captain. "Your channel is open."

"All hands currently EVA, you will report to *Chrysalis*, the aft cargo bay. There is a Malibor out there somewhere trying to infiltrate one of our ships. He must be discovered and secured. All hands will be personally identified by our crew and they will wait until all hands are accounted for. Alby, I need you to bring your people together in a location of your choosing. Once you have them, we'll scan the hulk for an extra body. Make no mistake, we will find this individual. We don't believe he is armed, but he should still be treated as dangerous."

"Channel is closed," Amie stated.

"Crip, you better get down there. You know everyone. Clear them through and we'll scan the area. Shoot for thirty minutes from now to have the space cleared between us and the other ships."

Crip jumped out of his seat and shot toward the overhead. He curled up to hit feet first and pushed off toward the corridor.

Jaq clenched her fists.

"Jaq, it's Bec. I'm going to take the engines offline. We'll be operating on battery only for the next seven days. Take care with energy usage since we won't be able to bring the engines up on an emergency or other basis. We're going to be rerouting systems and replacing parts. They'll be hard down. Seven days, Jaq. It's what you promised me."

The last thing Jaq wanted was to get into an argument with Bec. "Run us up to ninety percent and then take the engines down. I'm not good with starting a weeklong run at seventy-six percent."

"Without the ion drives or the E-mags or any system besides environmental control, we shouldn't use more than twenty percent the whole time. You're demanding a greater margin of error than is necessary."

"And I'm okay with that. Like you said, whatever we

have, that's what we're stuck with. Humor me, Bec. Be a scooper."

"What's a scooper?"

"It's a person who gives their captain ninety-percent power. A big healthy scoop of joy. That's what you want to give me."

"It's not, but seven days starts from whenever we take the system down, not now. You don't get to shorten my timeline. I get seven days."

"Yes, of course, Bec. The number of days shall be longer than six but less than eight."

"Did you hit your head?" Bec asked snidely.

"Which time?" Jaq replied. "Ninety percent and then power us down. You don't need to hear from me."

Jaq closed the channel before she could say anything else since he heard what he wanted.

She accessed the ship-wide broadcast. "All hands, when we hit ninety-percent power, we're going to take the engines offline for a complete refurbishment. They'll be offline for seven days. Restrict your power usage during the next seven days. Fabrication projects will be approved on a case-by-case basis. Run them through your department head to Commander Crip Castle."

Jaq smiled at the corridor down which Crip had disappeared. She knew he would be rolling his eyes and grumbling.

Taurus watched, mildly entertained.

Jaq winked at her.

"You enjoyed that too much," Taurus said.

"Is it that obvious?" Jaq's smile slowly faded. "He's the

right person for the job and with the ship on low-power restrictions, you'll have plenty of downtime."

"We have a great deal of work to do," Taurus replied. She nodded toward the two working on the calculations for the new high-speed E-mag targeting system. They programmed variables and jammed calculations. It was slow going, but they were working tirelessly, an aged man with the wisdom of years and a genius youth with an engaged mind.

At the moment, his eyes were closed and body slack as he napped. Dolly made random corrections in a screen full of code.

Jaq eased over to the position and spoke softly. "When's the last time you slept?"

"Last down shift. I'm fine." Dolly nodded toward Donal. "He didn't take the time off."

Jaq poked the original. He jerked awake. "Seven. Try base seven," he blurted.

"We'll try that later," Jaq replied. "Right now, you're off shift for six hours. You two are the only ones who didn't take twelve hours off when we were underway."

Donal blinked to clear his eyes. "You didn't either."

"But I did. And now it's your turn. Go get some sleep in your own cubicle. Turn off the lights and check out."

"Can I grab some chow first?"

"Always recommended. I sleep so much better with a full stomach."

"Maybe they'll have some spaghetti and meatballs available." Donal waggled his eyebrows. He untethered himself from his seat and casually flew out of the command deck.

"That was easy," Jaq mumbled. She turned her attention back to Dolly. "Are you making any progress?"

"So many variables... Streamlining their inclusion into a targeting solution is not yet obvious."

Jaq put her hand on the diminutive shoulder. "It will be, in time. It will appear, and then you'll wonder why you didn't see it before."

"That's what Donal said."

"Elders have a tendency to know stuff because they've learned lessons the hard way—over time through a lot of errors."

Jaq returned to the captain's chair. She forced herself into it so she could sulk in peace. A Malibor was out there causing grief by his absence alone. He could hurt them badly if he accessed a communications unit or detonated a power source.

Jaq tapped her comm screen to activate the broadcast channel. "Alby, put security on your communications equipment and your power generator. Same for you, Max and *Cornucopia*. We'll do the same here on *Chysalis*. This Cryl Talan cannot be allowed to send a message to the Malibor or to destroy one of our power sources. We need to find him. Tram, are you there?"

"I am listening. We're almost to *Cornucopia's* aft airlock. I'm working with Kelvis to bring *Matador* up to full operational capability. Can you send some food and water over, maybe even chernore? I could use a steaming bag of the good stuff. And please don't tell me that we have to turn around and go to *Chrysalis*. We have parts to find."

"Continue to *Cornucopia*. Max, meet them at the airlock. I'll see what I can do about food once the operational pause is lifted. We'll account for all of our people and then we'll get the resupply and repair done. *Chrysalis* will lose engines in a couple hours. Then we'll be on minimal power for seven days, but when we come out the other end, we'll be ready to depart for our high-speed pass of Septimus."

"We'll be right with you, Jaq. *Matador* will be ready."

"We'll talk about that later. We have time," Jaq replied. "Get your parts and bring our gunship up to speed."

"Roger," came Tram's reply.

"Did we lose Tram to the necessities of war?" Taurus asked.

Jaq didn't see it that way. "We need someone to fly that gunship. It's what's known as a force multiplier. If the Malibor expect one enemy ship, the second one comes as a surprise. That means we might get a shot off before them. Killing Malibor ships before they kill us is what we'll do until they stop fighting. I hope that's soon. I don't enjoy killing Malibor ships, because they could have people like Deena on board, those who aren't fully bought into why the Malibor are at war."

Taurus left her seat and activated her magnetic boots. "We should tell them that, you know, the Malibor, those on the space station in orbit around the moon they call Malpace."

"What are you thinking?" Jaq wondered aloud.

"We tried it with the armada, disinformation to make them think we're something we're not. What if we tell them what we are? The Borwyn have returned, and half your fleet is already destroyed. We will destroy the other half one by one until you stop fighting. The Borwyn have come home. Prepare to meet your maker."

"That's pretty dark." Jaq smiled. "But I like it. Indirect threat that we're going to turn all their ships into expanding clouds of space debris and their crews will die with them."

"We want them to decide to surrender as if it's their idea," Taurus explained.

"We want them to surrender regardless of whose idea it is. But you're right that we need to use every weapon at our disposal, even those things that may not seem to be weapons. Keep in mind that they're a patriarchy."

"Which means we record our message with the manliest of man voices?" Taurus chuckled.

"And a second, subliminal message with our most alluring feminine voice. There's no sex if you're dead."

"Jaq!" Taurus continued to laugh.

Jaq waved over her shoulder as she walked slowly off the bridge. "I'll be in my quarters."

She continued her short walk down the corridor. Once inside her room, she sat and strapped herself to her chair. She activated her communication console. "Give me a person to person with Alby Risor, please."

It took no more than five seconds before Alby answered.

"Tram is going to captain the gunship," Jaq said without preamble.

"Good. It was going to be uncomfortable with both of us sitting in that one seat," Alby replied.

"How many of your people want to come back to *Chrysalis*?"

"Eight will be staying. I don't want to force anyone to stay here, so we'll need a new chief and eleven volunteers."

Jaq stared at the bulkhead while gathering her thoughts. "I wish we could have brought more from New Septimus. They are good workers and motivated, too. They've integrated well with the ship's crew."

"The battle is joined, Jaq. They're believers in our cause because it's a dream that can come true. They can help it come true. I believe, too, Jaq, but I want to be at the spearpoint, striking a blow at the heart of the illegitimate Malibor empire. We can do that from *Chrysalis*."

Jaq nodded her agreement even though it was a voice-only channel.

Alby wasn't finished. "I wasn't sure what we could do. I figured the Malibor had fifty years to rebuild their fleet, just like us, except they had resources, a shipyard, and a population to draw on. What I didn't count on was that they'd tear themselves apart with civil wars. They didn't advance, the opposite, actually. We are the dominant force in the Armanor star system, all because of *Chrysalis*. It's crazy that we continue to grow. We've added capabilities while the Malibor continue to lose ships. We can end this war and reclaim Septimus. That's what I believe and so does everyone else. Thanks, Jaq."

"Let's see what our trip to Septimus brings," Jaq conceded. "Thank you for your kind words, but we have a lot of work to do to realize a free Septimus. The Malibor might have a million people on the planet. That could be a problem."

"A problem we'll deal with when we have cleared the

space above the planet. I'm ready to go, Jaq. I'm ready to fight the bad guys. We have six missiles ready to load aboard *Chrysalis*."

"I like missiles," Jaq replied. "Good work, Alby."

"The whole team worked on them, but we have a few other things, too. Spare parts, cabling, and more from the ship. There are two more missiles and most of the ship left to dismantle. There's a year's worth of work."

"We'll get volunteers to keep your work going. Is there enough food and water?"

"Both are good. We could use some fresh water to give us an emergency backup."

"I'll see what I can do," Jaq said. They were danger low on water. They needed to visit the asteroid belt to resupply. "After the high-speed run, we'll continue to the asteroid belt and find a source of ice."

"I look forward to getting home. When will this EVA group grope end?"

"We have a Malibor out there somewhere. Watch *Butterfly* and make sure no one sneaks aboard."

"Not possible to get to our power supply. We control the airlock from the bridge. No one comes in or goes out without us knowing. We have two remaining here. Me and Godbolt. Everyone else is between the ERS and *Chrysalis*."

"Can someone do damage if they only have access to external areas?"

"That's where the missiles are currently stored, but they'd have to know an awful lot to get themselves into that space, plus we can see it from here. We'll take a look. Godbolt!"

"Don't yell into the microphone," Jaq warned. "I'll wait."

"We'll be right back."

Jaq had nothing to do while Godbolt and Alby looked out the window. Her thoughts descended to what a saboteur could do. She wanted to talk with Max and ask what kind of spacesuits the crew of *Cornucopia* had. They had to be of Malibor make, but with the recovered suits from *Butterfly*, Jaq had people in those suits operating outside. No. Chasing someone based on the suit alone would result in upsetting the wrong people and possibly hurting one of her own. They couldn't risk that. They had to continue doing it the way they had planned. Funnel everyone through a known point and hold them there until *Chrysalis* could scan the area.

"Nothing, Jaq. Space is clear in all directions. The missiles are secure," Alby reported.

"Prepare to bring them over here as soon as possible. Who do you think can take over as chief of the ERS?"

"Give it to Godbolt, even though I selfishly want her to come back to *Chrysalis* with me. She can continue the work here uninterrupted if she agrees to stay."

"What do you think, Godbolt?"

The engineer spoke into the microphone. "That was unexpected, especially since I was one of the twelve returning to *Chrysalis*. But stay here and be responsible for the continued operation? That's hard to turn down. We're going to take over the cargo ship, aren't we?"

"That will add a level of difficulty that will challenge anyone who is in charge or even works here. That means you'll have the Malibor crew, too."

"Will I get a bunch of soldiers to help?"

"I'm afraid not. Did you find any landers on board?"

"We did. Two are still intact."

"Send the crew to Farslor. Give them extra jackets to keep warm."

"That's pretty harsh," Alby interjected. "According to Max and Crip, conditions are grim on the planet."

"At least the crew won't be causing us any problems as evidenced by what we'll call the great spacewalk interruption. I may look calm on the outside, but having a Malibor out there somewhere is scaring the crap out of me."

"Us, too, Jaq. We'll keep our eyes peeled and be ready to move the missiles as soon as our people make it back. We'll need eleven volunteers to backfill if you want to maintain the same capability, more if you want us to work with the cargo ship, fewer if you need less from us."

"Put together a proposal and we'll talk when you get back." Jaq closed the channel. She activated the ship-wide broadcast. "Crip, contact me in my quarters."

It took a full minute before Crip called.

"We've been through everyone, and we know them all. No Malibor sneaking around that we've found. Fire up the radars and let's see who's still out there."

"Consider it done, Crip."

Jaq hurried to the bridge. "Sensors, scan the area around all the ships. No one should be left outside."

"We've been scanning," Chief Ping replied. "There is no one left outside."

"Give me Max on *Cornucopia*," Jaq requested.

Max responded immediately. "We haven't found our man, have we?"

"No. Is there any chance he jumped while you were still underway and he's somewhere in space between here and Sairvor?"

"He was on board during the final approach. I'm almost positive of it," Max replied. "We've gone through the ships systems but in our rush to eliminate external signals, we disconnected the airlock tracking details. We have no idea when he left. He's somewhere around here, Jaq. We have to stay vigilant until we find him."

"We'll post a watch at all the airlocks, but otherwise, I'm standing down this exercise in futility. All hands, get back to work. One person from each department report to Crip in the lower cargo bay for a special assignment that also comes with an additional Malibor ration."

Jaq tried to incentivize tasks that were less than savory. An extra ration was the best she could do at the moment.

"Where did you go?" she wondered aloud.

CHAPTER 6

One may know how to conquer without being able to do it.

Max stared at his comm device. Tram and Kelvis watched him stare. When he looked up, they tore their eyes from him.

"What? Don't you two have parts to look for?"

"You lost a Malibor?" Tram quipped.

"Looks like it. Could you make me feel worse about it?"

"I didn't mean..." Tram scowled while focusing on the deck.

"Find your parts and get back to the gunship. You have work to do." Max hip-bumped Tram to let him know it was okay.

Kelvis threw his hands up in the air. "Where do we start?" The cargo bay was intimidating since it was filled floor to ceiling and side to side except for the area where they'd pulled crates to send to the troopship.

Deena laughed. "I'll show you. I was in there trying to figure out what was what but didn't succeed."

"This way." Max waved for them to follow. He released his boots and took the easy route. Deena pulled herself along behind him while Tram and Kelvis followed.

When they reached the area, Deena produced a tool to release the crate and handed it to Tram. "These six here." She waved her hand. "Good luck."

Kelvis took the tool and opened the first crate. He immediately whooped and pulled out two clear packages. "We need both of these." He kept digging while Tram tried to corral the growing bundle.

Max pulled a small cargo net off the nearby bulkhead for the very purpose of collecting and holding small bundles while in zero-gee.

Tram stuffed the parts inside.

Max and Deena stood nearby and watched.

"Don't you have anything better to do?" Tram asked pointedly.

"We don't. We're waiting for a linkup so we can return to *Chrysalis*. That's how we got onboard before the troopship tried to ram us."

"I remember. No spacesuits. It's clear. We're going to take our parts and haul buttocks back to *Matador*. Once we get this stuff installed, we'll have a modern gunship as part of our fleet."

"That's what I hear. It'll be nice to add extra punch," Max replied.

Kelvis sorted through three of the crates to get what he needed. Tram thought they had too much, but Kelvis wanted spares for the spares. The engineer beamed with his recent acquisitions.

"We'll be on our way." Tram tapped his nose and pointed. It was a dig at Max. *I can leave and you can't.*

Max wrapped his arm around Deena's waist while she clung to his neck.

Tram's smile disappeared.

"We'll have to make do."

Tram bowed his head at Max's countermove, forcing checkmate. The two shook hands. "We'll be ready soon, Max. The battle is joined."

"Victory is ours, Tram. We're so close, I can taste it. Fifty years to prepare and bending the Malibor to our will over the course of just a few months. Vengeance and justice."

Deena shifted uncomfortably. She had been raised as a Malibor. Talk of vengeance was unsettling.

"Freeing our people and all people who don't want to be in a perpetual war," Max added. "You better get back to your ship. Get it in fighting shape. The better we're prepared, the less chance we'll have to keep fighting. The Malpace fleet will be brought to its knees."

Tram nodded. Kelvis was already moving toward the airlock dragging his net filled with spare parts.

"Do you have any extra food? Sometimes we work through lunch..." Tram hinted.

"I'll grab some and meet you at the airlock." Max vaulted into the air and flew down a walkway between the crates.

Deena stayed where she was.

Tram waved over his shoulder while hurrying to catch up to Kelvis. They had kept their spacesuits on for their trip into the freighter. They recovered their helmets in the airlock and snapped them into place.

Max appeared with two hands full of Malibor food packets.

"That's it?" Tram groused.

Max laughed. "Aren't you in our spot at the port roller airlock? That means you have access to Chef's fine dining."

"But Malibor rations are better…" Tram made his best sad face.

"We'll bring more if you promise us a tour," Deena suggested from behind Max.

"Deal. Lots more. That ship is really big. It'll take two meals' worth of time to show you everything."

"It's tiny inside," Kelvis corrected. "If it takes longer than a minute to show them the ship, you're doing something wrong."

"What I'm doing right is trying to get us a stock of good food. What you're doing wrong is letting the truth get in the way of a good negotiation."

Max and Deena laughed. "We'll bring some more. No conditions. Get out of here, you goofballs." Max secured the inside hatch and cycled the airlock while Tram strapped on the mobility pack and Kelvis kept a tight grip on his spare parts.

When the external hatch opened, the two men disappeared through it into the darkness beyond.

"Why didn't you bring more of the food pouches for Tram and Kelvis?" Deena asked.

"It's important to keep Tram guessing. You can't just give him everything he wants when he wants it," Max replied matter-of-factly.

Deena shrugged. "That's it?"

"Yes, that's it. Spare the rod, spoil the child."

"What philosophy are you spewing?" Deena pushed him.

"From the old teachings of Septiman." Max clumped down the long walkway toward the bridge. He wasn't sure what he would do when he got there, but the missing Malibor was grating on his soul. "Where would Cryl Talan go that would avoid our sensors?"

"Inside. He didn't stay outside for long," Deena replied.

"How would he get in?" He caught Deena's look. "I know. It would be easy with the crush of activity that happened the second we got here."

―――

Alby suited up. Godbolt helped him. "Are you going to come back to say good-bye?"

Alby shook his head. "No. But you can come over to visit me before we go." He winked at Godbolt.

"You're leaving me with a mess and triple the workload."

"Unintentionally, mind you, but we know how well this place can work, and you're the right person to build on what's there."

"That's what I hear," Godbolt replied. "Go back to *Chrysalis*. Get yourself set up, and also, while you're relaxing, maybe you can find me eleven volunteers."

Alby shook his head but said, "No problem."

Godbolt threw her hands up. "You're not only leaving me, you're abandoning me."

"Aren't they the same thing?" Alby clapped her on the

shoulder. "I'll see you real soon. Send me out the airlock, Godbolt!"

She returned to the bridge, and he moved to the poor man's airlock. She opened the bulkhead, and he stepped inside. She closed the bulkhead and removed the air. When the outer emergency bulkhead opened, Alby stepped through, walked down the corridor, took a left, and found his way to where the ship was open to space.

Chrysalis hovered right above them. Alby knew the cargo ship was on the other side but just as close. He'd spot it as soon as he was on his way to the cruiser. He bunched his legs and pushed off toward the center of *Chrysalis*. He floated free through space.

It would have been easier with a mobility pack, but he didn't have one and wasn't about to wait.

The flight across represented the epitome of peace and freedom. He relaxed his arms and legs to fly spreadeagled. He rotated slowly to look around.

The cargo ship loomed, bigger than the cruisers but not streamlined to minimize its radar cross-section nor bristling with weapons.

It was filled with spare parts and food and things that the Borwyn couldn't have imagined in their wildest dreams. Alby couldn't wait to see what was available.

Crew zipped back and forth across the open space using mobility packs and tethers.

One individual flew past, stopped, and eased back to Alby. The individual gestured toward *Chrysalis*. Alby gave her the thumbs-up. She grabbed an arm and accelerated jerkily using the mobility pack. Once she got them straightened out, she let go. Alby was on course for the cargo bay, although he was heading in a little quicker than he found comfortable.

He had about thirty seconds to reconcile himself with his inevitable crash landing.

The cargo bay opening swallowed him as he rushed through. Crew dodged out of the way as Alby raced into the cargo netting at the back. It cushioned his impact. He hung onto the netting for a long time before a voice came through his earphones.

"Alby, is that you?" Crip pulled him sideways. "There you are. Stop goofing off and get to the bridge before they shut down the power."

"Thanks for the warm welcome, Crip."

"I'd go with you, but we're still looking for an errant Malibor." Crip scowled. "Go on."

"Holy Septiman's bad graces! Everyone is trying to get me to go somewhere else."

"I'm sure that's it." Crip touched his face shield to Alby's. "It's good to have you back, my man. I have to get to work, and so do you."

Alby moved to the airlock and departed the cargo bay. He stripped out of the spacesuit as quickly as he could and handed it to the crew member who was responsible for running it through the cleaning system and operational check before returning it to the rack for someone else to use.

Down the corridor and up the central shaft he went. He wasn't enticed by the smell of food as he would have been before, but he was drawn to a shower. He stopped two decks below the command deck and dove into the communal shower, happy to find one empty. He hung the jumpsuit he'd been wearing for the last month on the ultraviolet cleansing rack while the small jets of water pulsed over his body in little more than a mist. It stopped while he scrubbed with a bar of reclaimed soap made from algae. He floated in the warmth of the shower while waiting to hit himself with the last of the cleansing rinse. He wasn't as refreshed as he wanted to be, but he was happy that neither he nor his clothes smelled. He dressed and casually pulled himself to the bridge.

He stopped short and activated his boots so he could walk in.

Jaq waved to him and then went back to what she was doing. Alby looked around. Gil was the same, and Taurus was in the seat where he had recommended her, but there was a new guy he didn't recognize working with Dolly Norton. A stranger was at the comm station, too.

Alby instantly felt uncomfortable. He stood at the entrance to the bridge with a face full of fear and shock.

Jaq finished what she was doing and launched herself toward him. He didn't have time to step out of the way before she rammed into him. Jaq wrapped Alby in a quick hug and then let go.

"I had to finish some calculations I was in the middle of. I wasn't blowing you off," she apologized.

"It's odd seeing people I don't know."

"The volunteers from New Septimus. Amie Jacobs is on the radio. Donal Fleming is a math genius. He and Dolly are working on the problem of high-speed targeting. We flew past an armada of eight Malibor ships and only hit one. We have to do better than that."

"Did they hit you?"

"Not with anything that mattered." Jaq waved dismissively. "With some adjustments, we can improve our first strike rate. We'll need to have that in place when we run past Septimus."

"May Septiman steady the hands of His children in their quest to return to His glory," the shepherd intoned from the rear of the bridge.

Alby lowered his voice. "And some things never change." He glanced at the shepherd. When the shepherd caught his eye, Alby gave him the thumbs-up.

"May Septiman's peace calm your troubled soul."

"I'm good, Shepherd. All good here."

Jaq had to look away.

Alby and Jaq stood there in uncomfortable silence.

Jaq finally said, "We split the offensive weapons into two positions, targeting and trigger. Defensive is still one. We lost a few chain guns. You wouldn't have happened to pull any off *Butterfly*, did you?"

"They used lasers for close-in defense. Short burst, but they were busted up pretty badly in the ship's demise. Plus, we don't have the schematics for them in the first place, so we can't repair them without time to do some trial and error."

"That means you hand it over to Godbolt. We need defensive weapons. They still have an arsenal of missiles on their seven remaining cruisers." Jaq checked the main screen to confirm nothing had changed except the energy gauge, which was up to eighty-eight percent. She wasn't looking forward to powering down, but they needed the engines in top condition.

"Do we know that for sure?"

"We know they have seven cruisers remaining. Are they operational? Maybe? Probably? We have to assume they are and that their missile tubes are full and ordnance is ready to launch."

"That's why we're revising our targeting protocols. Take out the cruisers on the pass. Lessen their ability to fight us."

"At least remove their ability to fire missiles at us."

"I'll take that. Targets and triggers. Let me see how we can best work with that." Alby offered his hand. "Don't forget the gunship, too, which will be a surprise the Malibor may never recover from."

"Figure out the best time and way to deliver the surprise."

Alby grinned. "I would love to. When will Crip be back?"

Jaq shook her head. "He's looking for the Malibor."

"I'll call Tram." Alby nodded and then moved into his old seat. He caressed the frame and gel before settling in. He tapped the comm channel for a point-to-point with the now former battle commander. "Tram, this is Alby coming to you from your old chair. I need to talk about gunship deployment. Are you there?"

CHAPTER 7

Compassion separates the conqueror from the leader.

"Don't answer that," Cryl Talan said from the hatch leading into the gunship's bridge.

Tram lifted his chin to look as defiant as possible while making no move to answer Alby's call. "He'll get suspicious if I don't answer and he'll send people to check on us."

"I've secured the airlock, and you're going to release us so we can float free."

"Are you sure you want to do that?" Tram stared at the meter-long metal rod sharpened to a blade point.

"Very sure. You see, I used to serve on one of these monstrosities with seven of my closest friends. I love space. I don't love cramped space, if you know what I mean."

"I do. It's nice to be alone sometimes. Is that what you're looking for? We can find you a nice place to be free, like Farslor's surface. You could go down there and be free as a bird."

"You misunderstand what I'm doing here. I'm going to take this gunship and I'm going to destroy that Borwyn cruiser. I'm a patriot, Malibor through and through. Those other scumbags are in it for themselves, no matter what they say about their patriotism. They wouldn't risk getting hurt. They're perfectly happy sitting out the rest of the war in a Borwyn prisoner camp."

"We don't have any prisoner camps," Tram replied. "Prisoner camps? How many of us do you think there are?"

"Millions. In every shadow. Behind every tree. On Septimus and in space, too." He pointed toward where *Chrysalis* was holding station.

"Yes. It's important you believe that." Tram held steady. He made no move to release the airlock clamps.

Cryl hadn't lost his focus. "Step aside, Borwyn." He stabbed at Tram.

"How did you evade the radars?" Tram stepped back to stay out of range of the ad hoc rapier.

He pointed to Hammer's spacesuit. "It's a little big, but it made me look like your people. Evading radar? All I had to do was listen as your people told me everything they were doing." He jabbed at Tram, driving him far enough away from the console to give Cryl access.

The Malibor slashed back and forth as he looked down at the console. His erratic swings kept Tram from attacking.

Cryl tapped two buttons. He looked up, smiling. A thunk signaled the gunship's release of the airlock clamps.

"Lead the way to the engine room, please," Cryl directed, waving his makeshift rapier.

Tram released his boots and floated into the air. He

kicked off the front screen toward the hatch.

"Easy!"

Cryl jabbed Tram as he passed. Not hard but enough to tear through his clothes and slice into the flesh beneath.

Tram curled into the wound, holding himself until he hit the frame and stopped.

"Use your boots."

Tram activated his boots and they hammered into the deck. He grunted with the pain of the movement. A trickle of blood bubbled into the air.

Cryl watched emotionlessly.

"I need to bandage this," Tram said, trying to control his voice to keep it from pitching high. He had to show the courage and strength of the Borwyn. "You're Cryl Talan."

"Yes. You've announced me throughout your fleet. Everyone knows who I am, and more importantly, everyone will know who is behind the Borwyn's failure to retake Septimus."

Tram clutched at his abdomen. The cut burned as if it were filled with acid. "How many Malibor have you killed?"

"What?" Cryl waved his weapon and motioned toward the corridor.

"During the civil wars. You had what, four, five of them in the past fifty years?"

"Those were rebels. Not real Malibor. We fought for the sanctity of our way of life."

"You fought for a government that vilified its own people and is still doing that. Why were you on your way to Sairvor?"

"Put down another insurrection. They were raising their

ugly heads against their rightful leaders."

Tram nodded. "Sairvor didn't do anything. Your leaders confused us with them. We raised our ugly heads against you, not those on Sairvor."

"Bah!" He threatened Tram with his poker as he eased closer. "They still needed to be put in their place, just like you. The only thing this universe understands is power. You took over *Bessie Mae* because you had your pulse rifles. You overwhelmed us with your power. Now it's our turn, since we have the power."

"We don't have anything. A ship that isn't operational because we've taken the engines offline and even if they did work, the railguns are empty."

"Not anymore. The first order of projectiles was delivered while you were gallivanting aboard *Bessie Mae*. I've taken the liberty of inserting a minimal load in both cannons. At this range, we don't need many shots to make a big impact."

Tram's breath caught in his throat, and he forgot about his own injuries when he thought of the damage the gunship could do. The Malibor could destroy everything they'd worked for.

"I need a hand," a voice called from the corridor. "What are you doing?"

"Come where I can see you, please," Cryl called.

Kelvis looked over Tram's shoulder. "Our missing Malibor, I presume."

"I was never missing." Cryl smiled in a way that sent shivers down Tram's spine, reminding him of the pain that returned in a rush. He doubled over.

Kelvis grabbed him but immediately pulled back when he saw the blood. "You're hurt," he said, stating the obvious.

"My man, Cryl has a death saber."

"I thought it was an actuator rod," Kelvis replied. "We could use that, by the way."

"Shut up!" Cryl shouted. "Borwyn are idiots. The unwanted stepchildren of the Malibor. Now, we're going to the engine room."

Tram snorted. "Because you wanted to collect Kelvis. Since he's here, why would we go to the engine room?"

"I said shut up!" Cryl's face twisted through various levels of anger until he settled on a simple snarl. "Because I want to see how far your engineer has gotten in fixing the systems. I need to see what is at my command."

"What did you do when you served aboard one of these?" Tram asked. He continued to hold his side, but the pain was subsiding to a dull throb. His fingers were sticky with blood. They had minimal water on board, not enough to completely clean the mess.

But that was secondary to his main concern. The Malibor had a gunship that was marginally operational. He wanted to see for himself about the projectile loadout. Nothing should have been delivered, but the Malibor said it had. Did he have reason to lie? Of course. Maybe he intended to ram *Matador* into *Chrysalis*. That would cause a great deal of damage, but not as much as hitting the cruiser with railguns from a range of a hundred meters. Those would rip completely through the ship, destroying anything within.

Kelvis held Tram as they moved slowly to the ladder shaft. Zero-gee made it easier on Tram and his injury. He released his boots and floated along while Kelvis pulled him. They moved downward.

Tram tried to make eye contact with Kelvis, but the engineer was focused on getting Tram to the engine room without too many bumps. There would be no ambush of the Malibor. Tram couldn't manage it alone, and Kelvis wasn't a fighter.

They slipped into the engine room where Kelvis had already installed two of the modules. The others floated within the netting attached to the bulkhead.

"You've been busy," Tram whispered.

"When you have the right parts, a job goes quick and easy. We've grown accustomed to fixing the ship through ingenuity and innovation, which requires a greater level of understanding than just swapping out parts. Maybe we're better engineers because of it, but the ship isn't better off since everything is a compromise. Maintaining electrical flow without risking a surge through the wrong system. The right switches activate when needed. It's not straightforward."

Tram nodded. He didn't need the explanation.

Cryl waited inside the hatch, almost patiently. "Please continue," he said.

"Continue what?" Tram said.

"I'm talking to him." Cryl pointed his makeshift rapier at Kelvis. "Continue fixing my ship."

Kelvis straightened and shook his head. "I don't know why I'd want to do that."

"So you don't have to watch me slice this man into a thousand little pieces. Slowly, with much screaming."

"And you called us the unwanted stepchildren. Do you hear yourself?" Tram countered.

"I know that you're the enemy. Period."

"Just like you subverted *Bessie Mae's* crew to fly the ship for you, I'm doing exactly the same to you. You will help me fly this ship."

"Is this about us or you?" Tram tried.

Cryl lashed out, swinging wildly with his weapon. Tram tried to push closer, get beyond the sharpened end, but he wasn't able to push hard enough. The blade sliced into his uniform under his arm, creasing his rib cage. Tram clamped down with his arm to hold the blade in place. He gripped the shaft and pulled, trying to punch the Malibor in the face.

But his move was stilted, great in his mind, but poor in execution. He wasn't secured to the deck while Cryl was. The Malibor raised a foot and kicked Tram in the chest. He pulled free, the blade cutting into his arm and tracing a gash along his ribcage.

Tram screamed from the pain.

Kelvis covered his ears and closed his eyes as if that would make everything stop.

The Malibor laughed. "Now you understand what real power is. It's not technology. It's not these ships. It's attitude. Malibor have it, and Borwyn don't. You don't deserve to rule over your fellow man. That takes an iron fist!" He shook his weapon in the air. "I said, get back to work."

Kelvis held up his hands in surrender. He moved to the bulkhead like that, sufficiently cowed to not resist the Malibor.

Tram grunted as he tried to overcome the pain. He clamped his left arm against his side, hoping to staunch those wounds, while holding his stomach with his other hand to stop that bleeding. He didn't feel like he was going to die. His wounds weren't that bad, but they needed to be sewn up to stop the bleeding and start the healing process. Antibiotics to stop an infection. And fluids. Using the Malibor bathroom hadn't been pleasant, so he was half-dehydrated. He regretted that.

The only thing he could hope for was that Jaq and Crip recognized the unanswered comm for what it was. He also knew that hope was a lousy plan.

"Why is the gunship disconnected from the airlock?" Jaq asked.

"And why didn't Tram answer?"

"We found our Malibor. Bring the defensive weapons online and prepare to fire," Jaq said, focused entirely on the external view showing the gunship drifting away from *Chrysalis*.

The energy gauge ticked over to ninety percent. The power systems instantly shut down.

"Defensive systems will not energize!" Gil shouted.

Jaq hammered at her comm screen. "Bec! We need power. Give us the defensive systems." She activated the ship-wide intercom. "We need power! Bring defensive weapons online right damn now! Crip, get to Engineering. Prepare to fire on that Malibor gunship."

Alby shot upright. "Tram is on that ship. And an engineer."

"And a Malibor intent on doing us harm. Tram may already be dead."

"How did he get on board?" Alby wondered aloud.

"None of that matters right now. Tell me how we can take that ship out without power to our weapons." Jaq clenched her fists and glared at the ship on the main screen.

"Infiltration team. Send in the combat team," Alby suggested.

"They're on board *Cornucopia* and don't have any suits," Jaq replied.

"Then someone else is going to have to do it. Request permission to leave the bridge." Alby stood from his position.

Jaq glanced at him and tipped her chin.

Immediately releasing his boots, he pushed off and flew through the hatch.

Jaq added to her announcement. "Danny Johns, report to the port airlock in a spacesuit and with your gear."

The power remained off. The energy gauge had already dropped to eighty-nine percent. It wasn't that the usage was excessive, but that ninety percent was ninety-point-zero. Not one degree more. Bec had been literal in his application. She expected he'd written a subroutine that shut everything down that wasn't a critical system to prevent accidental power waste.

"Bec!" she grumbled, but it wasn't his fault. It wasn't anyone's fault. They were at war, which meant the enemy would make countermoves that were sometimes predictable and sometimes not. Just when she thought she was in front of the Malibor, they surprised her. Surprises in war were never a good thing.

Crip would be in Bec's face shortly, getting him to turn the defensive weapons power on. Then she'd give the order to take out that gunship. Remove the threat.

What if Tram and Kelvis were alive? She'd be ordering their deaths. Would the crew follow such an order?

Yes.

She hung her head and whispered, "The battle is joined." A tear dripped from her eyelash and into the air before her.

———

Max punched the bulkhead.

Brad grabbed Max's arm while talking over his shoulder. "Hammer, give your suit to Max. He has a Malibor to remove from existence."

"He took my suit. There's only one Malibor suit remaining in the aft airlock, and I'm not sure it's any good."

Brad clenched his teeth. "Get the emergency repair tape and meet us aft."

Max nodded and pushed off, moving as quickly as he could. Deena raced after him. Brad followed his son.

"Are you sure you want to do this?" Deena asked.

"I have to. It's my screwup."

"It's nobody's screwup." She caught his leg and pulled herself even with him. "How dare you try to treat them like decent people!"

Max winced at the acerbic tone. "How else would we treat them?"

"Exactly," Deena said softly. "It's their choice to act like this. They'll get smacked down until they decide to stay down, and then what will you do? You'll help them up, because that's what decent people do."

Max didn't have an answer because she was correct, even if treating them with respect had been costly. He stopped at the airlock but didn't enter.

He pulled Deena close. "My entire life has been limited to what I and my team could accomplish. I never realized how incomplete I was until you came along."

Deena pushed him. "And don't you forget it. Go take care of Mister Talan without getting yourself killed. I love you, Max Tremayne, so don't make me continue without you. I might end up with Bec."

Max laughed despite the gravity of the situation. He kissed her, longer than he should have. Cryl and the gunship were out there. He let her go and dove into the airlock to pull himself into the suit. She helped him snap the helmet in place.

"Test, test. Am I live?"

Deena pointed to her ears and shook her head. She checked the electronics package contained within the chest. It had been cannibalized and was nothing more than the shell. She gave him a thumbs-up and a smile.

The last thing he wanted to do at that moment was launch out the airlock and leave her behind, but he had a job to do.

For all the Borwyn.

He checked his pulse rifle to make sure he could operate it with the bulkier Malibor gloves. It was tight but doable. The trigger guard rotated away to give a gloved hand more room but for Borwyn gloves.

Max pressurized the suit and watched the stats come to one hundred percent, then start quickly dropping because of an air leak.

Deena grabbed the suit and tilted her head sideways to listen. She followed the suit to one spot and then a second. She pressed down on them with her hands and the rapid decline stopped.

Max tried to tell her that was it but couldn't broadcast his voice outside the suit, so he settled for the tried-and-true method.

He shouted as loudly as he could. She yelled back at him.

Brad and Hammer arrived with the tape. Deena directed them to the offending spots. They sealed them and also taped several questionable creases. They taped the remainder of the roll to the outside of his arm.

"Just in case," Brad told him.

Max gave them the thumbs-up, and they cleared the airlock. He accessed the control panel, and the air was sucked into tanks, equalizing the airlock with the vacuum outside the ship. He opened the outer hatch to study the trajectory he needed to take to get to the gunship.

It was drifting away from *Chrysalis* but was in between the Borwyn cruisers and the cargo ship. Max moved outside and closed the outer hatch. He used the suit's magnetic boots to move down the hull until *Chrysalis* was fully behind the gunship in case his attempt to launch himself at the gunship failed. Flying in space wasn't as easy as pointing at the target one wanted to hit.

He bunched his legs, released the magnetism, and pushed off.

CHAPTER 8

Sometimes, war becomes nothing more than one person against another.

Danny Johns pulled himself down the corridor, climbed into the first suit on the ready rack, and pushed toward the central shaft. He raced upward to the airlock deck. He maneuvered into the corridor and flew down it until he reached the airlock.

He found his former patrol partner already there, suited up and waiting. Instead of a pulse rifle, Carlow had a fire axe that was more pry-bar than axe, but it was a weapon worthy of close-quarters combat.

"Ready?" Danny asked.

"As ready as I'll ever be."

They entered the airlock and cycled it.

They popped the outer hatch and found the gunship farther away than they liked but not so distant it would prevent them from crossing the gap. In the distance, the cargo ship loomed as a backstop if they missed their target.

"Wait for me, you knuckleheads!" Alby said over the short-range radio.

Danny and Carlow turned to find the window in the interior hatch empty. "Where are you?" Danny asked. "Who are you?"

"Alby. Battle Commander. And I'm on my way. I heard you were heading out and wanted to wait until all of us are together. Three heads are better than two."

Danny assessed the distance once more and caught a glimmer of reflected light. "Looks like four instead of three. We'll intercept whoever is coming from the cargo hauler and wait for you on the outer hull of the gunship."

"Roger. I'm on my way. Don't enter the gunship until I get there unless you have a clear advantage. We need to stop this guy before he does any damage. Four of us could make the difference." He didn't count Tram or Kelvis because he didn't know their status. They could already be dead.

Danny Johns gestured to Carlow. They both gripped their weapons and pushed off gently, making sure they were on a direct line toward the drifting gunship.

They moved slowly through space, much more slowly than the individual approaching from the cargo ship.

"Is that tape all over his suit?" Carlow said into the silence of their travel from *Chrysalis* to *Matador*.

Danny squinted in his effort to better see the inbound individual.

"I bet it's Max," Danny replied. "We better catch him."

They had no way to increase their speed, but they were close.

"We'll hit and move hand over hand to intercept Max. We'll lock our boots and make a basket with our hands interlocked."

"He's going to blast all three of us off the hull," Carlow suggested.

"A glancing blow! But then he'll continue to *Chrysalis*. Maybe we just need to slow him down so he doesn't splatter against the big ship. It probably won't hurt him, but it won't blow his suit open, either."

They reached the gunship and gently caught an external protrusion. The heavily armored hull wouldn't transmit sounds like a thinner skin that would vibrate, but the pair didn't want to take any chances.

They pulled themselves into the line of flight of the inbound individual. Gripped a rail in one hand while clamping their boots down. They leaned into the impending impact as much as possible.

Max's face was clear through the face shield, illuminated by lights from *Chrysalis*. He reached out to catch hold of the two-hand trap set up for his arrival.

He slammed into them, chest high. Danny and Carlow pushed him toward the deck, trying to change his trajectory as much as attempting to stop his forward momentum. The two men grunted with the impact.

Max spun backward and hammered his helmet on the hull. A grasping hand caught the rail as he ripped away from the grips of his fellows. He bounced once and settled back against the gunship. Max closed his eyes for a moment before pulling himself upright and attaching his boots to the hull.

"Are you okay?" Danny asked.

Max shook his head and pointed to the side of his helmet. He then gestured toward the airlock.

Danny pressed his face shield against Max's and shouted, "Alby is coming. That will give us four. There are two airlocks. One on each side. I suggest we access them simultaneously."

Max perked up with being able to hear. "Good plan, Danny Johns! Thanks for the assist. Not sure how I got going so fast, but here we are. I don't have comm in this old suit, but I have my pulse rifle. Here's the deal. If we see this guy, we shoot this guy. We cannot have him threatening everything we've accomplished. Kill him and be done with it. Try not to destroy any equipment on the ship, but if you do, that's better than letting him go."

Danny relayed the guidance to Carlow and Alby.

They both concurred. "I'll wait for Alby on this side. You go to the other. We'll simultaneously enter the airlocks when Alby arrives."

Danny replied, "Alby says less than a minute."

Max took a step backward and gave Danny the thumbs-up. He stepped slowly across the hull to a point amidships where the airlock frame stood out. He stayed clear of the window and waited.

The Borwyn cruiser's airlock cycled, and the outer hatch opened. Alby stepped out, aimed himself, and gently pushed off. He was off course but would still hit the ship. The gunship was floating free without using thrusters.

Maybe that was a good sign that Tram and Kelvis had kept Cryl from taking over an operational gunship.

Max could only hope. He gripped his pulse rifle tightly, impatiently waiting to take off the Malibor spacesuit so he could move freely.

Alby approached the aft end of the ship. He rolled to land feet first, bending his knees to absorb the impact. He locked his boots upon impact and settled with his arms wide. He steadied himself and stood up, like he'd meant to land that way. He walked slowly toward Max.

When he arrived, Max used the manual override and opened the outer hatch. The two squeezed into the space, their bodies intertwined, head to toe. Alby cranked the outer hatch closed and activated the pressurization.

Max couldn't get out of his suit, and his pulse rifle was pressed against the bulkhead. He could rely on one thing: fury of action. He made sure he could reach the clasp on his helmet. He'd release it and rip it off the first moment he could. He needed to be able to talk with the others. A light beyond Alby's suit turned green, and Max popped his helmet open, but there wasn't enough room to take it off.

"Alby, prepare to go. Violence of action will win the day. Open the inner hatch and go. Push in and go right. I'll go left. Tell Danny and Carlow to do the same thing."

"Danny is in the airlock, but Carlow is outside. He couldn't fit."

"I guess my Malibor suit is smaller, but I wouldn't recommend it. We'll make do with three. Tell Danny to go to his right toward the engine room. That's where the work will be ongoing. I'll take the bridge. You go forward toward the weapons space."

Alby cranked on the inner handle to release the airlock but didn't have enough room to do it quickly.

He jerked away from the inner hatch. "We've been seen," Alby announced.

"Tell Danny to move. He's got a flank shot on this guy!"

Alby relayed the message.

"Stop cranking and show your hands."

"I have and I am. One hand anyway."

The airlock began to cycle. Max fought with the space to reattach his helmet but couldn't get it lined up. "Alby, you have to lean toward the inner hatch. I need to get my helmet back on."

Alby twisted, but it was no use.

"I can't get it." Max's voice was calmer than it should have been.

Alby started cranking on the manual lever to counter the Malibor's actions. They wouldn't be jettisoned into space, but they also wouldn't have any air. Alby punched at the face in the window, who started to laugh. He kept jamming the button to cycle the airlock, and Alby kept resetting it from inside. He punched feebly at the window once more.

Cryl's smile was plastered against the window as he was slammed forward with a great thump. His eyes shot wide and froze in place. He started to drift away.

Danny Johns tapped the window. He reestablished the cycle and within a few seconds, the inner hatch popped.

He pulled Alby inside, freeing Max to take off his helmet.

"Check on Tram and Kelvis!" Max called.

Danny yelled and received a reply from aft. Danny was first down the access with Alby behind him. Max headed to the bridge, but he couldn't make heads or tails of the control systems. He didn't touch anything.

Carlow appeared with his axe in hand.

"Do you understand any of this?" Max pointed at the screens.

"I can figure it out." He locked himself into the pilot's position.

Max headed to the engine room, where he found Alby and Danny working on Tram. Blood floated everywhere.

Danny looked up and then pointed. "Give me your tape."

Max ripped it from his arm and handed it over. Danny used it to secure the bandages pressed against Tram's sides and left arm.

"We need to get him back to *Chrysalis*," Alby said.

"Can you fly this thing?"

Kelvis nodded. "Give me two minutes. I had it disabled so the Malibor couldn't fly it, but I can get it up and running."

"We want to connect to the port airlock."

Kelvis was already elbow-deep into an equipment panel, working quickly to restore engine functionality.

The others moved Tram to the airlock.

Kelvis yelled that the engines were online. Carlow activated the thrusters without waiting for the engineer to arrive. A few minor tweaks and the gunship was headed back to *Chrysalis*. Kelvis appeared and took the weapons seat.

"How much damage could he have done with this thing?" Alby wondered aloud.

Kelvis frowned. "He could have destroyed both cruisers

and the cargo ship. The efficiency of the fabrication shop worked against us. They had already put an initial load of obdurium projectiles into the railgun feeds. Weapons only needed power, which we have. The capacitors were charged, something Tram insisted on during the transit here. He wanted to be able to contribute to the fight as soon as possible. Little did he know that the fight was going to be inside the gunship and not outside."

Kelvis left the engine room.

Alby contacted *Chrysalis* to have a team ready to take Tram to Doc Teller.

Jaq replied, "Doc Teller will meet you at the airlock. Good job, you guys. I didn't want to kill that ship and the people on it."

"Only one person didn't make it, and that was the Malibor." Alby looked at Danny Johns.

"He was the enemy," Danny said. "He hadn't shown us any mercy, and it looked like he was trying to space Max who couldn't get his helmet back on. I couldn't allow that."

"I'm happy that you intervened." Max clapped him on the shoulder, but he wasn't making light of the situation. He stared at Tram, who appeared to be unconscious except for the soft groans with each breath. Together, the men helped move Tram to the airlock.

"Update," Jaq requested over Alby's radio.

"Moving Tram to the airlock." He released the microphone key. "Are we docked yet?"

"Ten seconds," Kelvis yelled back.

Danny replied over the radio, "Almost there. Be ready. Tram has a few cuts that need to be sewn up and a new uniform. We'll need someone to vacuum the blood out of the air in the gunship."

Matador thumped onto the docking ring that connected the airlocks.

Kelvis said, "I'll override the airlock safeties so we can open both doors simultaneously."

It only took a few moments before the airlock pressurized, equalized with *Chrysalis*, and opened.

Doc Teller and two crew members were there with a stretcher. The old doc hurried forward to look at the patient before moving him further, but with the bandages and uniform taped down, he couldn't do anything.

"Cut from here to here—" Kelvis appeared and pointed. "—and from here to here. Also over here, but this one isn't bad except it's into the muscle."

"How much blood has he lost?" Doc Teller asked while checking his pulse.

"The Malibor didn't cut an artery," Kelvis confirmed.

"Pulse is strong." The doc pushed Tram through to the waiting assistants, who quickly strapped him down. The group hurried away.

Alby activated his comm. "Tram is in Doc Teller's capable hands." He didn't make a prognosis. The doc didn't seem shocked or worried, but that was for Doc Teller to inform the captain.

"What's with the lights?" Kelvis asked, tipping his chin toward the overhead in *Chrysalis's* corridor.

"Preventive maintenance on the ion drives. No power for a week, they told us," Alby explained.

"I'm going back to *Matador*. I have a lot of work to do

before Tram returns. I want the ship to be up and running for him. Can you bring me some of those Malibor food packs so I don't have to leave the ship, and maybe water, too?"

Alby gestured to Carlow. "Can you hook him up?"

Carlow waved and flew down the corridor.

Kelvis asked, "And if anyone wants to help on a project, I could use an extra pair of hands."

Max stepped in. He didn't have any answers for Kelvis since he'd been trapped aboard the cargo ship since Sairvor. "Let me report to the captain and then we'll see what we can do." He turned to Danny Johns. "Welcome to the team. You've done some serious soldiering for us today."

"My pleasure. I'm ready to do more, whenever you need it."

"We'll need to hook up with *Cornucopia* and get the rest of our people to *Chrysalis*. I'm not sure what to do with the other seven Malibor we have. They are becoming more of a problem than they're worth." Max's tone was ominous. "We can't just space them, but we can't have them running free, either."

Alby replied, "We'll think on it. In the meantime, we'll keep them under guard. We need to bring the cargo ship to the starboard airlock. *Chrysalis* is going to become a space station. Once we're all linked together, we'll be able to better discuss options."

Max headed down the corridor. "I'm going to get rid of this suit by sending it through the incinerator so no one else will ever wear it. It smells and is falling apart, if you haven't noticed."

The suit crinkled and crackled as Max walked slowly

down the corridor. He stopped at a comm unit and spoke softly into it, requesting to be connected to *Cornucopia* so he could talk with Brad and Deena.

Danny released his boots and pulled himself down the corridor using the upper rail to get past Max.

That left Alby by himself. He watched the others for a moment before deciding that he, too, needed to be somewhere else. Being the battle commander entailed a myriad of responsibilities, the least of which was hand-to-hand combat against a Malibor saboteur.

He breathed deeply, happy that no Borwyn had been killed and that the second crisis under his watch had been handled, which was the best he could do. Address the challenges as they reared their ugly heads, one by one, until there were none left.

The radio crackled with the broadcast channel. Crip spoke slowly, "We cannot get power to the defensive weapons for at least a half-hour."

Alby started to laugh. He keyed his microphone. "We'll make do, Crip. Thanks for trying."

CHAPTER 9

Opportunities multiply as they are seized.

Jaq met Doc Teller in the corridor outside Medical. Doc raised a hand to forestall any questions, took Tram into the examination and treatment room, and closed the door.

Presently, Vantraub popped her head out. "Doc Teller will be cleaning and stitching the wounds shortly. Vitals look good. Tram isn't in any danger. He needs some fluids to replace the blood loss and to close those slices. I have no idea how they happened."

Jaq thanked the engineer, surprised to see her working in Medical when Engineering was conducting a thorough maintenance scrub of the engines.

Vantraub disappeared into the exam room before Jaq could question her about it.

"Go to the source," Jaq counseled herself. She flew down the corridor and dove into the central shaft to travel to the engineering level. She pulled herself out of the shaft and stopped before the closed hatch. She thought long and hard about entering before taking the big step.

Bec was going to be trying, but she'd let his verbal attacks flow past her like meteorites descending through the atmosphere of an M-class planet.

She was pleased to pass the first test of her resolve. The hatch to Engineering was unsecured. Jaq opened it slowly to not upset anything happening within. She found music playing and the lights bright, unlike the rest of the ship. She'd assumed they would be reduced, but it made sense that they needed to be able to see what they were doing.

Jaq didn't want to be angry, so despite summoning the courage to visit Engineering, she changed her mind and took the path of least resistance. She'd visit them in one week to make sure they delivered on time, while staying in touch with Teo for reasonably delivered updates. Jaq slowly stepped away from the hatch, but it was too late.

"Jaq! Come on in. This is where the party is," Teo called.

"There's no party. Go away," Bec grumbled.

Jaq started laughing, stepping across the threshold and into Engineering, but that was it. She didn't move any farther inside. "I only wanted to give you my encouragement and support. We can send down food and drinks. Everyone can use a bag of chernore to start their day or to make a bad day better."

"Not me," Bec snapped.

Jaq closed her eyes and thought of asking him what was wrong. When she opened her eyes, she found Teo staring at her, expression pleading for Jaq to stay. She rolled up her sleeves and clumped ahead.

Bec groaned and rolled his head like he'd been subjected to the worst news of all time.

Jaq had to bite her lip. She managed to say, "How's it going?"

"We have started the process. We also have a wish list of parts that we could use from *Cornucopia*."

"We're going to bring *Cornucopia* to the starboard airlock. You'll be able to look for yourselves, because no one else will know exactly what you want."

"What a waste of time!" Bec blurted.

"If this were a planet with a blue sky, green leaves, and joy, you would be the one dark cloud trying to rain on everything, but you know what? It takes rain for everything to grow. So, my rainy cloud boy, how about you take your happy hairy buttocks to the cargo ship and find what you need? If you have new stuff, then you'll spend less time trying to find creative ways to make the old equipment work."

"Happy hairy buttocks..." Teo repeated.

"What happened to food and drinks?" Bec asked.

"Since you'll be out, you can probably pick those up yourself. Make sure you get something for Teo."

Jaq waved and took a step toward the door.

"Hey!" Bec shouted.

"I'm sorry. Don't you have work to do? I'll let you know when the cargo ship is accessible."

"I'll go!" Teo called. She extricated herself from her work in a tangle of wires. She smiled at Bec. "You got it, Bec-man." She grabbed his collar and pulled to help accelerate herself over his head and toward the hatch. He feebly slapped at her as she passed.

Jaq hurried through the hatch, and Teo closed it once she was in the corridor.

"Is he insufferable?" Jaq asked.

"Nah. He's fine. You get under his skin, though, but big sisters have a tendency to do that. Those idiot brothers of mine were always fodder for my practical jokes." She shook her head. "They're not really idiots."

"Hammer took a pulse rifle." Jaq looked sideways at the young engineer.

"Oh, that. Maybe he fell on his head one too many times. We had gravity growing up, and in his case, that may have been a drawback. As for the pulse rifle, he should have known better. I should probably stop defending those two. They're old enough to make their own way."

"How is the rebuild going?"

"Just maintenance and streamlining. Bec is a little more aggressive than I would be."

Jaq recoiled from the revelation. "Keep your eye on him because we don't want anything to break. Our next run is going to stress the engines, plus we may take a great deal of incoming fire."

"Nothing we can do about that except pray to Septiman they don't hit the engines. The plan is to put in better circuit breakers to reduce the chance that an impact on the system would create an overload resulting in a cascade failure. We just want the system to shut down so we can replace the part. Those parts are what I have to find."

Jaq gestured for Teo to follow her down the corridor. She accessed the comm unit on the bulkhead to contact the bridge. "When will the cargo ship marry up to our airlock?"

"They are maneuvering it right now, but we have to adjust, too, so *Cornucopia* doesn't bump into *Butterfly*. We're close, but it'll be better if we create a little standoff distance," Crip replied.

"We'll meet the ship at the starboard airlock."

"Port. We're moving the gunship to the other side as the cargo ship will marry up better with the roller on the port side."

"A game of Jangle getting the odd bits and pieces to fit."

"We'll be done soon. We have expert pilots moving each of the ships."

"Who's flying *Matador*?" Jaq asked skeptically.

"Kelvis, of course, because Tram is hanging out in Medical acting lazy, getting bottle fed, and generally basking in the light of adulation."

"Envious?" Jaq quipped. "Tram is going to be okay. We're all worried about him, but back to Kelvis. He's the engineer who built the fissile capsule to power the engines on the Malibor gunship."

"He assures us he's an expert flyer."

"Why do you believe him?"

"Because there isn't anyone else. He's as expert as anyone we can find. Is there anything else? I should probably sound the collision alarm. Gotta run." The green light on the comm unit went out.

Teo chuckled while grabbing onto the corridor's center rail.

Jaq thought he was joking until a second later when the collision alarm arruga'ed throughout the ship.

Jaq grabbed the rail with both hands and extended her

body across the corridor to lock her boots on the far bulkhead. She flinched while waiting for the hideous sound of metal getting sheared from the ship.

But the impact never came. A minute later, Crip sounded the all-clear signal. He spoke over the intercom. "All hands, we are clear. The former Malibor gunship is now accessible at the starboard airlock, and the port airlock has the cargo ship attached. Anyone needing parts or supplies, please join me at the port roller airlock for accountable access to the cargo ship."

"That was exciting. Shall we?" Teo asked.

"I'm going to kick Crip right in his hairy buttocks." Jaq smacked one hand into the other.

"What is your fascination? Do you think my dad has those?"

"Your dad? What?"

Teo kicked toward the central shaft.

"What are you talking about?" Jaq pressed.

"You know he has a thing for you." Teo interlaced her fingers behind her head and floated toward the midship decks.

"I know." Jaq caught up with her. "What happened to your mom?"

"Killed in an accident setting up the production facility. When we tried to expand, things didn't go well. That's why we stopped at four scout ships. We didn't contemplate starting it up again until you arrived. It took a lot for Dad to change his mind on that."

"It took the possibility of defeating the Malibor and returning to Septimus."

"It took more than that, Jaq."

"We have a lot of work to do. Maybe we should focus on that."

"Maybe. You're going to have to face it. He'll keep giving you those big brown eyes of his."

"This is your dad we're talking about," Jaq replied. She pointed and dodged out of the shaft to join the random crew members queueing up at the airlock. She made her way to the front. "Engine parts."

The crew congenially offered for the captain and the engineer to take the first position.

The airlock cleared and the hatch opened. First person through was Brad. Jaq tried to step back, but Teo blocked her. She looked over her shoulder to see the young woman's infectious smile.

"Jaq!" Brad bellowed. He caught her in a hug and would have swung her around if her boots hadn't been rooted to the deck.

"Nice try," she told him. "Can you point us to where we might find electrical components? Better yet, take Teo and show her. I've got a combat team to recognize."

"Always the captain and never the voluptuous woman." Brad winked.

Teo made gagging noises.

Jaq replied, "If by voluptuous you mean short and blocky, I'm your girl. You two get to work. We've got to get those engines back online in a week. That means finding the parts soonest."

Brad waved and turned to head back into the airlock, but the combat team was pushing the Malibor crew through.

"Buster," Jaq said by way of greeting.

"You people are evil. Borwyn are the enemy!" he shot back.

"Blah, blah, blah." She jerked a thumb over her shoulder.

The combat team pushed the group toward the central shaft. The forward storage area awaited their arrival.

"Brad, you can fly this thing?" Jaq wondered aloud.

"How do you think we made it to the airlock? No need for the Malibor crew." Brad tipped his chin toward them. "They're not bad people, Jaq."

"They've only done bad things. We'll keep them on ice until we've won this war, although that's not optimal. Maybe your people on New Septimus can watch them," Jaq suggested.

"That'll be a hard sell, but it's better than keeping them on board the Borwyn flagship."

Jaq nodded.

Hammer stood in the airlock, watching sheepishly.

Jaq waved him in. "Join the combat team, Hammer, and secure the prisoners."

He grinned while racing after the group.

Deena was last out. Max rushed in, and they met in the corridor.

"Jaq, will you marry us?" Max blurted.

Jaq stared with her mouth open.

"We're going to look for those parts," Brad said. "Wish us luck."

Teo giggled at the look on Jaq's face. She and her father disappeared into the cargo ship.

"Wouldn't you rather marry each other?" Jaq replied once she had collected her wits.

"Funny, Jaq."

"Set it up with Shepherd and Chef. We'll hold the ceremony on the mess deck. Now get out of here. The rest of us have work to do."

"We'll point people toward the right cargo pallets," Deena said. "After ten days on that tub, I don't wish anyone to wander around lost."

That left Jaq by herself to conduct the orderly movement from *Chrysalis* to *Cornucopia*. "Let's go, people. Philo first. What are you looking for?"

"Food."

"That's easy. I think food is about seventy-five percent of the cargo. No matter where you look, you'll probably find it."

"Next!" Jaq pumped her fist in the air.

"Food."

She looked skeptically at the crew member looking at the overhead while keeping her hands behind her back.

"How many of you are here for food?"

All of them raised their hands.

"Make sure it gets to the mess deck, you bunch of knotheads." Jaq waved them through until she was alone.

Crip showed his face from the far end of the corridor.

"Aren't you grounded?" Jaq called.

"Alby's on the bridge. The parade between the ships has renewed without the threat of an infiltrator. We're doing everything we're supposed to be doing." Crip rubbed his hands together and waved away his responsibilities.

Jaq took a few steps. "Get someone to stand watch at the airlock."

"Why?" Crip asked. "If we're space pirates, then everyone gets an equal share of the spoils. And think about this. Nearly all of our crew have never stepped foot outside this ship. *Cornucopia* is an entirely new experience."

Jaq mulled over the insight. "Sometimes, I take things for granted. I'll make an announcement and encourage everyone to take some time, visit the gunship at the starboard airlock, and take a stroll through the cargo ship."

Crip nodded. "I think that's a good call. They may take a memento or two and so what? Let them have their spoils of war."

"You have a different perspective than I do. I want good order and discipline. I want the crew to stay true to their roles and responsibilities. But you're right. Let them live. Show them what their labors have produced. Give them a reason to keep driving themselves, above and beyond their duty to their fellow Borwyn."

Crip pushed back and floated toward the central shaft. "I think you're needed on the bridge."

"Why's that?" Jaq asked.

"Because I'm going to get some of that fine Malibor chow. Your orders, Captain. One of us is supposed to be on the bridge."

"I think it should be you, but since we have no power and there's nothing we can do, I'll join you. I don't remember the last time I ate."

They moved casually to the mess deck, greeting the crew they passed with smiles and kind words.

"These people will die for the cause, which has to always be clear. Free Septimus," Jaq whispered.

"The battle is joined, and we *will* win." Crip lifted his chin and clenched his jaw.

"It takes that attitude. I'm not sure we've been tested yet," Jaq said.

"We have been, but our people are so good that when we look back, it doesn't seem as bad as it was. The ship has two major repairs along the primary framing. We're lucky we can fly straight."

"Thanks to a thirteen-year-old welder, among others."

Only two crew were lounging at the tables when Jaq and Crip entered. They popped up to leave the second they saw who had entered.

"Don't leave on our account," Crip told them.

"We've been here long enough. I don't want Chef to kidnap us for kitchen duty. It's not our turn until next week."

"Married couples work together…" Jaq muttered.

"They always have." Crip didn't understand.

"You didn't hear?" Jaq chuckled. "Max and Deena are getting married. He's going to be working for Chef every now and again."

Crip joined the captain in seeing the humor. "Good for them. He was absolutely smitten. He needed to wear her down over decades like I did with Taurus. I thought I was being a good role model."

Jaq shook her head.

They reached the counter, where Chef stood with crossed arms. "No one wants our processed food anymore. We went from a shortage to a glut. What am I supposed to do with the excess? We've never had such reserves before. And where is my assistant, Deena? I heard you mention her name."

"She and Max are getting married," Jaq replied.

"Great! I get an extra set of hands. That young man goofs off way too much."

"He's not that young," Crip clarified.

Chef waved her hand to dismiss the information. She handed them greens and algae protein.

The captain tried not to look disappointed.

Crip took his while sticking his tongue out.

"No thanks. I use the bidet," Chef replied.

"Gross," Jaq mumbled at the old joke. "Thanks, Chef. We'll send packets over to *Butterfly* and *Matador*."

"We need more water, like a thousand cubic meters. Tanks are low," Chef said.

"I've been watching it," Jaq replied. "They're not danger low. We need to drag an ice chunk to the ship for reclamation."

"Do you think the gunship could do it?" Crip asked between sips from his microgreens bag.

"That is a great idea. We don't have to extend our presence here. Let's go talk to Tram."

"Isn't he still in Medical?"

Jaq frowned. "I better check in on him. And then on Kelvis, who is working on the gunship. And you can go back to the bridge."

Crip nodded and finished his meal. It had taken all of two minutes. That was the benefit of eating processed foods. They were easy to digest and quick to consume but eliminated the opportunity for recreational eating, a pleasure the crew of *Chrysalis* had never been exposed to.

The team working on *Butterfly* had started them. It would affect the entire crew and soon, mealtimes would take longer.

Jaq conceded the point. "We'll get to enjoy that good Malibor food soon. I'll call for a ship-wide feast as part of Max and Deena's marriage. They deserve it."

"We all deserve it, Jaq. Don't count yourself separate."

"I get to officiate. I'll definitely be there." Jaq headed out on a tangent. "We win together. All of us. This is another step forward. A Borwyn-Malibor marriage, and I hope it's not the last."

"That's a funny way to look at a war," Crip suggested. "Marry our way to the hearts and minds of the enemy."

"Make love, not war," Jaq quipped. "It shows that we have a lot more in common than different. There's no way we'll be able to remove a million Malibor from Septimus, so we have to find a way to live together."

"That's a big ask. Really big. We have to destroy their fleet to give us time to negotiate but, in the end, we're still a little over a thousand making demands of a million."

"Which leads me to our strategy. Think about this, but keep it to yourself. I want you to take the combat team to the surface and meet up with the Borwyn outside the cities. See if they can be formed into a ground army."

Crip winced at the suggestion. "We can't take a lander because it'll be ripped apart from the speed. You're thinking we'll take the gunship."

Jaq nodded.

"It'll be easier to pass ourselves off as Malibor until we can hit the ground and disappear. I want to talk with Max about this, and his bride-to-be. She knows more about the Borwyn who are living in the wild than anyone else we have access to. I wouldn't trust the crew of the cargo ship. Damn, Jaq. That's a bold move."

Crip stared at the table as he contemplated the impact.

"We're in this war to win, which means sacrifice. We've already lost too many people, and we're going to lose more. Whoever goes down to Septimus is going to be without support. We'll be flying away at a high rate of speed and won't be back for a long time even if we only circle Armanor and return. It'll be ten days, two weeks. I don't know. It depends how aggressively we want to decelerate."

"You've thought through this long and hard, haven't you?"

Jaq nodded again, tightlipped. She didn't need to tell him what he already knew.

"You lose the gunship to distract the Malibor."

"Not really. They drop you off and then head back to space. Will they escape Malibor control? That's the question. I have confidence in Tram and Kelvis and maybe one more. The rest of the space going in will be taken by the combat team, which will include Deena and you."

"Volunteer doesn't have to start with the word 'I,' does it?"

"Not when we need the right people to open a second front against the Malibor, bring all resources to bear against our enemy until they understand that peace is the better option."

"Like you said, you have a big ask. That's a lot, Jaq, but I understand. Let me think through it and see what kind of loadout we'll need to make this work. We'll need a radio, which means one big antenna to send signals into space."

"And there will be a massive time lag in comms, so we have to use a burst instead of having a conversation."

Crip stood, keeping his boots connected to the deck. He studied Jaq's expression, knowing that she wasn't kidding. This was as serious as she got. Life for the Borwyn had become a series of calculated risks, each with a greater and greater reward until the final payoff delivered a free Septimus.

Or death. It was the only way they would stop. As long as one Borwyn lived, the dream of returning to Septimus would remain.

CHAPTER 10

Every meal's a feast. Every day's a holiday.

Jaq leaned against the captain's seat and watched the main screen. The outside view had been replaced by a checkerboard of status updates. Energy had dropped to seventy percent, which left them using six to eight percent a day, well within what Jaq considered acceptable. If they maintained the same usage trend, they would have more than thirty percent remaining when the engines came back online.

The fabrication section was using the most to smelt fixtures needed to integrate the Malibor spares. Seizing the cargo ship had been their greatest victory in the war.

What to do with the crew, she thought. Maybe New Septimus. She'd have to bend Brad's ear, but when he was in a less amorous mood, which seemed to be never. Would she be like Taurus and get worn down over time? Or maybe she would select her time, like after Septimus was liberated.

A partial inventory of the cargo ship scrolled within its

own window on the screen. They'd been able to identify much, but some of the spares were for systems that the Borwyn didn't have, such as ground attack vehicles. The engines required air to operate, which then became polluted with exhaust, so they weren't useful on a closed system like a spaceship.

Still, New Septimus might find something to do with them.

Or the combat team once it was on Septimus. That thought kept her awake during her sleep cycle. She liked the people on the team and couldn't imagine a scenario where they weren't obliterated by a massive Malibor counterattack.

One thing Brad's people didn't know was what the Malibor ground forces looked like. That meant Jaq gave them superhuman abilities in gross numbers with unlimited logistical support, enough to turn the Borwyn-held areas into a desert wasteland.

The fact that the Malibor had not already done so should have given Jaq solace that her worst case was overblown.

"Looks like it's about time," Taurus said.

"Aren't you carrying the bouquet?" Jaq asked.

"Aren't you conducting the ceremony?" Taurus countered. She stood and straightened her uniform, but in zero-gee, it didn't stay that way.

Jaq did the same thing. "Look okay?" she asked.

Tram smiled. "The same as you always do."

"I'm not sure that's what I was going for. Maybe you could have told me that my face is extraordinarily ordinary."

"I can say it if you want." Taurus released her boots and pushed toward the corridor.

"No need. I'm good. I'll stop by my quarters first. I'll be along shortly."

"I'll let them know."

Jaq walked down the corridor, taking her time. In her quarters, she wanted to do nothing more than get a drink of water. They hadn't captured an ice chunk yet because the gunship hadn't left the airlock. Kelvis wouldn't take the ship out alone, and Doc Teller had not yet released Tram.

Time was ticking down. Jaq didn't want to give the Malibor time to regroup. Her strategy was to put them on their heels and keep them there. The added benefit was that they still believed it was a Malibor uprising and not the return of the Borwyn.

That was where the idea of landing a team and rallying those left behind had come from.

Jaq studied herself in the mirror. The uniform looked like it always had, but she looked older. An original's face stared back at her, and it wasn't a look that she liked. "When did that happen?" she wondered aloud.

Since *Chrysalis* returned to the active combat zone. It started with the first engagement around Farslor and continued to this day.

But this was a happy occasion. Chef was gaining a newlywed couple in her quarters, which made no sense, but the three got along and space was at a premium on board *Chrysalis* even with adding crew to *Butterfly* and *Matador*. The cargo ship would need a minimal maintenance team, but the crew aboard *Butterfly* could do that since they'd count on the ship for their supplies.

Jaq yanked her attention back to the matter at hand—a marriage ceremony.

She left her quarters before her mind could wander once more. The ship was completely shut down. They would squeeze the entire crew onto the mess deck level, where they'd fill the corridors. It would be a tight fit, but the celebration was something for all. Malibor food packs had been stockpiled and were ready to distribute. Two for each crewmember to eat now or later. It was a feast, a chance to do something to excess.

And to carry them through to a period of austerity, where they would travel to Septimus and deliver a blow of epic proportions.

That was the plan, anyway. She needed an original and a teenage prodigy to successfully deliver the calculations to the targeting computer. The E-mags were ready, they only needed to be pointed in the right direction at a very small point in the void through which an enemy ship would pass while both ships were traveling at a combined three hundred thousand kilometers per hour.

In the central shaft, Jaq found the crew overflowing the deck where the mess was located. She eased in over their heads and used the upper rail to pull herself to the mess deck. She took care not to kick anyone in the head, but the crew helped by holding their hands up. She could have surfed along them had she wanted.

Inside, she found a space had been cleared by the serving counter. She eased to the deck and activated her boots for the final walk to the front. She found Max and Crip and Deena and Taurus.

"Congratulations, you crazy kids." Jaq shook each of their hands in both of hers. She was always happy to see the crew commit to long-term relationships since the entire Borwyn population had consisted of those aboard *Chrysalis*. With the discovery of New Septimus and that Borwyn were still on Septimus, the necessity to continue the species was less, but Jaq was from a prior generation and her attitude was instilled deep within.

"What about you two?" she asked, pointing at Taurus and Crip.

"Sure, why not?" Crip replied with a sly smile.

Taurus shook her head. "You never even asked me."

Jaq crossed her arms and smiled while watching.

Crip caught her. "What?"

"Nothing like a good fight for pre-wedding entertainment." Jaq grinned.

Crip pulled Taurus to him and whispered in her ear. She whispered back. "Okay, we're in. Marry us, too."

"I was joking."

"We're not," Crip confirmed.

"Two for one. Sounds like a good deal." Jaq raised her hands to quiet the crowd.

Brad waved from the first row. He pointed at himself and then Jaq. "Three?"

"Cool your jets, mister." Jaq looked down to stare at her boots. "You may wear me down, but that's not happening today. We'll administer these two and then start the feast."

Amie brought up the comm system. "Ship-wide is live, Captain."

"I retain the hope for perpetual joy," Brad continued.

"You want me to marry some old guy?" Jaq countered.

Amie waved frantically.

"I'm not just some old guy. I'm a virile starship captain, emphasis on the virile part." He winked and smiled.

"Ship-wide comm is live!" Amie screamed.

Jaq assumed her best stoic countenance. "All hands, this is the captain speaking. We're here today to celebrate not one, but two marriages, bonding beyond a verbal commitment. It also gets them combined quarters, where they lose space to gain a partnership in Septiman's timeless embrace."

"Three weddings!" someone shouted from the corridor.

"Two weddings," Jaq emphasized. "And because we're all here for the feast, I ask Max and Deena to deliver their vows."

Max spoke first at the look of shock on Deena's face. "I am blessed to be your partner in life."

Deena leaned close and whispered, "Is that what I'm supposed to say?"

Max nodded.

"I'm blessed to be your partner." Deena said the phrase as if it was a single word.

Jaq nodded toward Crip and Taurus.

"In witness whereof, Taurus and I stand before all hands and make a commitment of love and a life shared, that we may face all obstacles in the future as we have in the past. I am honored to be your partner."

Taurus gave him the side-eye, a look that only a married couple could share, after his tedious deviation from the usual script. Crip beamed, and Taurus laughed.

Once she composed herself, she replied, "You'll do."

"And there we have it! Congratulate the happy couples, and let the feast begin," Jaq bellowed.

"Missiles are loaded," Alby confirmed. "New missile guidance programs are installed. I have high confidence that they'll kind of work. I recommend short-range employment only."

"It'll be your call, Alby. I'm not feeling a lot of confidence in your disclaimer of 'kind of.' Don't waste them and don't save them if they can keep us from getting killed," Jaq replied.

She drifted around the bridge as she did, never staying in her seat more than she had to. She felt like she spent too much time in it as it was.

"I'll do my best." Alby crossed his arms while staring at his screen. He frowned with the lack of revelation.

Crip fidgeted in his seat before sharing the bad news with the captain. "*Matador* has not found any ice."

Jaq calmly cruised across the bridge to settle at Crip's position. "Then we'll have to take *Chrysalis* in search of a supply." At Crip's look, she continued, "There is no other choice."

"It impacts our timeline."

"Only by a day or two. We'll deliver what excess stock we have, restrict water usage, and then go find it. With our sensors, I give it a day before we find what we need and can set course for Septimus. We can't head directly there, no matter what."

The Malibor would backtrack the course to find the

origin. Whether they could strike it or not was up for debate. Jaq didn't want to give the Malibor even a hint that the Borwyn had established a base beyond Farslor's moon. It was easier to avoid a battle than to hope it didn't happen. The Borwyn had no way to defend themselves if the ERS was attacked. They needed to make like a hole in the sky, and that meant *Chrysalis* had to fly perpendicular to their desired course before heading down the star's gravity well on a heading toward Septimus.

Jaq glanced at the clock on the screen that counted down the seven days the engine was supposed to be offline. She hadn't bothered Bec or Teo beyond turning Teo loose to find spare parts.

The clock ticked down to one, turned red, and started counting upward. The engines remained offline.

"Crip?"

"He responds so much better to you," Crip replied, smiling.

The lights dimmed further than they already were before brightening. The energy gauge had hit thirty percent but changed to reflect that it was charging.

"Bec will probably claim they finished early," Crip suggested.

Jaq accessed her comm for a direct link to Engineering. "Right on time, Bec, and thank you."

"We're early by nearly twenty-four hours!" he shot back.

Jaq closed her eyes. "Are you going to realize the efficiency gains you were shooting for?"

Bec replied, "The engines are protected from a

catastrophic disassembly. They will shut down rather than go critical and destroy the ship."

"I'll take it," Jaq said with her eyes still closed. "Thanks, Bec." She closed the channel before he could get any deeper under her skin.

Brad braced himself in the hatchway. "Let's go see them," he suggested.

"The last thing I want is to get into it with Bec. He sounded contented, and despite his claim of being a day early, seven days is one hundred and sixty-eight hours, not the seventh day which would be the eighth day. Sometimes, Bec's logic is not anyone else's logic."

"It has nothing to do with logic," Brad replied, nodding toward the corridor. "It's just Bec trying to play mind games."

She didn't want to respond to such a summons, but his daughter was in Engineering, too. Jaq could thank her for keeping Bec on track.

Jaq grabbed the mid-rail and launched herself toward the hatch.

Brad headed down the corridor. She followed him to the central shaft, where he executed a somersault, missed the rail, and slammed into the far wall. He rolled and kicked back to the guide rail.

Jaq executed the somersault, caught the rail, and redirected her momentum downward, flying like a missile and using one hand to keep pulling and increasing her speed.

Brad had no hope of catching up.

She waited for him at the bottom of the shaft. He showed up wearing a look of defeat.

"My ship. I've been doing this for forty years. You gravity weenies are spoiled."

"Is that all I am to you, a gravity weenie? I feel like there's more to me than that."

She chuckled. "You bring four scout ships and a thousand Borwyn, too. It's nothing to sneeze at. We need all Borwyn embracing this fight."

"They are," Brad replied. Her expression suggested that wasn't it. "What aren't you telling me?"

She looked around to make sure they were alone. "We're going to drop the combat team on Septimus to rally the Borwyn who have been left behind. Only then will we have all the Borwyn on board."

Brad stopped his posturing and playing. "I never contemplated that." His face fell when he realized what that meant.

His boys were on the combat team.

"All volunteers. No one has to go who doesn't want to, because this could very well be a one-way trip. First challenge will be to convince the Borwyn of who we are, and the second will be to start wreaking havoc in the Malibor backyard. They need to know they are at war with the Borwyn once more, and it's a war they won't win."

"Are you going to aim at the space station?"

"Killing their families won't get them to the negotiating table. We had better not destroy that station. I'll count on your people to send us updated intel on ship locations while we're inbound. If the entire fleet is attached to the station, we're going to have a big problem. We need most of the spacecraft to be separate so we can get shots without jeopardizing the station."

"Do you have confidence in the targeting program?" Brad asked.

"More than I had before. I'd prefer if we didn't have to make any miracle shots bending around the station. We need direct shots with deep space or the moon as a backdrop. No errant rounds peppering Septimus or the station."

"Makes sense. I suspect you have the angle of approach already figured."

Jaq nodded while turning the center wheel on the hatch to Engineering. Engineering was clean without a single tool floating or panel open. Bec looked to be asleep, even though he had spoken with Jaq not five minutes prior. Teo floated serenely with her hands behind her head.

"Good job, Proteus. I'm happy that you're able to expand your mental horizons," Brad told his daughter.

"I'm learning a great deal—most of all, how not to kill someone who's even more obnoxious than my brothers. I feel like I've been training my whole life to not kill people."

Jaq and Brad looked at each other.

"You're welcome," Jaq said, having nothing better on the tip of her tongue.

"What's your plan?" Brad asked.

"Sleep, eat, and sleep some more," Teo replied. "Everything is on automatic down here as an additional upgrade. Despite Bec's refusal to consider it, it's done. We'll watch to make sure nothing breaks, but otherwise, we could have the easiest job on the ship."

"I love it when the crew makes themselves obsolete," Jaq said. "I look forward to the day this ship becomes a museum.

Until then, *Chrysalis* is the most lethal warship in the system."

"When do we start the run to Septimus?" Teo asked while continuing to lounge.

"As soon as we've charged to one hundred percent," Jaq replied before adding, "and replenished our water supply."

"Sixteen hours."

"That's how much time you have until we get underway."

"Sounds like two sleeps and four meals. Perfect." Teo kicked off the overhead and inverted to land feet first, her boots thumping to the deck as the magnets engaged.

"I'll leave you to it." Jaq walked slowly from the engineering section. Brad hugged his daughter and whispered something in her ear before taking his leave. He secured the hatch behind him.

Jaq was halfway into the central shaft when Brad called, "Jaq, wait up."

"Are you going to make a pass at me, because if you are, save it for a better time."

Brad chuckled. "What I hear you say is I have a chance, even as an old guy."

"Of course you have a chance. Look at me and then look at you. I'd be a fool to not take a chance, but I can't right now. There is nothing more important than this ship and this crew. Don't make me say it again."

"We walk into the sunset on Septimus?"

"Together. And then we'll have lost time to make up for."

"Don't you dare die on me, Jaq Hunter. You win this war,

and do it while you're still upright so you can keep your promise to me."

She held out her hand, but Brad was having none of that. He gripped her by the shoulders and moved in. She nodded slightly, and he planted his lips on hers.

"Dad!" Teo called from behind him.

Jaq waved and headed up the central shaft.

"Look what you did," he told Teo, scowling.

Jaq's laughter echoed through the hatch.

CHAPTER 11

Power comes from the soul, whether an atom's or a human's.

"*Cornucopia* is detached with a skeleton crew aboard. *Butterfly* is staffed and continuing dismantlement. *Matador* is standing by to trail us on our secondary trajectory. Energy is at one hundred percent, and the board is green. We are ready to get underway," Crip reported.

"Move us away from the flight hazards," Jaq ordered. "All ahead slow."

Mary and Ferd bumped knuckles before engaging their controls. Thrusters angled the ship toward a clear route away from the ERS. The engines started at ten-percent thrust until they were ten kilometers away, then advanced the drive to thirty percent.

"Sensors outboard. Find us that chunk of ice, Slade." Jaq pointed at the sensor section.

"Dishes are directed and transmitting," Chief Ping

reported. "I see why *Matador* was unsuccessful. There's nothing close except bare rock. I'm extending the range."

Jaq waited.

"Still nothing," the chief said.

"Take us along the asteroid field, all ahead standard. One-point-two gee acceleration. Crip, set Condition Two throughout the ship. Let's practice with the new E-mag targeting program."

"I'm all over that!" Alby replied with the greatest enthusiasm. The ship accelerated.

Jaq sighed in delight with the return of gravity. It wouldn't last long as they'd have to slow to a stop once they discovered what they needed. In the asteroid belt, asteroids of ice were common following a comet's impact at some point in the distant past.

They had recovered ice in the past, as needed. Their tanks carried twice the capacity they needed with their closed system and filters that created a nearly one-hundred-percent efficiency resulting in minimal loss. When they supplied *Butterfly* and *Cornucopia*, they had depleted their excess. With the new crew members, there had been more waste than usual.

They couldn't continue the war without refreshing their water supply. They'd search as long as they had to. Water was life, no matter what the level of technology or where one was in space. No water. No life.

Jaq settled in. The sensors were pinging rocks more than two hours away at their present speed. They'd have to slow their acceleration soon to ensure they could stop when they needed to. Ice was out there. They only had to find it.

They were skirting the inside of the asteroid belt, which hid their radar signature and prepared them to head toward Septimus when they were far enough away from Farslor to make their origin unclear.

Misinformation and disinformation. Jaq counted on the gunship to help create confusion.

"Check on Max and his team. We probably have a couple days before they cross-deck to the gunship."

"I'm going, too, or did you change your mind?"

"*You* probably have a couple days..."

Crip smiled. Taurus was less than amused by Crip's insistence on joining the team. She couldn't go since she had no role on the team and added no combat value. Deena wasn't a soldier, but she knew the Borwyn on the planet and the Malibor. She would be their diplomat and negotiator.

Crip stepped to Taurus and kissed her on the head.

"Don't get yourself killed," she told him.

"I'll do my best while making sure Max knows he's going to get his ass kicked if I die and he doesn't." Crip laughed at his own joke.

"That's not funny." Taurus tried to shame him, but he was beyond that. He wouldn't be the butt of a sedate life.

"We're going to liberate Septimus," he promised.

"Yes, we are," Taurus agreed. She stood and hugged him tightly until he felt like the bridge crew was staring at them.

He gently pushed himself away. "I'm coming home to you. After all this time, I'm not going to screw it up by dying."

Taurus nodded, tightlipped.

Crip reluctantly waved to Jaq, the only one watching them despite Crip's discomfort.

She watched because of his discomfort.

Once he was gone, Jaq found her way to the offensive weapons officer. "It'll be worth it in the end," Jaq said.

"Doesn't make it any better now," Taurus replied.

Jaq found her ability to console was impacted by her focus on the mission. Would she sacrifice everyone on board to achieve victory? If not all, how many would it take before she couldn't justify the war?

Before they found the other Borwyn, they couldn't make the ultimate sacrifice. They couldn't trade lives for progress, but now they could. How many were too many?

That was the question Jaq would wrestle with until the war was over. "We can't allow any sacrifices to be in vain." The bridge crew watched her closely. She realized she'd spoken out loud. "Everything we do must be measured against that standard."

Taurus teared up but didn't break. She maintained her composure while returning to her screens.

Alby glanced at Donal. "Are we ready?"

"I want to stress the targeting program. We'll need to pick three asteroids and rotate back and forth between them. We aren't traveling very fast, yet, but we should get some good data."

"Fire it up," Jaq called out. "Set Condition One throughout the ship. All hands, battle stations. This is a drill. We're testing our new E-mag targeting system."

The departments reported in one at a time, not as quickly as Jaq wanted to see, but they were a long way from any known threats. Still, that was when they needed to respond the quickest.

Jaq jumped on the ship-wide once more. "Pick up the pace, people. Although this is a drill, we don't ever want to grow complacent."

The lights turned green, showing the ship was ready.

"Pick three, Captain." Alby pointed at the screen.

Jaq walked close to the main screen. She pointed at two that were close to each other and one about ten degrees offset. "A little bit of a challenge," she said.

"Refining the targets. Preparing to fire," Alby reported. "Fire."

Taurus tapped the 'fire' button, and the E-mags barked into the void. The rumble reverberated through the ship.

"Cease fire!" Donal called. "Need to recalibrate the aim. Dolly, forward the data showing impact points."

"No impacts. All rounds were wide right and high. Forwarding what I have."

Slade Ping chewed on his lip as he thought about the data. When he spoke, it wasn't good news. "There's a lag."

"I'm not sure what that means," Alby replied, getting out of his seat to join Slade at his position.

"Try it now," Donal said.

"Firing." Taurus tapped the button. The rest of the bridge crew watched the main screen. The rounds clipped the edge of the two asteroids that were close together and missed the one farther away.

"Recalibrating." Donal hammered at his keys, looked up to study the main screen and then returned to his computer. "Dolly." He waved her to him.

She climbed out of her seat and joined him. Together, they went through the calculations. It was much more involved than simply adding numbers to put the E-mags on target during this one exercise.

Chrysalis sped ahead, well past the designated asteroids. "Any idea when you'll be up for another test?" Jaq asked.

"We've got to do some reprogramming. It'll take a while," Donal admitted.

"Set Condition Three throughout the ship," Jaq ordered. "Stand down from general quarters."

She slumped into her seat. It was going to take longer than she wanted. It was distracting her from the high-speed pass of Septimus.

"Alby, you have the bridge. I'll be in my quarters."

Jaq left the bridge, happy to be able to walk under the one-point-two gees of acceleration. In her quarters, she did a series of pushups, sit-ups, and jumping exercises. It made her heart race, in a good way. She sat at her desk and pulled up the flight route to Septimus.

It was sixty million kilometers to the closest point of the orbital ellipse. Then it could be another two hundred and eighty million across the orbit past Armanor, depending on where they finally were able to find ice. A quarter of the orbit would be about a hundred and fifty-seven million kilometers.

They would have to accelerate to well over a million kilometers per hour to shorten the trip, maybe accelerate to more than two million KPH. At that speed, they better be pointed where they were going as it would take a long time to turn.

If they were able to find ice and calibrate the E-mags within the next day, they would be able to accelerate on an angle to intercept Septimus. If it took a week, they would best be served by turning around. It wasn't going to take a day.

Jaq called the bridge. "Bring us to a full stop and turn around. We're going the wrong way. We'll follow the asteroid belt in the same direction as our home orbital vector."

"Roger," Ferd replied.

"All hands, secure your tools and equipment. We'll transition through zero-gee while we turn around and head back past Farslor. We'll intercept Septimus and Arraslee coming in from behind as opposed to rushing toward the planet. Closing velocity will be impacted, but we'll just go faster because we can do that. *Chrysalis* is the fastest ship in the system by an order of magnitude. We'll continue testing and calibrating our E-mags throughout this evolution. We'll find ice and then we'll make a little visit to Septimus. Notify *Matador* of our plans."

Jaq strapped herself in her seat as acceleration stopped and the ship's orientation started to change.

The command crew would take care of it.

She returned to her console to make the calculations on when to best conduct their run. They wanted to pass the planet as the moon appeared from around the other side, moving toward them. The audacious maneuver would put *Chrysalis* between the moon and the planet. It would grab the Malibor's attention like nothing else, but it would also be high risk. Any hiccups in acceleration and the ship would crash into the moon. A flyby outside the moon's orbit would have to be sufficient. Eliminate the risk of hitting the moon or any shuttles moving between the planet and the station. Focus the ship's efforts on taking out Malibor cruisers. Seven of them remained, but not all could be operational. It would come down to the efficacy of rounds fired while traveling at high speed.

Jaq stared at her screen. She was in no mood to do the hard math and with *Chrysalis* maneuvering, it wouldn't be a good time to tour the ship.

Acceleration renewed with the ship facing opposite the direction of travel, but that made no difference to how it impacted the crew. One-point-two gees pressed her to the deck since the engines only accelerated in one direction, even if that acceleration slowed momentum they'd already established.

And that made it the perfect time to tour the ship. The crew wouldn't expect her. She released her belt and stepped out, looking for anyone and everyone to share a few kind words with. But it was mainly for Jaq to help her relieve the tension involved with this phase of the Borwyn return.

"*Chrysalis* is turning around?" Crip complained. "What for?"

"Something about getting too far past Septimus going the wrong way," Tram replied. He sat, instinctively draping an arm over his ribs where he was still healing.

"Bring up the tactical display of the star system and orbits with gridlines," Crip requested.

"Are you snorting pain relief mushrooms? This is a Malibor tub. We're lucky to get an outside view." Tram tapped on the control screen until a rudimentary tactical display appeared. "That'll have to do."

Crip used his short-range comm device to contact

Chrysalis. "Recommend we continue from this direction and turn in toward Septimus after twelve more hours. We'll be able to arc in to come in from behind, just like *Chrysalis*, but with a much greater lead time. We won't have to stress the engines."

Jaq replied, "Come at Septimus from two different main approaches. They shouldn't see the gunship for quite some time until you're already within their orbital plane. They'll see us sooner, but we'll be coming at them like a comet. We'll send our time of arrival so you can adjust your acceleration and deceleration appropriately. It's critical that we arrive at exactly the same time."

"I know, Jaq. We'll come in right on your tail and dive into the atmosphere as if running from your awesomeness. Then we'll land. If we think we can hide the gunship, we will, otherwise, it'll take off with just Tram and Kelvis to get it away from us since we won't want any attention brought our way."

"Roger. Plan approved. We'll transmit on a narrow beam once we know when we'll be able to turn toward Septimus. Send us your flight profile as soon as you have it. You'll disappear from our screens soon enough, and we want to know where you are for any communications we need to send."

Crip agreed and signed off. "That's it then. We're on our own to get to Septimus. Change course, Tram. Put us on a trajectory home."

"I used to be somebody," Tram grumbled. "I was the captain of this ship. I even named it, and here I am, taking orders from a ground pounder."

"Not for too much longer. We'll disembark, and you'll take off."

"But you told the captain we'd evaluate it once we reached the planet surface," Tram countered.

Crip tapped his nose with his index finger. "No matter what we do, this gunship will stand out. We'll never know if we were seen until ground and intra-atmospheric forces show up to destroy the ship and us. A quick drop-off and then get out of there. They may not know exactly where we stop, especially if it's in the mountains, but they will find us. Deena?"

"Your maps are aged, but the general topography is the same. I'll point out some potential landing zones away from population centers and urban sprawl. They could be a long hike from any Borwyn."

"We're okay with a long hike as long as it reduces our chances of getting killed," Crip replied.

"Who said anything about a long hike? I want to use the hammock I made," Max interjected.

Crip laughed at him. "This isn't going to be a picnic in hydroponics. The enemy is going to be looking for us."

"I still don't see a need to sleep on the ground. Deena told me about the bugs."

"Bugs?" Crip tried to visualize what that meant but came up short.

"Little gnarly creatures that attack exposed skin. They'll climb in your ears and go for your brain. They fly into your eyeballs and rip the jelly out."

"Stop it." Deena slapped at Max. "They will be annoying

and some of them may go after exposed skin and take a little bite."

"You mean Septimus has creatures that eat humans?"

"Just the bits and pieces you can do without," Deena replied. "Do you really not know anything about bugs?"

"No. How do you know about bugs?" Crip stared at Max.

"I'm married to the one who knows about bugs. We talk. What do you think we do?"

Crip stepped back.

Deena raised her eyebrows.

Crip needed to extricate himself from the verbal pit he had dug. "So, bugs. How big are they?"

"So small you can barely see them to about the size of your ears. They might get in your ears, but that's to be annoying. They aren't going for your brain. They do not eat the jelly out of your eyeballs." She turned to Max. "Why would you say that?"

"Because he doesn't know, and he's my best friend." Max nodded as if that explanation was final.

Deena leaned against the bulkhead with her arms crossed. She stared at the opposite wall before shaking her head. "I don't get it."

"No one does," Crip replied.

"One quick test of the railguns? Three rounds per barrel," Tram advised. He yelled toward the hatch. "Kelvis, we're test-firing the railguns."

"Go for it," the engineer called from the lower deck.

"This ship has an intercom, doesn't it?" Crip asked.

Tram laughed. "No." He pointed at the console next to the captain/pilot's station. "Crip, if you'd do the honors."

"All right! I get to shoot stuff." Crip sat and studied the console. It was self-explanatory, unlike the captain's position. He accessed the targeting program, locked in on an asteroid, and manually fired three rounds.

The main screen didn't show an impact.

"Anyone see where those rounds went?"

Tram had been tracking them with the forward radar. "All high, but directly over the asteroid."

"Adjusting." Crip accessed the calibration program and dialed the targeting down five clicks. "Firing."

The gunship thrummed with each round sent downrange. At first, it felt like power, but after the sixth round, it seemed to vibrate their organs, and not in a good way.

"This ship sucks," Crip said.

The impacts on the asteroid were nearly center mass.

"Picking a target farther away to refine the calibrations." He added a target that was more than ten thousand kilometers distant and pressed the fire button once more. He sent the obdurium projectiles into the void, enlarged the impact area on the screen, and adjusted once more. "A single round to confirm."

A direct hit. Crip grinned.

Max slapped him on the back.

"Left barrel, firing," Crip said. The two railguns were tied together, and the left needed no adjustments. It was dialed in with the right barrel.

"Bullseye," Tram said. "Go toss a few of the load on the left to the right hopper to balance them out. We don't want to be banging away with a single barrel when rapid fire is called for."

"You think those last few rounds will make a difference?" Max asked.

Both Crip and Tram nodded vigorously. "They could, and that's why we do all we can to edge the odds in our favor," Crip explained.

"I understand. A dual shot of those last five rounds or ten single shots. I think there's an advantage to getting more shots to adjust."

"Point to the ground pounder," Tram said. "But we can select a single cannon and fire that way. Better to bracket a target, except when there's no time. We don't plan to unleash the cannons on the run to Septimus. We're going to make believe like we're Malibor."

"If we have to fire, we're going to hit them with enough at the closest range possible to destroy them without giving them a chance to send a distress signal," Crip added.

Max and Deena left to balance the ammunition. Crip played with the controls to familiarize himself even more, minimize his reaction time if they did have to unload on a target.

"Once we get the thumbs-up from Max, I'll alert the crew and adjust our heading. We're going to Septimus, my friend." Tram reached over to grip Crip's shoulder, but he stopped when his stitches pulled.

"Still hurt?"

"A lot," Tram admitted. "Damn Malibor."

"Look for the time when we'll have to shake hands with them. If we win this war, we'll have to rise above the animosity or past harms."

"Will they?" Tram was skeptical. He expected the

average Malibor to never surrender, even after they'd been soundly defeated. Getting them to consider surrendering with anything other than the complete annihilation of their armed forces seemed impossible.

"We have to convince them. Me, Max, Deena, and the rest of the team."

"All million?" Tram couldn't believe it was possible.

"As many as we have to. I know, it's a longshot, but all of us are willing to take it. The most reluctant is Deena, because she's already lived there and doesn't want to go back. She knows how evil they can be, but she's also said that there are normal Malibor, too, those who just go about their business without hating on people. We may have to kill a few of the evil ones to get everyone else's attention."

"I'm not opposed to you killing bad Malibor, but I am opposed to them killing you."

"I appreciate the sentiment." Crip would have said more, but Max confirmed the railguns were balanced and ready for action.

"Brace yourselves as we change course," Tram shouted. Crip climbed into the acceleration couch, the Malibor's version of the gel seat. Tram tapped the controls and thrusters changed the ship's orientation. He accelerated to two gees to decrease the amount of time it would take before the ship assumed the new course. Somebody grunted from the crew quarters on the deck above.

Tram chuckled. "Spoiled by Borwyn technology. They'll get used to *Matador* in the two weeks it takes to get to Septimus."

"I hope not," Crip replied. "I want them in a hurry to get off this tub the instant we touch down."

"Now you're talking. That'll put them on edge. Also, Jaq made us take the leftover food packs from the hydroponics bay. We didn't get the good Malibor food."

"I didn't know that, but I like her style. I have my stash, of course, because we had free access to *Cornucopia*..."

"And you like to share," Crip suggested.

"I do not." Tram accelerated to two-point-five gees. "Hold onto your guts. I'll keep increasing speed until your people stop complaining."

"They're soldiers. They'll never stop complaining."

Tram laughed while shaking his head.

"Yeah, baby! Give me more!" Hammer shouted from the deck above.

CHAPTER 12

A plan is a star chart to success, with many ways to go.

"It's about damn time!" Jaq snapped. It had taken eight days to find a chunk of ice. Jaq relaxed. "Slam on the retroboosters and declutter the power menagerie."

"What's a retrobooster?" Ferdinand said from his thrust control station. "And what's a power menagerie?"

"I'm just making up words that sound impressive," Jaq said. Her attempt at humor had fallen flat despite the quality of her jibe, at least in her mind. "Settle us next to the ice and bring it aboard."

"Recommend seven-gee deceleration for four minutes." Ferd leaned out of his seat to look at the captain.

Jaq nodded. "All hands, this is the captain. Into your seats for a seven-gee burn. Four minutes and then we're going to recover enough ice to fill our tanks to bursting. It'll be nice to have full showers again. Set Condition One throughout the ship. And get that scout ship off the airlock so it doesn't get ripped free."

Brad jumped up from the deputy's seat and ran for the corridor.

When the board showed green that all hands were secured, Jaq stabbed a finger at her flight crew.

Ferd announced, "Inverting the ship." The nose rotated through one-hundred-and-eighty degrees until *Chrysalis* was flying tail first. Ferd slowly increased the power to the ion drives until the ship was decelerating at a steady seven gees.

"Increasing to seven-point-five gees to stop forward momentum closest to the asteroid," Ferd grunted.

The only thing for the crew to do was focus on their breathing and let the gel do its job of squeezing their limbs to keep their blood from pooling away from their hearts. It was only four minutes, but it was right at the edge of where some would pass out—the older crew members and those with maladies. Still, it had to be done.

Jaq justified it all with the war. Her fear of losing momentum following the battle above Sairvor could have been overblown, but she was already concerned that they'd taken too long. That a new armada was on its way to Sairvor, and any time the Malibor were in the sky above the planet, they could stumble across New Septimus. Jaq couldn't risk exposing Borwyn survivors.

The two scouts currently deployed to gather intelligence about the disposition of the Malibor fleet hadn't reported anything untoward. Jaq had to embrace that, but they were also used to radio silence, making like a hole in space.

Even a narrow-beam message to them would risk getting

intercepted since they were located between *Chrysalis* and Septimus.

No news was good news, Brad kept telling her, but the only news that made sense to her was where she could ask questions. News was useless in a vacuum. She remained at loggerheads with Brad over that issue.

The clock counted down until it hit zero, at which point the engines cut out. Energy showed ninety-seven percent, which pleased Jaq. They wouldn't lose any time recharging after securing the ice ball.

"Team is ready to deploy. Grapples are ready," Alby said.

Jaq floated free from her position. Alby currently filled the role of deputy while also filling the position of battle commander. She thought about making Brad her deputy but was reluctant because of his attempt to take charge when they'd first met.

She worried about what the oldsters would do. They were prejudiced against the Malibor as the Malibor had shown their systemic hatred of the Borwyn. She wanted the Malibor to negotiate after the bloody nose she was about to deliver.

Jaq activated the comm-link to the scout ship. "Brad, I'll need your people to relay any comms the Malibor may attempt with us after we've made our pass."

"Why do you think the Malibor will attempt to contact us?" he asked.

"I have a hunch that they'll be confused and intimidated. They'll start with threats and maybe that will lead to a conversation, just like we had with the Sairvor Malibor."

"That was one unarmed scout ship staring at the business end of sixteen E-mag cannons."

"What good is firepower if you can't use it to force people to talk? I sure can't get them on the radio using my good looks."

"Self-defecating humor. Delicious!"

"Deprecating," Jaq corrected. "You're incorrigible. I was going to ask you to be my deputy, but you're going to leave, aren't you?"

"Someone has to fly the scout ship. You've taken my crew, so I'll be flying solo."

"It'll fit in the cargo bay."

"That's filled with pallets of food and equipment. There's no room," Brad countered.

"Move as many pallets as necessary into the corridors. We'll give your little ship a ride. Alby?"

"How did I get roped into this?" Alby replied.

"By being the acting deputy, of course." Jaq pointed to the empty seat.

"Make me do the dirty work while you're angling to replace me."

"Not as the battle commander. I'm relieving you of the burden of having to do jobs like move pallets."

"I see the wisdom in your ways, Captain." Alby stood and bowed. He released his boots and flew to the corridor.

"When you get here, park in the cargo bay," Jaq transmitted.

The scout ship wouldn't be able to sustain a seven-gee burn like *Chrysalis*. He wouldn't decelerate as quickly and then he'd have to fly back to the cruiser, but the operation to collect the ice would take hours. There was plenty of time.

"Watch for crew outside the ship with and without mobility packs. Ease in opposite the asteroid belt."

"Will do, Jaq. It was a pleasure taking this little fella for a ride. It handles like a dream but can't accelerate like the big ship. Is there any way we can install an ion drive on a ship this small?"

"Maybe sometime in the future when we have a space dock and are building ships for exploration and not war."

"That is a might lofty goal, Madame Captain," Brad replied. "I hope I live long enough to see it come to fruition."

"I hope we all do." Jaq closed the channel.

The bridge crew went about their duties. The first four crew were already in space, heading toward the ice chunk nestled between two large asteroids. There was at least a kilometer between the objects, but in space, that wasn't excessive. One small impact from another asteroid could kill everyone involved in the recovery.

The asteroid field had been there for billions of years, and casual impacts almost never happened because a certain equilibrium had been established.

The crew was ready for what had been a rare but routine exercise. With improvements in recovery and water treatment, they had to snag ice about once a year. With the influx of additional bodies, they were nine months ahead of schedule for recovery.

Will this be the last? Jaq wondered. She wanted it to be. Plan for success, prepare for failure.

If it wasn't, she wanted to remember where the

remaining ice was. Next time, they might not have eight days to search.

It was more than a week's travel at relatively slow speed from the Expeditionary Resupply Station. That wasn't prohibitive. *Cornucopia* gave the ERS crew a means of transportation. They could fly anywhere they needed without leaving anyone behind.

It was an added bonus. With the removal of a section of pallets, it also gave them extra space in which to live and work, if only *Butterfly* had a working airlock by which to attach the ship to the remains of the cruiser. That was one of their tasks. Godbolt would figure it out, and the two ships would become one. The crew would want for nothing but gravity.

"Make sure we tag the leftover ice, in case we need a refill," Jaq instructed.

The comm officer contacted Alby to pass the order.

"Way ahead of you. They have a transponder with them. They'll be cutting into it soon. It's a big one. We only need a quarter of it, if that much," Alby replied.

The captain nodded. She would have left the bridge, but with no deputy available, she needed to stay. She was grounded—as she'd told Crip and yet, there he was, on a Malibor gunship headed to Septimus.

Jaq had no choice. She'd make Brad the deputy to fill the ship's role. She'd appreciate his insight into the Malibor since he'd been watching them for decades.

Time moved slowly until it almost stopped. Jaq's continual chronometer watching didn't hurry things. She fell asleep, only to be roused by Alby. "Cargo hold is clear, and Starstrider is moving in."

"Alby! Thank you. I was thinking."

"That's what I say when I sleep for half an hour, too."

"Has it been that long...and obvious?"

"So they say." He gestured toward the weapons team. They nodded back. "I'll watch the bridge in case any Malibor pop out of nowhere. Go meet Brad and take him to lunch."

"Microgreens and algae," Jaq declared.

"If you feed him that stuff, he'll be back on board his ship and off like a projectile shot out of an E-mag cannon."

"Am I supposed to be upset if he makes an adult decision?"

"I'll be upset enough for both of us since I don't want to be the guy responsible for moving pallets around."

"Maybe you can take him to lunch," Jaq countered.

He locked his boots and assumed a loose position of attention. "Permission to leave the bridge?"

"No. I'll go. You watch for invisible Malibor." Jaq back-flipped toward the corridor, laughing at Alby's discomfort, although he may have had the last laugh because Brad would stay and fill the deputy's seat.

"Bring us about and get under way, one-point-two gees until everything is settled and then we'll alternate between three gees and seven gees. Times?"

Ferd had already run the calculations. "Seven gees for thirty-two minutes, then three gees for seventy-nine minutes to take us to one million KPH. If we continue accelerating at one-point-two gees for six and a half hours to reach two million KPH, nine hours of acceleration and then more than twenty-two hours of coasting."

"Contact *Matador* and inform them of our arrival time. Give it to them in minutes and seconds. We want our arrivals at E-mag firing range to coincide so *Matador* can peel off and head toward the planet while we have them distracted. A little more than a day to prepare. Targeting. Are you dialed in for a couple million KPH? We're going to hit them with everything we have, but we'll barely have a few seconds of firing time. You know what that means?"

"Sixteen cannons jamming at the max rate of twenty rounds per second for three seconds comes to nine hundred and sixty rounds. The ability to retarget during that time frame is zero. We'll have to direct the E-mags to their exact aim points before we pull the trigger. One shot, Jaq," Donal explained.

"You know our limitations. Make every shot count. We'll get the exact location of the Malpace fleet not long before we arrive. You'll have to come up with your targets quickly and aim the E-mags based on where we'll be when we reach optimal firing range."

"*We* know, and we're ready. Can we get the good food once we're accelerating at a reasonable pace?"

"I guess so," Jaq conceded. "Brad, ask Chef to make it so. When did our food become bad? We should feed people a steady diet of New Septimus offal." Jaq looked at Brad. "No disrespect intended."

"None taken. Our food is horrible. Your food is better,

and as much as it pains me to say it, Malibor food packs are better than anything you can produce on this ship."

"It's simply the ability to grow food on a planet, a planet they stole from us. It's payback time, and then we'll grab our own damn food."

"Not this time, but soon," Brad replied.

Jaq simmered but agreed. "Let's go ahead and eat the Malibor stuff. We know where there's more."

"Yeah, in the lower corridors," Alby offered.

"Thanks for that. Give me ship-wide, please."

Amie signaled that the intercom was live.

"Attention, all hands. Into your seats for two hours of hard acceleration, then we'll draw back to one-point-two for nine hours. That's when we'll make sure we eat and rest. After that, we have about twenty-two hours of coasting before we reach Septimus. The last two hours, we'll set Condition One throughout the ship and assume battle stations. Into your seats right now. We'll begin our acceleration in two minutes. Next stop, Septimus. We'll take a good look at our home and let it know that we're coming back."

Jaq crawled into her seat and belted herself in. It was going to be a hard burn. They only needed to weather the gee forces for the next two hours, then it would be smooth sailing.

"Prepare for a burst transmission to *Matador*," Jaq said. Amie nodded, and Jaq continued, "Tram, Crip, Max and the team. Best wishes for success. Land where Deena instructed and make contact. Convince the Borwyn survivors that we are going to liberate Septimus, starting with destroying the Malibor fleet. We'll do our part. You do yours. We'll meet on the planet after we've taken control of the sky. This is the last transmission before you go in. Do us proud. Captain Hunter out."

Brad nodded approvingly. "I'll get the latest from my people before we are on terminal approach."

"We'll need it as soon as they can provide it, and we'll also need any updates once their fleet starts moving around, and they will. How far out will they see us? That's the big question."

"Once we have that answer, we'll hammer out an attack plan with Alby and his team. It'll all work out, Jaq."

Jaq worried about when the Malibor would see them coming and then how would they respond. If they scattered, it would make hitting them far more difficult than it already was, but she didn't expect them to stay in place. Maybe they would come at *Chrysalis*, use their ships to stand in the way and defend their station. Jaq hoped they would do that as the direct shot down the line of travel was the easiest for the E-mags.

"You Malibor need to do that," she muttered to herself.

CHAPTER 13

Build your opponent a golden bridge to retreat across.

"All hands, battle stations. Set Condition One throughout the ship," Jaq announced. She stood in front of her seat, boots locked to the deck as *Chrysalis* raced toward Septimus at a blistering two-point-one million kilometers per hour. At four million kilometers away, the planet was little more than a blip in the void before them, but it was the biggest and brightest, a gibbous view, growing with each passing minute.

"The latest disposition is in," Brad started, "and you're not going to like it."

Jaq would have rather simply had the information than the assessment of whether she'd like it or not.

The main screen populated with a close-up tactical display of the space station above Malpace, the Malibor's word for the moon orbiting Septimus and the name the Borwyn had taken to calling the enemy who occupied Septimus.

They were looking for seven cruisers and eighteen gunships.

Alby studied his screen. "Where'd they go?" he wondered aloud.

Two cruisers were attached to the space station along with six gunships. One cruiser was in the shipyard dock along with a new ship under construction. One gunship was in the dock.

"I'd like images of the ships attached to the space station." Jaq stepped closer to the main screen, which was filled with grainy images a moment later.

"It's hard to make out," Brad said. "That's the best we have. I didn't want our scouts getting too much closer as we didn't want to rile the Malibor fleet, especially since they're still reeling from the damage you've done to them."

"Your scouts had to see where the other ships went. So where are they?"

"Give me a narrow beam to *Starstruck*," Brad requested. At Jaq's look, he explained, "They will know we're coming even if they intercept our transmission, but I doubt they'll be able to decode it before we arrive—if they ever decode it. They'll be scrambling enough as it is."

"Concur," was all Jaq said. "We need the information more than we need to remain invisible."

Alby returned the main screen to the tactical display showing their course past the station and the moon. Their closest point of approach was going to be five hundred kilometers. Not as close as Jaq had wanted, but it was a safety margin she could live with. She wanted a more aggressive attack profile.

"Lateral thrusters, please. I'd like to close the distance to two hundred and fifty kilometers. That still keeps us clear of Allarees while giving us a better shot at anything they have."

"What are you going to shoot at?" Alby asked.

"You're going to pick those ships off the side of the space station." Jaq squinted at Alby as if ready for a rebuttal.

"I can't guarantee that we won't hit the space station." He tapped his screens. "The angle on one cruiser will give us a decent shot. The other is behind the station as we approach but we might have a shot once we pass, but the rounds will lose some of their momentum. The cruiser in the shipyard is a clear target, and I'd like to designate it as priority one."

"Pri two," Jaq countered. "Pri one is the cruiser at the station where we have a good shot. Pri two is the ship in the yard. Do not attack the one under construction. When we defeat the Malibor, we might want to take over that ship. It puts us ahead for future space exploration."

"What about the second cruiser at the station?" Alby asked.

"It's my understanding that you'll have to already have the E-mag cannons targeted before we arrive, which means they'll be facing aft since we can't redirect them that far in under two seconds."

"That's correct."

"Are any of the gunships a target of opportunity?"

"They are too small. To hit them, we'll have to hit the station."

Amie interrupted. "*Starstruck* is on the channel."

All conversation stopped as the initially garbled voice of the scout captain came through. The decryption software cleared it up. "This is *Starstruck*. Four cruisers and twelve gunships departed for Septimus yesterday. They disappeared behind the planet shortly thereafter and have not reappeared on our scopes."

"They could be positioned behind the planet, or they could have gone to the planet surface."

"There's no way they can catch us," Ferdinand stated.

"What could they be doing? Ambush, hide, run, something else completely?" Jaq looked at Brad and then to Alby. Both shook their heads. "Then we have to plan for the worst case. What is the worst case?"

Brad offered, "Ambush. They drop mines or fire into our line of travel. Hitting something at two million KPH will leave a mark, a big mark."

"We're doing our best not to hit anything," Mary replied.

"Not a question about your abilities. We're looking at an enemy who might fight back. What can we do about mines?" Jaq wondered aloud. She straightened her jumpsuit, a constant fight in zero-gee.

"Hit them going so fast that we shatter their very existence, blow them up before they blow themselves," Alby declared while pumping his fist.

"We'll do that without damaging ourselves?" Jaq asked.

"We blast them with our E-mags or even defensive weapons fire. I recommend we fire right down the nose no matter whether we see something or not. We're ready."

"Concur." Jaq gestured toward Gil Dizmar.

Gil nodded. "Proactive fire is programmed and ready to go. Firing four banks of chain guns directly in front of the ship for two seconds preceding and the three seconds of the proposed engagement."

"Sounds good, Gil. Taurus, give me two E-mags, too."

"Directly down our line of travel. Are we going to be shifting sideways with thrusters?"

"Ferd?"

"Passing distance is four-fifty. We are still moving sideways but not fast enough. Estimate we'll pass at three hundred. I'm sorry, Jaq. We won't get to two-fifty before we pass."

"It's my fault I didn't recognize it early. Three hundred kilometers will be the optimal firing range for a fraction of a second. That's where your targeting solutions need to be optimized. We need to hit what we are trying to hit. That means they lose two cruisers and get a wake-up call. What about civilian vessels in the area? Are there any cargo haulers or troop transports? Shouldn't that trooper we sent from Sairvor be back?"

Brad contacted the scout and started to give him a hard time, but the scout reported that they'd reported the location of every ship in the area.

"Where is that troop transport?" he demanded.

"Still in orbit over Sairvor," *Starstruck* replied.

Brad looked at Jaq. "I guess we hurt them as bad as they said."

The captain unhooked her boots and floated free. She pulled herself along the mid-rail until she reached her deputy. "Looks like they'll have to land on Sairvor. Why didn't your people tell us they were still there?"

"Because they're not!" Brad didn't need to access the

latest report. He'd read it. They had taken a scout ship into orbit for five trips around the planet before returning to the surface. "The troopship isn't in orbit."

"Contact *Starbound* and find out if it's somewhere between Sairvor and Septimus."

"Hook me up, Amie," Brad requested, putting his attention on his screen while he re-tallied the total number of ships. Cargo haulers were plentiful in the system, dozens of them, but many had the ability to land on the planet if booster rockets were available to lift the ship back into space. Others were only used in space, like *Cornucopia*.

"Where is *Matador*?" Jaq asked.

"Ahead of us by nearly three million kilometers. They have been slowing for the past two days using minimal thrust to maintain a low profile. They are twenty thousand kilometers abeam, on the planet side. They will enter orbit approximately thirty seconds before we pass our closest point," Slade reported.

"Exactly as we want. How many orbits will they make before they clear into the upper atmosphere?" Jaq knew but wanted everyone to be certain.

Mary had the answer. "One."

"Then they'll see what's hiding behind the planet. That could be a bad thing, because whatever is back there will see them, too." Jaq rubbed her face. She'd run through this plan a thousand times. She knew every step of every second. Where people were supposed to be. What they had to be doing. It was a slow build-up to a chronology of rushed actions.

"They'll be skipping across the upper atmosphere. They can take a steeper angle if the situation warrants. Gunships are tough. Did you see the amount of armor plating on that thing?" Brad replied.

"Armor won't help you if it gets melted away. How steep can they go before the ship comes apart?" Jaq hadn't thought about this contingency.

"As steep as they need to. The armor is interlaced with ceramics. It's made to enter the atmosphere."

"Then why didn't they put their old gunships on the ground instead of in orbit around Farslor?" Jaq wondered aloud.

"If they're in orbit, then no one can get to them who doesn't already have a spaceship." Brad tapped his nose.

Of course he was right. The Malibor fleet had to be paranoid about losing control, which also accounted for why the ships were over Farslor instead of in mothballs at the Malpace shipyard. They didn't trust their own fleet.

"What a way to live," Jaq muttered.

"Not us, though," Brad said. "Everyone is here for the right reasons and committed to freeing Septimus. Maybe we won't clear the skies above Septimus right now, but we'll get one step closer."

The trial of patience. Jaq tried not to stare at her feet and make faces. Patience wasn't her strong suit. She'd never thought it would be easy, but she had lulled herself into believing it would be quick. That was a failure of expectation. She vowed to herself to live more in the moment, or the next nearly two hours' worth of moments.

"If we can wipe two cruisers off the board, we'll call that a win. We're also putting the Malibor on notice that the

Borwyn have returned. Amie, are you ready to broadcast our message?"

"I am. I'll burst it as well as send it. Transmission time is thirty seconds, so I'll start broadcasting the second *Matador* begins its atmospheric entry, which is thirty seconds from our closest approach."

"I like the timing," Jaq replied. "Play the message, if you would. We have time to redo it if necessary."

Amie tapped two keys, and Jaq's voice sounded throughout the bridge.

"People of Septimus. This is Captain Jaq Hunter, Commander of *Chrysalis*, flagship of the Borwyn fleet. We have returned to liberate Septimus and all territory that's been seized by the Malibor. You have two choices. Fight us and die or talk to us. We will continue removing Malibor ships from your fleet until you realize you cannot stand before us, but you can stand beside us. I offer you my hand to stop a war started fifty years ago. Understand that we'll negotiate on my terms, since we are in a position of strength. How many more ships and people must you lose before you realize that? In the end, the only choice you have is how many of your people you will let die. Contact us on this open channel. We'll be around."

Brad chuckled lightly. "That last part cracks me up. *We'll be around.*"

"Too casual? Too threatening? I want to set the tone that we're in this war to win. They've grown complacent and will pay the price."

"They'll be thinking that, especially after they start asking questions, like how many ships have they lost," Alby offered. "Will they rise up when their government doesn't give them straight answers. Everyone will know someone who has been lost. The constant messages will stop, and the leadership will be silent. It will foment discontent."

"Over time. We'll keep hitting them where it hurts." Jaq shrugged. "Anything I need to change in that message?"

Brad shook his head. "You gave them what we're doing and an alternative along with consequences for their continued resistance. You have already delivered on your threat. Maybe you can ask them what happened to *Hornet* and her crew?"

"I like that. Plant the seed of suspicion." Jaq rolled her finger, and Amie nodded. "Ask your leadership about your most-powerful warship, the one called *Hornet*. Why hasn't it reported in the last two months?" She drew a finger across her throat.

"I'll insert that after where you ask them to talk to us and before you tell them you'll continue removing Malibor ships."

Jaq gave Amie a thumbs-up. "Anything else?" Jaq scanned the command deck, looking from face to face.

No one had anything to add.

"Targeting, are you ready?"

"Not yet, Jaq," Donal replied. "Still crunching lots of numbers. Ludicrous amounts of numbers. The math is staggering!" He waved his hands erratically.

CHAPTER 14

Trial of the soul starts with a trial of the mind.

Dolly stopped what she was doing to watch. Alby twisted around in his seat to look at his team member. Taurus chuckled to herself. Her role was nearly nonexistent. The firing points were so precise that they were programmed. The E-mags would fire themselves, once Donal plugged the exact aim points into the computer along with the ship's location. The aim points would micro-adjust as they got close to firing, taking into account any updates like sideways drift from the predicted firing point.

It was complex, but the prodigies had been working on it for nearly two weeks. One old and one young, committing the entirety of their intellect to the problem.

"I have faith in you, Donal. They're just numbers. Nothing to be afraid of." Jaq delivered her best maternal smile.

He continued waving his arms around.

"Don't make me come over there," she added.

He started to laugh. "My mother used to say that to me." He sat down. "We'll be ready, Jaq. No fear."

"I miss the droning of the air handler," Alby blurted.

"I don't." Jaq glanced in the direction of the previously offending vent. She sniffed the air to find it clean. The old air handler left a slight smell of ozone, like it was on the edge of failure when it wasn't. The droning interrupted anything and everything on the bridge until it was done with its cycle.

They would have no time to interrupt necessary bridge chatter during the new tactics pioneered by Jaq and her team that now included a number of originals. They believed they could win by taking advantage of what *Chrysalis* was better at than its predecessor, the same ship with a different drive and different crew.

The Malibor were different back then, too. Ruthless and efficient. Since then, *Chrysalis* had been rebuilt while the Malibor had fought five civil wars. They were weaker, and the Borwyn were stronger. The Borwyn also had nothing and everything to lose. The Malibor would continue to fight if Jaq tried to make peace without using sufficient violence to establish the superior negotiating position.

It seemed to be the message that the Malibor understood the clearest. Peace through force of arms.

Jaq would make sure the Malibor were on the receiving end of the bad deal this time.

Since they'd been coasting for days, they'd had time to rebuild their power supply. They were at eighty percent, which was more than enough since they couldn't conduct any radical maneuvers and had no plan to try any during the three seconds of the E-mag barrage. The ship would continue on a ballistic trajectory toward Armanor and then slingshot around it to put themselves on one of three courses: back to Septimus, to Sairvor, or to Farslor.

Brad bumped her with his shoulder, startling her.

"What's bothering you?" he whispered.

"I wanted the totality of victory, right here, right now."

"The longer we fight, the more we're exposed. I get it. We're at risk of dying every moment we're at war. Fifty years ago, the Malibor attack was devastating because we didn't realize how much or even what they were capable of. Maybe we believed we were invincible. How many ships did we have to lose before our ancestors realized we were not?"

Brad gripped her shoulder. "I know the answer because I was there. We lost all of them, including this ship. When *Butterfly* and *Chrysalis* were destroyed, that was the end of it. The rest of us flew for our lives. As it turns out, neither cruiser was destroyed. Was it a disinformation campaign?"

"*Chrysalis* would have died if not for the heroic efforts of our forebears. *Butterfly* was probably in the same shape. Not disinformation. It was the reality of our mortality. We went from invincible to terrified in a single heartbeat. I want the Malibor to feel the same as we did back then."

"Vengeance doesn't suit you, Jaq. The fact that you're not attacking the station is proof of that. You'd lob a couple missiles at the government buildings on Septimus, too, if you wanted the Malibor to pay. Although the average person may appreciate the removal of a corrupt government, the majority will treat it like their sister."

Brad studied the tactical display on the main screen.

Chrysalis was quickly closing on Septimus. Soon, they would be able to see features on the planet with their naked eyes.

"What do you mean by your sister?"

"*I* can call my sister ugly all day long, but when *you* do it, we're gonna fight. The Malibor might get defensive about their government, even though they know it's bad. It's still theirs. That's why I fully support your decision not to attack anything other than their military fleet."

"Tell me something I don't know." Jaq studied the screen.

"If you chew gum while peeling onions, you won't cry." Brad watched Jaq for a response.

"Is this what life with you is going to be like? I have to try and make sense of your nonsense?"

"Sense of nonsense. That's funny. It's going to be a glorious life!" Brad declared. "Did you know about the trick with onions?"

"I didn't because we don't have gum, even though I know what it is. Onions are something completely different. We have them in hydroponics, but why would peeling one make you cry?"

Brad shook his head. "All my best material is wasted. You know how many decades I've been planning these one-liners? This is good stuff."

"It's not." Jaq looked back and forth, checking his pupils to see if he'd gotten into a batch of painkillers.

Alby thumped his boots to the deck to interrupt Jaq and Brad in the least-intrusive way.

They both turned their attention to him. "The targeting is ready. I've passed the exact vector we have to travel to Mary and Ferd. We cannot be off course by more than the cross-section distance of the target hulls. That means thirty meters. Our aim points are center mass, stem to stern. A direct hit will rake the ship and split it open like a pressurized can in space."

"Take us straight down that line, no more than fifteen meters' deviation," Jaq said loudly.

"Separation from target one is three hundred and four-point-two-one-two kilometers. Target two is four hundred and eight-five-point-six-one-one meters. Distance measured from *Chrysalis's* central axis. Our flyby orientation must be ninety degrees negative roll," Mary confirmed.

Alby clarified, "That roll brings the most E-mags to bear by putting the ship's spine facing the station and yard."

The ship was mostly cylindrical but could have been declared a lifting body had it gone intra-atmospheric, which it was never designed for. It was built with an orientation in mind, where the weapon systems would be concentrated to simultaneously bring more of them against single targets. It made it easier to service and reload those weapons by having their internals on a lateral track.

"And two E-mags firing straight ahead, just in case the Malibor try to put something in our way."

Jaq stared at the board, even though there was nothing new to see. The energy gauge increased to eighty-two. That made Jaq happy. She feared attacking the Malibor and running out of power. She had nightmares about the one time that had happened over Sairvor. They had made it through, thanks to Bec, but she didn't want to relive it.

Power was the asset that determined their fate. Without it, they were doomed.

Jaq tapped her comm unit. "Bec and Teo, Jaq here. Thanks for everything you've done for us, keeping us flying at the fastest anyone has ever gone before while keeping our power up, so we can fly and fight as we have to. Ninety minutes to contact with the Malibor."

She closed the channel before they could reply.

Brad smirked. "I don't know how Teo does it."

"She's an angel," Jaq said. "There's no other explanation."

"Hammer and Anvil are her brothers. She's tougher than them," Brad suggested.

"I'm sorry that your boys are on the mission to Septimus."

"Don't be. They are part of the vanguard. My children get to step foot on Septimus, something I've been denied for the past five decades. It's an honor to be a part of that. We will all die, Jaq. It's what we do while we're alive that matters. What they're doing matters. What we're doing will make a difference. Me and my children are involved. I can ask no more from life."

Alby clumped to his position and strapped into his seat.

"Give me a narrow beam to *Matador*," Jaq requested.

Amie gestured to indicate the channel was open.

"*Matador*, this is *Chrysalis*. We wish you the best of luck, and if you need anything, we'll be back, but not for a while. Make contact and rally our people to the cause of freedom. They'll rise against the Malibor when they realize they haven't been abandoned and that they are not alone."

"Thanks, Jaq. We'll do right by all Borwyn. This time, we win," Crip replied.

"You know what we're trying to accomplish. We'll position a scout closer to pick up a microwave burst transmission that they can then relay to us. I would like to hear updates just to make sure you're okay."

"We will be," Crip replied. "Love to Taurus. Out here."

The bridge crew avoided looking at the offensive weapons officer to give her a moment alone.

Jaq contemplated the transmitter the team would use. Two-point-four gigahertz and a portable dish to send the signal into space. The scout ship would have to be close and tuned to the bandwidth, which they would be if they weren't discovered. Jaq planned on losing contact with the team on the ground. Once *Chrysalis* passed and the message was delivered, the Malibor fleet would be stirred up, looking for enemies behind every hunk of space debris.

The plan was for the scout ship to close in after a week's time, once the fleet settled into a predictable routine of patrol routes and times.

That was the hope, anyway. They had a backup to that plan, and a backup to the backup.

But the soldiers on the ground wouldn't know that they hadn't been abandoned if there was no one left to respond.

"Update on our targets?"

"No change," Amie replied instantly.

"Where is the bulk of their fleet? Where is that troopship?" Jaq muttered. She would have stomped her feet had they not been magnetically attached to the metal deck. Instead, she shifted back and forth. The unknowns occupied too much of her headspace.

"We'll figure it out, Jaq. There's nothing we can't handle as long as we can see a couple million klicks in front of us."

Brad stepped to the deputy's seat and climbed in. "Take a load off and relax."

Jaq was in zero-gee. There was no load except for the self-induced kind. Three million kilometers and ninety minutes to showtime.

CHAPTER 15

If you want a message to be heard, send it in a way that it's never been sent before.

"I was worried about pulling high-gee maneuvers, but the extra time allowed us to do things more casually," Tram stated, sitting in the captain's chair of the ship he had named *Matador*.

Crip was in the weapons seat, but their primary plan didn't include lighting up the sky with railgun rounds. "I have to say I'm happy about that, too. How are you feeling?"

"Good as new. It reinforced my decision *not* to do what you do. I'm not a soldier type, and I'm afraid I'll freeze up if threatened. Getting chopped up and left for dead scared me. I'm happy to fight them, but from behind the controls of the ship." He shook his head. "That's not the right word—I'm not happy about it at all—but I want the Malibor to end their attacks. No one deserves to go through what I went through."

"This could be the beginning of the end, my friend," Crip

said. "You're helping us make it happen. Maybe they'll name a school after you."

"That's exactly why I'm doing this," Tram scoffed. "Don't you get any of these good people killed. And you!" Tram pointed a finger at Max and Deena standing in the hatch to the bridge. "Newlyweds. Why are you doing this?"

"Because we have to. It's every decision we've made in our lives that have delivered us to this point in time. There's no one who can do what needs to be done, no one besides us."

Tram frowned. "Are you sure there's no one else?"

"Who else has been on Septimus and knows how modern life is? Who else has trained to lead the combat team? No, Tram. There is no one else, and we're good with that. This is what we were meant to do. And I find the thought of a school getting named after me to be quite compelling. Max and Deena's school for miscreants and vagabonds."

"I'm not sure that's the kind of school I want with my name on it," Deena said, "but I'll take it."

"No one is getting their name on a school." Crip pounded his fist on his console.

"Take it easy," Tram cautioned. "This ship's old. We fixed it better than it was, but it still belongs in a museum and not on the front lines of a war."

"You said there was no problem taking it to the ground. Don't tell me you were prevaricating." Crip's lip twitched. Like Tram, he didn't want to die, especially not as part of a fireball that ended in a huge crater.

"We shouldn't have any problem. We decelerate and fly as normal. This ship is built for it. We have plenty of fuel. We'll be fine. We'll enter the atmosphere nose first, then rotate and use the main engines to decelerate. Thrusters will keep us oriented. It's standard stuff, exactly how the lander delivered your team on Farslor." Tram smiled. "Strap yourselves in. We need to decelerate at two gees for eight minutes, and then just under one gee until we reach the atmosphere. That's when *Chrysalis* will pass us and take on the Malibor fleet."

"They won't have their hands full. The majority of the fleet is gone."

"I bet Jaq is beside herself." Tram checked the gunship's sensors once more. Nothing new was on the scope. "Why aren't there any weapons platforms over Septimus?"

"Five civil wars. They probably used them to fire on each other, making the space above Septimus a dangerous place, no matter which side you were on. I'm guessing, but thinking about the Malibor, I bet I'm not far off."

"I wouldn't doubt it. It doesn't really matter except that it makes it easier for us. We don't want weapons platforms unless we can steal them and dismantle them for parts and metal." Tram checked the clocks. "Five minutes to final deceleration. I'll need everyone to strap in."

Crip leaned toward the corridor and made to yell, but Max and Deena stood there. "Pass the word. Strap in, decel in five."

Max nodded. He yelled down toward Engineering before climbing to the next level up where the team waited and informing them.

"You like the comm system on this ship," Tram said at the look on Crip's face.

"It has a certain attraction that I find comforting, familial even."

"You belong with them." Tram tipped his chin and eyes upward.

"I think so. I understand them." He reached across to poke Tram's arm. "Don't worry about us. I won't let us stick our necks out too far."

"Make sure you don't. Those are good people. Take extra care with Deena. If the Malibor find her, they'll declare her a traitor and her life will get real bad, real quick."

"We have to protect her. She hasn't trained with the combat team. She'll advise us and help with negotiations, but exposing her to the Malibor wouldn't be good."

"One minute." Tram checked his systems. Everything was working as it was supposed to.

Crip tested his straps to make sure he was tightly in his seat. "Railguns are loaded and ready to fire, for what it's worth."

"Unless we turn around, there's nothing to shoot at except *Chrysalis,* and I suggest we don't do that."

"Let's not. This is going to be hard enough without our own people shooting at us."

Tram shrugged. "So far, it's been easy. We flew to Septimus, and there aren't any ships waiting for us. If they interrogate us, we ignore them. The old tech on this ship probably was inoperable more than it worked."

"And we're back to hoping for the best. I liked this plan better when we weren't so close to Septimus. There's a lot to be said for imminence. It makes the heart race. So, your crash landing will be a relief that we'll happily run away from."

Tram laughed. "I'm not going to crash my ship. I have my own command. I can't squander that, because I'm not going to get another." He tapped a key. "Starting decel."

Two gees weren't an extreme amount. It weighed on them but not like the seven-gee burn that Jaq had been forced to use.

The ship vibrated gently. "We better double-check that nothing is loose. There will be intense turbulence on the way in. We don't need anything flying around, neither your people nor tools flying into your people."

"When we drop to one gee, we'll do a quick search," Crip replied. "We need our people to get their packs on and grab their weapons. We'll be ready to disembark the second we touch down since we won't know if we've been followed. I think we'll be far enough away from the Malibor, but we aren't sure of that, either. We have a lot of unknowns on this op. The strategy is sound, and we need to do it, but damn!"

"Planner's remorse," Tram suggested. "It's a great plan until you realize you need more information than you have available that you happily filled in with assumptions. It's great until you're in the middle of it. I've heard that no plan survives first contact."

"We'll be winging it from the second we hit the upper atmosphere. We're surrounded by good people, Tram. It'll all work out in the end. If it doesn't work out, then clearly it's not the end."

"Aren't you a bright ray from Armanor?" Tram tapped his controls. "Three, two, one. Reducing thrust to one gee."

Crip jumped out of his seat and headed up the ladder. He bellowed orders the entire way. A mad scramble on the level above suggested the combat team was gearing up, putting on their body armor, equipment vest, and strapping into their packs. Last thing issued were the pulse rifles and hand stunners.

"Upper atmosphere in thirty seconds!" Tram shouted. "Hey! Need you on the weapons."

Crip slid down the ladder and dove into his seat, strapping in and checking the scope.

"Just in case the Malibor fleet is hiding in the sensor shadow."

"Right." Crip studied the screen while dancing his fingers across the controls, ready over the targeting and firing options, in case he needed to do it quickly. "I'm not going to shoot them if they're there. If they shoot first, I'll fire back."

"That's the plan." Tram pointed at the screen. "*Chrysalis* is going to ruin their day. Five seconds."

"Active sensors at full power," Chief Ping announced.

Jaq couldn't stay in her seat. There was no maneuver they could make at this speed that would require her to be instantly secure within the gel's firm embrace. She needed to see everyone and everything.

The Malpace space station and moon rushed toward them.

"Ready to fire!" Taurus called. The targeting and firing systems were slaved to computer control, so there was nothing the crew could do but watch.

The main screen popped with a new contact in the

planet's shadow, confirming in Jaq's mind that the Malibor had seen them coming and hidden where the Borwyn sensors couldn't reach. The positioning of the New Septimus scouts prevented a view into the shadow because they had to have a line of sight for best communication with *Chrysalis*.

They needed a third scout ship looking behind the planet. It also suggested the Malibor were aware of the general direction from which the Borwyn would come. Jaq knew for certain that a fleet was not on a direct heading to Farslor. The Malibor ships were slower. If they took a circuitous route to get there, *Chrysalis* could return before the fleet arrived after a slingshot around the star.

All this flashed through Jaq's mind in a millisecond. Time was compressed as they approached faster than any comet.

One gunship, two gunships, and then a cruiser appeared on the screen in a low orbit, keeping the ships away from most sensor sweeps except the ones made from danger close.

They had not shot because the space station and the moon were in the way. This also meant the Malibor had no shot at them. Jaq wanted her shot. *Chrysalis* was moving too fast for the Malibor to target their weapons effectively. Risk was low. It made her angry that they would survive this confrontation.

"Any way we can get a shot at them?"

Alby replied, "We don't have time to retarget the E-mags before we're almost out of range, and then by firing backward, we lose just enough that the rounds could be ineffective. If we launched a missile, it would run out of fuel before it could turn around. The only shot is if you want *Matador* to take it."

"What's more important: getting to the surface or killing a Malibor ship or two?"

"That's a rhetorical question," Alby replied. "We'll go after those ships when the time is right. E-mags are hot."

The chain guns created a slight hum, but when the electromagnetic launch cannons kicked in, they droned throughout the ship and drowned out all other ambient noise. Two E-mags cleared the space in front of the ship with a sustained rate of fire of ten shots a second, increasing to twenty each one second before the ship reached the closest point to the station.

The speed at which the station rushed at Jaq made her question their ability to get a shot without hitting the station itself, but that was a risk Jaq was willing to accept.

It was war, and the Malibor had been the aggressor.

The Malpace station was huge, a solid cylinder that rotated like a spinning top. The interior had to be open, based on the outside surface area. Unlike a central spindle with supports leading to a surrounding circular tube that would have been more efficient from a construction materials standpoint, this looked more like a skyscraper in space. A city in and of itself.

Jaq could only watch as *Chrysalis* reached its closest point. The sudden cacophony of fourteen additional E-mags engaging at the cyclic rate of fire filled the bridge. The crew winced as one with the assault on their eardrums. One cruiser attached to the station. Another cruiser within the lattice work of the shipyard along with a new ship, twice the size and bulk of the cruiser.

It wasn't a troopship or a cargo hauler. It was the next

generation of warship. Quantity of ships hadn't helped the Malibor. They wanted one ship, a dreadnought to menace the system and deal with upstarts like *Chrysalis*.

Jaq vowed that it would never go to space. They hadn't targeted it this time, but there would be another opportunity. It was farther along than they had expected based on the grainy images they'd looked at, but they were collecting their own data now.

Chief Ping was head-down at his station. His entire team pecked rapidly at their systems, keeping every tool at their command engaged.

Even with their speed at two million KPH, the E-mags fired at one-tenth the speed of light. The impacts were nearly instantaneous.

Images of the impacts on the station rocked Jaq back on her heels. The first round put a hole into the structure near the end of a gantry that connected to the ship. The rounds danced down the gantry, making it look like it was being sequentially exploded. The cruiser started to twist with the jerking of the gantry, but the rounds shattered the ship. It didn't blow up, only vented atmosphere and split along both longitudinal and lateral seams.

The rounds impacted so quickly that Jaq wondered if they hit in a sequence or all at once.

"Transmitting," Amie reported. Jaq's message would flood the Malibor airwaves.

"Bullseye!" Alby said.

Jaq didn't consider it a bullseye. She hoped that section of the station could be closed off by emergency bulkheads to limit the damage and loss of non-fleet lives.

She turned her attention to the shipyard snapshot, but the pre-programmed rounds had already impacted the cruiser undergoing overhaul.

It would never fly again. It was nothing more than a cloud of debris and disparate sections, torn apart by the violence of obdurium projectiles hurled at one-tenth the speed of light.

And just like that, the firing stopped.

The silence seemed loud, a ghost of noise from the symphony of destruction. Jaq turned to thank the battle commander and his team.

Then it started anew. Jaq nearly jerked her neck out of joint rocketing her attention to the main screen.

"I added that in, just until we clear this sector of space," Alby explained.

"You about gave me a heart attack." Jaq clutched her chest to emphasize her point. "Good shooting. Chalk two cruisers off the Malibor order of battle."

"Something ahead, one million kilometers," Chief Ping reported. An indistinct icon appeared on the tactical board.

"Set course for a slingshot maneuver around Armanor. Get us off this vector," Jaq ordered.

"Course laid in."

The ship changed its orientation to fifteen degrees off the nose.

"Accelerating at one-point-two gees," Ferd said.

Jaq welcomed the apparent gee forces and released her boots to walk around with a sense of normalcy. She glanced from position to position. "Damage report."

Brad looked askance before checking his screens. "All

departments are at one-hundred-percent combat effectiveness."

"What's ahead of us?" Jaq asked, looking to Slade for the answer since the main screen was uninformative.

"I believe we'll find the Malibor fleet waiting for us," the sensor chief said nonchalantly.

"The what? All their ships? Donal and Dolly, dial up your programming to get quality shots at that mob."

"They are scattered and maneuvering," Slade announced before updating the main screen to show two cruisers and six gunships.

"We're still missing two cruisers and eight gunships, if my math serves me correctly," Jaq replied.

Alby reported, "Current order of battle is five total cruisers remain and eighteen gunships. Disposition is one cruiser at Septimus and two in front of us, leaving two unaccounted for. Two gunships are attached to the station and two are in a low orbit of Septimus. Six are in front of us, which leaves eight gunships unaccounted for. Your math is correct, Captain."

"See what kind of shots you can make on these ships."

Donal pumped his fist. "The program was written for this type of engagement. The Malibor ships are linked from sensors to the targeting computer. Our offset angle is accounted for, recommend roll five degrees starboard and yaw of ten degrees."

"Adjust ship orientation," Jaq ordered.

The movements were miniscule and done quickly. "We'll need to compensate more to get onto the right vector around Armanor."

"I understand. We have a ways to go before we need to worry. We have three days to make more adjustments. Let's take care of business right here and right now. Nothing would make me happier than destroying every ship in this defensive armada. And, Brad, why didn't your people see these ships setting up to ambush us?"

"I can't answer that. I would have thought they'd have been visible departing or getting into position. A million kilometers is nothing. Our scouts should have seen them."

"Fire all batteries you can bring to bear, sustained rate of fire, not cyclic." Jaq pointed at Alby to implement her order.

Cyclic burned energy a great deal faster than the sustained rate of fire of ten rounds per cannon per second.

With all of the firing, the energy gauge had already dropped back to ninety percent. Jaq would only worry if they needed to start maneuvering away from the Malibor ambush.

"Obstacles in the line of travel," Slade said, speaking softer than the emergency warranted. "Incoming railgun fire and missiles."

"Missiles! Taurus, send four at their cruisers. Give them something to worry about besides us."

"Targets identified. Launch!"

The missiles jumped from their tubes, traveling at over two million kilometers per hour at a yaw of thirteen degrees off the travel vector.

"Nose first, Mary. Present as little of a target as possible."

"Adjusting." The ship rotated the rest of the way to continue on the previous vector at one-point-two gees acceleration.

"I believe they are lobbing ordnance in our flight path.

Their targeting isn't up to the task like ours," Slade guessed.

Jaq nodded. She crossed her arms and glared at the screen. The sensor systems were trying to keep up with all the junk in space before them.

Outbound rounds tracked green toward the Malibor cruisers. The targets were microscopic at that range, but they didn't need to pepper the ships. They only needed to send a few rounds down the length of the hull.

That was the same thing the Malibor were attempting to do to the Borwyn.

No longer a game of tactical micro-moves, it was now a slog between behemoths where each tried to hit the other harder until one fell.

It wasn't an analogy that Jaq liked, but it was what came to mind. Whoever could survive the other's barrage would be the winner, not the one who delivered more accurate fire.

"Side thrusters, please. Move us away from where they're predicting we'll be. Star angle plus three. Accelerate to seven gees for..." Jaq did the math quickly in her mind. "...four minutes. Then return to nose forward and one-point-two gees."

"Roger," Ferd confirmed.

Jaq gestured to the comm officer for ship-wide.

Amie gave her the thumbs-up.

"All hands, into your seats. Seven-gee hard burn for the next four minutes. After that, damage control teams rally to your equipment locations and prepare to respond to damage."

"We can escape it. You're already making them look like fools."

The E-mags hammered away, vibrating the entire ship.

Eighty-eight percent energy.

Jaq hated seeing it drop, but they were in good shape. They'd exit the engagement with plenty of energy remaining.

The ship angled away from the orbital plane, and the ion drives powered toward a new vector. The crew pressed deeply into their seats.

"Take us to nine gees!" Jaq shouted.

The compression grew more intense to the point where their vision narrowed as blood struggled to continue flowing to their brains.

Jaq gritted her teeth and bore down as she'd been trained. Her heart raced, thumping heavily in her chest with each beat, but it kept pumping. The gel squeezed her legs and arms until they hurt.

After four minutes, acceleration eased back to one-point-two gees. Jaq panted to recover her wits along with her mobility. She eased out of her seat and wobbled as she stood. "Sensors?"

"We're away from the vast majority of it."

"But not all?" Jaq was surprised to the point of being shocked. "How much did they throw into our flight path?"

"Everything they had," Slade replied.

"Missiles are flying true," Taurus interjected. "Targets are two missiles at four different gunships."

"Why didn't we target the cruisers?" Jaq asked.

"Because the cruisers have defensive weapons that would kill the missiles. They wouldn't have a chance."

"Do they have a chance against the gunships?" The gunships were small and wouldn't have to maneuver much to avoid the missiles. But if it took their eyes off the attack, Jaq would consider it a win.

"Our guidance system inside is much better than what the Malibor use. Terminal approach is different than what they're expecting," Alby replied. "We did that at the ERS because the Malibor will know they are Malibor missiles, so they'll try to avoid them using the methods they've grown used to in their training scenarios."

"Why wouldn't they train against Borwyn missiles?" Taurus said.

Jaq intently watched their closing speed.

"They fought one war against the Borwyn fifty years ago and five wars against themselves. Their bet is that we're their own ship. Even though we transmitted a message declaring ourselves as the Borwyn," Jaq explained, "they may not believe it. Give me a channel to those ships."

The E-mags shut down.

"Keep firing!" Jaq snapped. "Brad? You'll sound more like the captain of *Hornet*."

"Broadcast is open."

"This is *Hornet*. You will stand down immediately," Brad said in his deepest voice. "I say again, stand down."

Amie signaled that the channel was closed.

"We'll see if it gives them pause." Jaq pointed at Brad, who nodded back.

Inbound projectiles tracked across the tactical screen.

"Ship-wide broadcast. All hands, brace yourselves for impact."

Jaq dove toward her seat as the ship screamed with the first impact that came from overhead, same as the second.

CHAPTER 16

The battle of wills starts at the top but ends with the most junior member of the crew.

"Damage report?" Jaq demanded. Two impacts, no more, both in the decks above.

The damage control board flashed red for decks one through five.

"Loss of atmosphere on Deck One. Impacts on Decks two through Five. Damage Control is already working. Automated systems sealed breaches on Decks Two through Five," Brad reported.

"Malibor cruisers are taking damage," Taurus interrupted.

Jaq rapidly glanced back and forth between the two screens. The inbound ordnance was scattered far and wide, and they'd passed most of it.

The E-mags adjusted and renewed firing.

Chrysalis closed on the ambush armada heading for the

closest point of approach of five thousand kilometers. The Malibor ship-to-ship missiles arrived before *Chrysalis,* and three of them were promptly shot out of the sky. Fire from the cruisers and railgun fire from the gunships hammered at the big, slow missiles until they exploded harmlessly. The last one kissed a gunship's outer hull and skipped but blew up without penetrating the armor. The ship bucked and started to spin.

Donal adjusted the E-mags to fire at the gunships.

The E-mags droned on. Three gunships disappeared into debris clouds. A fourth jerked and bounced, then started to drift. The final remaining gunship continued on a course to take it behind a cruiser.

The E-mags tracked toward the gunship heading for the cruiser, but they suddenly stopped firing.

"Hit it!" Jaq shouted an instant later, but the E-mags didn't start firing. Jaq threw up her hands in frustration. "We had them!"

Chrysalis raced past, increasing the distance between it and the Malibor fleet. Both cruisers were streaming atmosphere. One gunship continued to maneuver to keep a Malibor cruiser between it and *Chrysalis*.

The Borwyn accelerated away from the engagement zone. No one fired at them, and they didn't fire back.

"What happened to the E-mags? We left two cruisers alive!"

"Or did we?" Alby asked. "We hit them hard, and five gunships are gone. Those cruisers are flying junk. Maybe they're dead on the inside."

"Like your girlfriend?" Brad joked.

Alby stared. His lips moved but no sound came out.

"Damage control?" Jaq was serious. Her mouth fell open, and she stared.

Brad left his humor behind and got out of his seat. "What?"

"*Bessie Mae's* crew was in the forward storage space." Jaq ran from the bridge, but she had to wait for the elevator. She tapped a staccato beat with her boot while waiting, checking through the cage for the elevator's location.

She skipped past the elevator and climbed into the narrow tube beside it with a vertical ladder. She would have only been able to take the elevator upward a short way before checking on the progress of repairs on Deck Five.

After two decks, she started to slow. At the third deck above, Deck Five, she climbed out to find a damage control team from the lower decks working to seal the penetrations and replace the affected equipment—cabling on one side of the corridor, an air diverter on the other. But thanks to *Cornucopia* and *Butterfly*, spare parts were available, which made repairs go far more quickly with more assurance of permanence.

Jaq didn't distract them. She returned to the ladder and found crews working just as diligently on Decks Four through Two.

The top deck was closed off by emergency bulkheads. She stood there wondering why she climbed up there without a spacesuit, knowing that there was a huge hole in the ship.

A tap on her shoulder announced the arrival of the team that would work the first deck repairs. She stepped back to find Teo looking at her through the clear face shield of an old

Borwyn environmental control suit. "We've got it, Jaq, but we'll need to use this section as an airlock as soon as we can take the foot off the accelerator and move our equipment up here."

Jaq accessed the comm unit on the bulkhead. "Announce to the ship we'll be at zero-gee for five minutes. Idle the drives, and let's move our heavy equipment around the ship. Clear it with me before reengaging the drives."

Brad's voice announced the move over the ship-wide intercom. After two minutes, zero-gee brought a respite to those moving steel, welders, and heavy parts throughout the ship.

Jaq stayed back from the second emergency bulkhead. Teo with a team of four stepped inside and closed the bulkhead behind them. Emergency bulkheads had no windows, so Jaq had to guess that they had cleared the atmosphere and walked through to the first deck.

She contacted the bridge. "Brad, send me a spacesuit."

"I'll bring it myself."

"Deputy is supposed to stay on the bridge when the captain is away." She waited, but there was no response. "Brad?"

She shook her head but liked that the leadership team was hands-on. They needed to be comfortable throughout the ship with the crew. It was less of a family with the new additions, but with each passing day, they became closer.

The curse and blessing of life on a starship.

Jaq found her way to the repair crew working on the second deck. The damage up here was more cosmetic than structural and had impacted no systems. The only equipment the team had was an arc welder and rods. The thirteen-year-old was there, filling the holes caused by the railgun impacts.

He looked up to see Jaq watching him with shielded eyes.

"Just burning steel, Captain!"

"And doing it well, too. Where's you dad?"

"Next deck down. I got the number one job!"

"You've earned it, but it's more dangerous up here. You probably should switch places."

He shook his head. "Pops is gonna spacesuit for the repairs on the next level up. He's got the tough job. I can't wait until I get bigger and can fit into a small suit. Welding outside would have to be the ultimate bonzo!"

"I'm sure it will be. Did I miss the class where they taught new words?"

"Nope. Me and the boys came up with them ourselves," the young man replied.

"I don't know if I'm more bothered that I hadn't heard them before or that I already know what they mean." She clapped him on the shoulder. "Get back to work. I want to check on the people forward."

His face dropped. "That's another reason why Pops is going. He said there's dead people up there, and it wasn't my time to deal with that. A dad has to protect his son from the evils that are out there. Do you believe that, Captain?"

Her voice caught in her throat. She settled for a nod. "We all have to protect each other the best we can. We won the battle we just fought. We won't have too many more to win before there won't be any more to fight. This is our strategy, and we're doing extremely well. Soon, we'll be able to do things like normal people and not be fixing battle damage. I promise."

The young man dropped his face shield and turned back to the task at hand.

The dexterity of youth belied his wisdom. Another element of being trapped within the hull of a ship condemned to an eternity in space.

It was Jaq's mission to give the crew a future. The Borwyn on New Septimus settled for hiding. Those on board *Chrysalis* didn't have that option until recently, and Jaq didn't give them a choice to go to New Septimus.

She was afraid some would choose the easy way when there wasn't a choice to be made. Their parents had committed them to this war, and they were all in, even if they didn't want to be. They had been raised without knowing another way.

There was no reason to plant the seeds of discontent. The captain trudged toward the bulkhead sealing the ladder tube. She would have normally floated free in zero-gee, but not right now.

The burden of command. She had approved putting *Bessie Mae's* crew forward. She knew the risk, and they paid the price. Their transgression? They were Malibor. But they were survivors. They had made their lives aboard an old freighter. She held out a glimmer of hope, like a bright light to guide her toward a friendly home.

Brad appeared out of the elevator, wearing a suit and carrying another. Jaq took it without comment and climbed into it. She checked the fit of the gloves, and Brad helped seat her helmet. It snapped into place, and the suit filled with air.

She checked the suit's status. It was good. She accessed the manual override panel next to the emergency bulkhead. She secured the next bulkhead and then turned a hand crank to refill the space with air. When a light flashed green, she opened the bulkhead before her.

Once inside, she reversed the process.

Jaq steeled herself for what would be on the other side. The emergency bulkhead lifted to reveal far more destruction than she had guessed. The round had penetrated the gap between the hardened nosecone and the hull, which had then ripped open, creating a three-meter-by-one-meter opening. There were no bodies. When the atmosphere explosively vented through such a tear, it took everyone in the forward compartment.

They went into space without environmental containment suits. Jaq leaned against the bulkhead while Teo and the crew took measurements and relayed instructions to the fabrication team. Thanks to the weapons platform and the hulk formerly known as *Butterfly*, they had plenty of metal plates to create both internal and external patches.

They wouldn't make external repairs until the ship stopped moving. The vacuum of space wasn't complete. At their speed, it wouldn't take much to lose a person forever if they were stripped away from the hull. She didn't want to trust a life to a tether. Until then, they'd keep the first deck off limits, fill it with ballast and other material to prevent further penetration into the ship if another lucky shot hit the same place.

"Anything?" Jaq finally asked.

Teo clenched her jaw and shook her head.

"We need to let them work," Brad said, urging Jaq toward the ladder and makeshift airlock.

Jaq straightened and walked slowly with her head up. She climbed down at a measured pace with Brad climbing after her.

Once returned to the serenity of the ship, Jaq removed her helmet as if it were stifling her ability to breathe. She drew a long breath. The damage control team joined them.

"Well?" the young welder asked.

"Your dad was right. It's best that you don't go up there, even if you had a spacesuit, but we'll get it fixed up good as new for our next strike on the Malibor. We're going to win this war, and you'll be working in the shipyard, if that's where you want, bringing that new ship—twice the size of this one—online and operational. It'll be a ship for exploration and not war. Would you like that?"

The boy frowned. "I like the action the way it is now."

Jaq winced. "The invincibility of youth. I'm sure we'll find something exciting, but you'll be able to do what you want. Freedom is what we're fighting for."

The boy smiled. "That's what Pops says."

The elevator arrived, and two crewmembers stepped out. One was Benjy, the lander operator and teacher. They each carried two suits. The ship's best welder appeared in the ladder well. He stepped onto the deck and waved to his son.

"Pops!" the boy called.

Jaq pointed upward. "There's a lot of work to do up there. There's a big hole in the ship."

"So I heard. That's why we brought this along." He looked around, but the rest of his team was far behind, straining, despite the zero-gee, to guide the metal patch up the ladder.

When it appeared, the team made eye contact, snapped their helmets into place, and stepped into the makeshift airlock. The last thing the welder did was point a finger pistol at his son.

The young man clutched at his chest as the bulkhead lowered, which put into place a blocking plate in the ladder well. When it depressurized, it opened the emergency bulkhead to the deck above.

Jaq waved to the damage control team. Their exuberance made her feel better, even though she would torture herself to her end of days for losing the cargo ship's crew.

"You didn't kill them," Brad said after reading the expression on her face.

"We didn't have to put them all the way forward. We could have put Malibor food up here and the crew on the lower deck."

"Moving everything up here would have been time consuming. No. Once their guy tried to sabotage us, they lost their ability to be free. There was no other choice than to paint them with the same brush. All they had to do was nothing, and they wouldn't even be here. They'd be on the cargo ship still, hanging out, playing cards. But no, they had to let one of their own go rogue. The captain should have known that he was responsible for everything his people did."

"I know, but it's hard to reconcile. I will always consider it a mistake."

"That's your prerogative. I think it's wrong, and I'm not going to lose any sleep over it. I could have talked you out of it, but did you see what their guy did to Tram? I wasn't inclined to speak on their behalf."

"Tram was in pretty bad shape. Thanks for talking your Doc Teller into joining us."

They cycled the airlock to open the bulkheads to the lower deck.

"Leave the suits, if you would," one of the damage control team said.

Jaq and Brad removed the suits and left them standing for the next user. "Lots of air left," Brad said, then asked Jaq, "Talking about Tram, when are we due to hear from them?"

"Not anytime soon. And this will be the longest wait. I want to know that they're okay. I want to know that they've made contact with our fellow Borwyn. And I want to know what it feels like to stand on Septimus."

CHAPTER 17

Any landing you can walk away from.

The buffeting started the instant they hit the upper atmosphere. They lost sensors shortly thereafter. The ship tossed like it had zero aerodynamics built in.

Because it didn't. Landing the ship on a planet took the engines managing the heavy lifting. The thing was little more than a block of metal with nothing in the way of lift. Had the engines not been driving it forward, it would have plummeted out of control until it crashed into the ground at Mach Twenty-five.

As it was, they were riding the turbulence.

"The good news is that the Malibor ships didn't seem to take any notice of us," Danny shouted.

Deena had her eyes jammed shut. She clenched her jaw and maintained a death grip on her seat.

"We're not going to die," Max said loudly but calmly.

"Who are you trying to convince, us or you?" Danny laughed almost maniacally. "Riding the drop can to the trenches. Oorah!"

"Is he okay?" Crip asked out the side of his mouth.

"I think he might always be like that," Deena managed to reply. "You have to do a better job of vetting people."

The ship jerked and twisted, slamming everyone against their restraints.

Hammer and Anvil stopped smiling and kept their mouths shut to keep from chipping a tooth, straining to get through the worst of the buffeting. They'd taken a steeper angle to start, to get away from the ships in orbit, but Tram lessened the angle to decrease the friction to what the gunship's structure could handle.

Ninety seconds later, the pain of entry stopped as the ship plummeted in freefall.

A voice from below shouted up the stairs. "Clearing the turbulence. Skies over Septimus are clear. Hang on, we need to slow down."

"No kidding," Danny yelled back.

Matador inverted, and the engines kicked in to both stabilize the ship and slow it down. Compared to the power of gravity, human bodies were soft. With deceleration, they were slammed into their seats once more. Deena started gasping for air.

"Just a little bit more," Max told her. "We'll come out of it soon."

She nodded with her eyes still closed.

Danny coughed. "Feeling my age," he grunted.

Max held Deena's hand. She squeezed it like she was

giving birth. His fingers went numb. He suffered through it like she was and shared her anguish.

The landing on Farslor was nowhere near this rough, but the lander had been built for it. The gunship was capable but almost as an afterthought.

The rocking and yawing continued as if telling the live beings that their deaths were imminent. They were being rocked to a permanent sleep.

"Crip!" Max blurted.

"All good. Landing zone is on the screen. Mach five and slowing," Crip shouted from below.

That little bit of information was all it took to calm everyone's nerves. Deena relaxed her grip. Hammer and Anvil shared a laugh.

Even Danny Johns relaxed. He swallowed hard. "It's been fifty years since I last stepped foot on Septimus."

"Your wait is over. We'll be standing on it soon enough, as long as Tram figures out how to land this thing, otherwise we'll be splattered on it."

"Don't say splatter," Deena begged. Her stomach started to heave.

"Babies and fuzzy bottoms!" Max shouted.

Danny started laughing.

The ship bucked one last time, lifted them out of their seats, and then settled them back in. With a soft thump, the ship stopped, and the engines shut down.

"Hi, sweetie pies, we're home!" Crip called from below into the instant silence. "Get your trash and prepare to disembark."

Crip was first to the airlock. He overrode the controls and

opened both hatches at the same time, flooding the ship with scents that most had never smelled before.

"What is that?" Max said.

"Wildflowers, the likes of which only grow outside the city," Deena replied.

"It smells funny." Max wrinkled his nose while gesturing for the team to follow him out.

Crip extended the ladder from the hatch to the ground. Once it was in place, he scanned the area slowly, looking for any sign they'd been spotted. Rapid movements drew his eye. He recognized them as birds. Not a threat. Active wildlife would indicate that no people were nearby.

At least, that was what he had read. Wildlife and the smell of a warm planet were new to him. Farslor bordered on being a dead world, cold and unfeeling.

He climbed down, the first Borwyn of the new generation to return to Septimus. His reverie almost got him kicked in the head.

He shuffled away, making room for Max and the others. "Defensive perimeter!" Max shouted, pointing the soldiers into positions fifty meters away, forming a semi-circle with the ship at the central point.

Crip, Max, and Deena took a knee. "Which way to the city?"

Deena threw her hands up. "I've never been out here before. I have no idea."

Crip realized the error of his pre-conceptions. Just because she was from Septimus didn't mean she could navigate her way around the wild parts.

"From the map," Max said, referencing the memorized terrain. "If we landed where we were supposed to, we move in the opposite direction of the mountains behind us." He slashed a knife hand at the open area opposite. "We go down that valley and take a left when we hit the forest below. After about fifty klicks, it'll turn into a plain for another twenty klicks and then we come to another forest, sparse, mixed with rolling hills that borders the grasslands outside the city. We're about a hundred klicks from the city."

"Sounds like an easy day's walk," Crip replied. At Deena's look, he winked. "Where do you think we'll find the Borwyn?"

"They could be anywhere between here and the city. I suggest we walk and if we see sign of them, we start an outreach."

"What do you mean by that?" Max asked.

"You yell that you're Borwyn and ask for a parlay."

"Will that work?" Crip wondered aloud.

Deena shrugged.

Max snorted. "I hope so, otherwise we're going to have real problems."

"Business as usual. We came down here with an objective but no real plan." Crip shook his head and stood. "Prepare to move out. That way." He pointed down the valley, a wide natural ramp, kilometers long, lined by hills as it descended toward the trees below.

"Crip," Tram called from the hatch. "We have a problem."

"Hold up," Max called. He turned his head when he

caught a sound. Birdsong. Chirping and whistling. It was mesmerizing.

"I hear it, too," Crip admitted.

Deena smiled.

Crip returned to the ladder. "What's the issue?"

"We don't have enough power to break out of the atmosphere." Tram's face twisted and creased with the strain.

"That was always a possibility. Grab your trash. You're coming with us." Crip twirled his finger in the air.

"We should stay with the ship, just in case."

"Just in case a magic space bug delivers a new power supply?" Crip taunted.

"No!" He made a rude gesture at his fellow command officer. "In case you need supporting firepower. We can get off the ground and fire the railguns. They'll shake the planet itself. I would think you can hold us in reserve and use us to pack a punch, deliver the winning blow!"

"The Malibor are going to be all over this ship in no time. All you'll get is captured and tortured. You've personally seen the vitriol within the Malibor soul. How much more of that do you want?"

"I don't want that. I don't want to walk a hundred klicks either."

"Pick your poison, Tram, but I would prefer they not capture you since you know things I would prefer the Malibor didn't learn."

"I won't tell them anything!" Tram thrust his chin in the air and stuck out his chest.

"From what I read, everyone breaks, so we'll assume that

you'll break after three days of intense interrogation. But what you'll tell them about *Chrysalis* will be timeless and help to get them killed. You can't hold out. And then the Malibor will learn how to kill our people. Let's remove that possibility by taking you and Kelvis with us. Grab your packs. We don't know how long it will be before the Malibor show up to check out the errant ship they tracked to this part of the world."

Tram looked like he was going to cry. He hesitated, standing in the hatch, staring down.

Crip waited.

"Maybe we can hide the ship," Tram suggested.

Crip looked around and threw his hands in the air. "Using what?" Their immediate surroundings were devoid of growth, a primary reason they'd selected this spot to land.

The team members glanced back and forth between their overlapping arcs of fire and the gunship.

Tram nodded and disappeared inside.

Crip cupped his hands around his mouth. "Hurry up!"

It took two minutes before Tram and Kelvis appeared with their packs on. They slowly descended the ladder.

"Close the hatch, otherwise we'll be learning about the birds and bees the hard way."

Kelvis climbed up and tapped on the pad. The hatch rotated into place and sealed.

"I coded it so no one can get in. It's four, five, six, seven, eight, nine, eleven."

They reached the ground and stood beside the ship.

Kelvis waved a small part. "The Borwyn integrated

circuit. With the modifications I've made, no one will be able to get this ship operational without a major refit." He stuffed the part into his pocket.

"Got it," Crip confirmed. "Welcome to Septimus. Now, if you don't mind, we need to get out of here."

Max brought the team to their feet, signaled a two-by-two formation, and they took off at a brisk pace that made Deena and the two engineers run. It was downhill and they kept up without huffing and puffing, even though they weren't used to such physical activity.

Septimus was one gee. It was the scientific standard that the Borwyn used. They'd become accustomed to acceleration at one-point-two gees, and that made the movement down the mountain pass less strenuous.

Kelvis and Tram kept looking back at the gunship. It presented as both severe and lonely against the mountain backdrop.

Crip and Max didn't relax until they reached the woods.

"Inverted V, five meter spacing, Danzig on point. Binfall, Barrington, Hammer, and Larson on the left wing. Johns, Zurig, Anvil, and Tomans on the right. Crip will ride the center with Kelvis, Tram, and Deena. Finley and I will take Tail-End Charlie."

The soldiers moved into their positions quickly and with little sound. The group walking in trail of Danzig made the most noise of all, even though Crip glared with each broken twig or scuffed boot.

"Pick up your feet and watch where you step!" he cautioned.

"I'm not supposed to be here," Kelvis whined. "I'm a power engineer."

Crip called a halt. He turned on Kelvis. "You *are* here, and we have a mission to bring all Borwyn on board with the final campaign of a long war."

"What if they don't want to fight our war?" Kelvis countered.

"It's going to get real old, real quick, if you keep whining. We came to Septimus to start a new front in the war, pull their attention away from how to defeat *Chrysalis*, and we're going to do just that, whether we get the surviving Borwyn to come with us or not." Crip clenched his fists. "We're here to win the war, Kelvis. Whether the Borwyn want to fight or not, war was inevitable. Where could we have gone and not continued the war?"

The engineer shrugged. "Nowhere. The Malibor hate us."

"If they didn't, then we could have returned without our cannons hammering away. No one wanted to deliver mass destruction, but it's what we had to do. They believe they're still at war with us. Good thing we believe it, too."

"That's a lousy explanation about why Tram and I can't stay with the ship. Maybe you could have told us, 'because I said so'."

"I need you to believe in the mission. For all Borwyn. That's why we're here, and that's what we're willing to sacrifice everything for. And if you find a power source somewhere out here, you and Tram can return to the gunship. I promise."

"I'm going to hold you to that," Kelvis replied. He perked up. "That's all I needed to hear."

Crip shook his head. He looked at Max, who shrugged.

"Any words of wisdom in how we can contact the locals? Do we look Borwyn?" Crip asked Deena.

"You don't look Malibor, which will hopefully give them pause. Otherwise, you're going to have problems." Deena smiled while tilting her head back to catch a light beam penetrating through the branches above.

"So we landed without a plan," Crip reiterated. "I really thought we had a plan."

"It sounded like a plan," Max said, "but it wasn't. We have ideals with objectives and goals with steps. Have we ever had a plan?"

"You guys are killing me. I used to think I knew stuff, that I was ready to conduct any operation." He dug his toe into the ground and kicked away a small clump of earth. "No matter. We're on Septimus, my friends. If I die here, I'll be happy."

"There you go, talking doom and gloom again!" Kelvis sniped. "Who wants to die?"

"Of old age." Crip gave the engineer two thumbs up.

"Soldiers," Kelvis grumbled.

Crip twirled his finger in the air. "Let's put a couple more klicks between us and the ship before we settle in for the evening. Danzig, be on the lookout for a place where we can shelter."

Gentle foothills rose on their left while the other three sides were filled by a thick forest, which slowed them down. Slow was better than exposed. They stayed within the confines of the cover.

"Stay alert. Call out if you see any sign of our fellow Borwyn. Doubly so if you see any Malibor."

"The silence is silent," Kelvis noted.

"It's called nature. Listen for what's not normal," Max explained.

"None of this is normal!" Kelvis threw his hands up.

Max started laughing and continued to chuckle to himself as they moved slowly through the underbrush.

Birds flushed out in front of Danzig, making a commotion as they panicked to flight. The combat team instantly stopped and dropped to one knee, ready to engage an enemy made aware of their presence. After a few heart-stopping moments, Danzig rose and continued ahead.

Crip wanted to talk to someone about the vegetation and the birds and the bugs and the air and everything. He was nearly bursting with excitement, despite the nature of their mission and the inherent risk in contacting their fellow Borwyn.

Max drifted back and forth across the back, stopping occasionally to watch and listen before hurrying to catch up. Danzig also meandered and varied his pace. They acted as consummate professionals.

Crip berated himself for being distracted. They'd take it slowly to begin with and not press for maximum distance. They also needed to find supplemental food. They had a week's worth of rations. Ten days if they rationed what they had.

That was enough to get them to the city, but they weren't going to the city. Their so-called plan was to wander around the bush looking for their blood relatives. Maybe Danny

Johns would personally know some of the survivors, but with a rough life, none of the previous generation would be alive. That was what had happened aboard *Chrysalis*, and it was probably what had happened on Septimus. Only New Septimus was spared the shortened lifespans.

They'd find out for sure when they ran into the Borwyn.

If they ran into their fellow Borwyn.

CHAPTER 18

The power in a great team is found in their ability to work alone.

Jaq scowled. She leaned on the corner of her seat. They'd already passed Deltor on their way toward Canton and ultimately the Armanor star, but only as a halfway point.

"We've gone over the data and the images we were able to collect, and I can say with relative certainty that the space station is a tube, hollow in the middle. It's only one level, and the benefit is that it'll only have one force that feels like gravity, independent of changed diameters. Centripetal force will be nearly identical at every location throughout the entire station."

"That's interesting, but how can we use that information?"

"Some of their fleet assets are inside."

Jaq snarled. She looked at Brad's seat, but he was out touring the damaged areas as the crew finalized repairs—all except for the first deck, where Teo and her chosen team were still sealing the tear in the hull.

"What have the scout ships missed? What is the real order of battle?" Jaq snapped her fingers. "You have the estimated size of the station and the interior. How many ships could reasonably fit in there? Include unreasonably, too, so I have a number range to work with."

Slade checked his screen. He presented what he had to Dolly with Donal looking over their shoulders. The three returned to their terminals and tapped furiously.

She would eventually get an answer. This was another lesson in patience. Haranguing them would get her no closer to her answer. She'd already done the eyeball math in her head and come up with four cruisers and ten gunships or six cruisers and two gunships. It changed the dynamic, but not by much. If they wouldn't come out and fight, then she'd deliver an ultimatum. *Evacuate the station or your families will die when the Malpace station is destroyed.*

Then they would also be able to count the number of shuttles and personnel carriers available. Get a more complete picture of what the Malibor were capable of doing.

Jaq activated the ship-wide comm channel. "Brad, please return to the bridge. We have new information I'd like you to look at."

What she wanted Brad to look at was how the scout ships were employed in delivering incomplete information. She wanted an accurate assessment of the enemy. She couldn't get that with half the information.

It sent her stomach into somersaults. What didn't she know about the Malibor?

Jaq drummed her fingers on her seat's armrest until she caught people staring. She cracked her knuckles, smiled, and nodded.

During the high-speed pass, energy had dropped to seventy-six percent. It was one of many things that had gone right. She needed to embrace that instead of dwelling on the shortcomings that led to the loss of *Bessie Mae's* crew. The Malibor never embraced the new ship name, and Jaq wouldn't tarnish their memories by equating them with it. *Cornucopia* was a Borwyn ship, just like *Butterfly* had become *Hornet* but was *Butterfly* once more.

The captain should have set a higher standard for his crew. Don't mess with the Borwyn. All you'll do is make them angry and get yourself killed.

Her thoughts wandered until Brad tapped her on the shoulder.

"New information?"

She resisted the temptation to vent at him. "Our scans have revealed that the space station is hollow. It's a cylinder and not a spindle. Inside, there are ships, possibly an entire fleet."

Brad rocked back, flowing with the zero-gee while his boots held him in place. "And you're wondering how we missed it?"

"At first, yes, but now, no, because that part doesn't matter anywhere near as much as figuring out what we're going to do about it."

"Another high-speed pass?" Brad offered. "And this time, take out the space station. We send a warning right now and give them plenty of time to evacuate."

"I'd like to do that, but all they'll do is fill our return course with garbage that we'll run into, including missiles, mines, and railgun ordnance. I don't want to give them a week and a half to set a trap for us."

"They won't know how far away we'll fire from," Brad countered.

"At our speed, we can't change course significantly. Giving them a long lead time can't benefit us."

"We'll do nothing?" he asked.

"Of course not. We'll do something, but what and when? First and foremost, I need one of your scout ships closer to Malpace. We can't get surprised by fleets running around the system and hiding or worse, waiting to ambush us."

"They've lost a lot of ships trying to confront us." Brad held up his hand to forestall an argument. "They can't stand up to *Chrysalis*. We only need another engagement or two where we destroy all of their ships, and they won't sally out to meet us. They'll run, every single time."

Jaq gazed at the tactical screen showing the relative location of the planets orbiting Armanor, the star they raced toward. The flight path was projected but only so far as it began the slingshot maneuver. Their next destination had not yet been decided.

That was on the captain and her trusted advisors.

"I want to return to Septimus, hit them again while they're still regrouping. By my count, they're down four more cruisers and five more gunships. I want to hit them again while they're still reeling from the overwhelming force of our last attack. Four cruisers and five gunships. They paid heavily for trying to fight us. Maybe you are right."

"Maybe?" Brad countered. "I concur. The best time to hit them is right now. We should slingshot around Armanor and return to Septimus to hit them again."

"What if they run, as you said?"

"Then they won't be there when we arrive, and we'll end up doing a high-speed flyby."

"Alby." The captain motioned for her battle commander to join them. "What do you think?"

"I've been listening, and I agree. If we can hit them now, we may deliver enough destruction to force them to the table."

"Brad, get your scouts closer, danger close. We need to know how the Malibor are responding. I want their communications between the ships and the station and the station and the planet. I want a good count and location of every ship they have available, plus their tracks since we passed. I see four gunships and one cruiser ready to engage. We have two unknowns. Where did the rest of the fleet go, and how many ships are inside the station? If we can figure out if the ships inside the station are the same ones that were outside, then we don't double count. While your scouts are at it, I want to know what happened to that troopship we left above Sairvor."

"You don't want much, do you?" Brad asked.

"It's for the survival of the Borwyn." Jaq furrowed her brow and cocked her head as she questioned Brad's willingness to put his people in harm's way.

"I know, Jaq. I'm not arguing, but if we overextend ourselves, then we risk losing one or more of our scout ships, which means we risk losing my friends. Did we have enough information to effectively conduct the last battle?"

"Barely," Jaq admitted.

"That might be the best we can do. We use all passive sensors as well as visual. That's it. We can't irradiate the entire area. That would turn us into a Malibor missile target. I don't want my people to die doing something they were never intended to do."

"Why did you develop the scout ships and the scout program?" Jaq relaxed and let her body flow in the zero-gee even though she remained rooted to the deck.

"To do something. Most of us weren't ready to surrender completely to living inside a moon. The scout program gave us hope. And now you're telling me it wasn't good enough." Brad hung his head. "We did the best we could with what we had available to us. And we're still doing the best we can."

Jaq squeezed Brad's shoulder. "I appreciate it, but I'm asking for a little bit more. If we're going back to Septimus, then we need an up-to-date and detailed disposition of Malibor fleet assets. We need it in four days after we've rounded Armanor, and then we need it updated every couple hours so we can adjust our course to give us the best firing solutions. They may try to intercept us, but their weapons can't target us at speed. They could try to seed our flight path with mines and debris, but that's why I want tracks on their ships. Space is a big place. If we can adjust a few hundred kilometers, they'll miss us. When we hit them a second time, we'll bring their dominance of space to an end."

"I think their dominance is already at an end." Brad nodded tightly and held Jaq's gaze without blinking.

She stared back until she realized a contest of wills was better fought between adversaries and not friends. She didn't need to win anything with her crew. "I only need to keep them alive until they stand on Septimus."

"Who?"

"Did I say that out loud? Sorry." Jaq looked away. She spoke loudly for all to hear. "Set course for a return to Septimus. What is our centripetal limit?"

"With Armanor's gravity, we need to slow down. At our current speed, centripetal acceleration is over forty-five gees. We need to slow to seven hundred and eight-six thousand KPH to reduce the centripetal acceleration to seven gees."

"Forty-five gees is a bit extreme. It would rip the ship apart and kill everyone before our catastrophic demise. When will repairs be finished to the first deck's cargo hold?"

"Soon," Brad replied. At Jaq's look, he took a different approach. "I will personally verify and get back with you." He released his boots and launched himself toward the corridor.

"Prepare to slow the ship. Recommendation?" Jaq asked.

Ferd tapped his screen to make the calculations. "Three gees for about three hours or one-point-two gees for eight hours."

"I like the one-point-two gee option. Time to Armanor?"

"Forty-four hours," Ferd replied.

"Lots of time. Begin slow down at thirty-seven hours and thirty minutes. Mark."

"Roger. And we'll need to continue the deceleration as Armanor's gravity will attempt to accelerate us. We'll have to fight it until we circle the star and are launched toward Septimus."

"We'll pick up speed as we accelerate at one-point-two gees until we've returned to two million KPH."

"Do we want to go that fast this time? I recommend a slower approach," Alby replied.

"Slower increases our risk."

"It makes us far more deadly. We can slew the E-mags and deliver death left and right, above and below." He made finger guns and mimicked blasting everywhere in a way that looked like a spastic fit.

Jaq stared. "Do we look like that when we're shooting in all directions?"

"For Septiman's sake, I hope not." Alby holstered his finger pistols. "At a million, we may be able to target gunships attached to the station. Our ability to hit what we aim at is greatly improved at half the speed. Even though Dolly and Donal have reduced our margin of error by about ninety percent, we still have room to improve, and that comes from a reduction in speed. We'll find the sweet spot, that point where we're going too fast for the Malibor to hit us while putting maximum number of rounds on target."

Jaq moved around the command deck, mumbling to herself as she worked through the various options.

The air smelled clean, despite how long they'd been in their seats. It had been six hours with a significant battle during that time. No one had swapped with their replacement to get some rest. They were still at it to see what was going to happen next.

The battle had unfolded quickly, as Jaq had known it

would. Then, it was over in an instant, but it wasn't because there was a second phase to the battle. That, too, ended almost as soon as it started.

Jaq returned to her seat. "Give me ship-wide, please."

Amie confirmed with a thumbs-up.

"All hands, this is your captain. I want to thank you for how you've acquitted yourselves during the demands of combat. This has always been a warship, but it's also our home. We have to remember both roles that it plays for us. We use it to fight, and we use it to eat and then relax. Get some of that good Malibor food and then get some rest. We have two and a half days before we reach Armanor for a slingshot maneuver to take us back to Septimus, where we will wreak a little more havoc on Malibor fleet assets. We're going to keep hitting them and keep knocking them down until they reach a point where they don't get up. Take care of yourselves. We have farther to go."

Jaq closed the channel.

She told Alby, "We don't have to make the decision now regarding our passing speed. We have plenty of time, and not enough information. If Brad's people improve what they see, then we'll adjust accordingly. Whatever gives us the most positives and fewest negatives."

"Are you okay with forcing the scouts outside their safety zone?" Alby wondered aloud.

Jaq didn't like the pointed question, but she'd already asked herself exactly that. "Am I uncomfortable with that decision? Yes, of course I am. It's hard sending people where they could get hurt. Even the repairs on the first deck. We sent people to a place where the structural integrity of the hull could have been compromised. Everything we do is dangerous. We can't put this ship and its two hundred and fifty crew at risk to keep a single ship with a crew of two or three safe. I don't want to lose anyone, but least of all *Chrysalis*. Without this ship, we lose the war, and we fail the Borwyn."

"No one wants to lose the ship, any ship." Alby knew there was nothing to dispute. The logical decision removed the emotion. They couldn't be afraid of loss, except that which hampered their ability to fight. They needed the information that the scout wasn't able to provide by staying too far away.

It could have gone home for all the good it was doing, but no one wanted to say that.

Brad was adamant that they were doing the best they could.

Jaq wasn't so sure, and neither was Alby.

"Once Brad gets back, we'll send the message. Danger close, figure out the secret of the space station, and send that information to us. That's not too much to ask, is it?" A rhetorical question. Jaq wanted the answers to her questions, and only the scouts could find them.

CHAPTER 19

There is no silence in the peace of the wilderness.

Crip looked to Max, who nodded. Crip circled his arm in the air. "That's it for today. Establish a security perimeter fifty meters away from center, that's me. This will be our camp for tonight."

"Darkness is coming," Deena said in a voice that drew everyone's attention. "It's something that is replicated on a starship by dimming the lights, but on the planet, the darkness is total. Your eyes will adjust, but you'll hear more than you see because your ears will adjust, too. Your imagination could run wild."

"We saw the night on Farslor, and it was terrifying," Max said, "because the Malibor were out to get us. Here, if anyone is watching, it will be the Borwyn, so whatever you do, don't shoot first. And once it's completely dark, pull back to a secondary position of thirty meters. Soldiers will be on watch, two on, two off through the night. Dig in."

The soldiers paired off. Max worked his way around the perimeter. He had twelve soldiers, including himself and Crip. Add in Deena, Kelvis, and Tram, and they had a walking menagerie of talent. He questioned leaving Hammer and Anvil together until they kept whispering to each other.

"You two, split up. No sound when on watch." He pointed to his ear and back at the pair. "Anvil, join Danny Johns, and tell Zurig to come over here with Hammer."

"Sorry. If we—"

Max cut him off. "No. Maybe later. You have a lot to learn when it comes to ground combat tactics. Being big and strong isn't going to help you if you're in the wrong place or doing the wrong thing."

"I don't feel so strong," Hammer said softly. "Gravity is different here than home."

"It's heavier. That's why Jaq prefers one-point-two gees on the ship. Keep everyone strong enough to make the return here more comfortable. The plan has always been for every member of the crew to walk on Septimus."

Hammer took a deep breath. "I like the air here. Better than New Septimus and definitely better than recycled scout ship air but not as good as what's on *Chrysalis*."

"We like being spoiled," Max replied, "but it was all for a good reason. We needed people to be at their best, and they wouldn't be if life was pain and discomfort. Despite the relative small size of the ship, we had enough space and we had what we needed to be comfortable."

"You have a good captain." Hammer looked around to make sure no one else was listening. "Nothing against my dad. He was fine, but the others seemed to take pleasure in bad food and everyone's misery. Like that elder you met, Bill Macturno. That guy hates everyone and everything."

"But he supported the mission."

"He's probably getting soft in his old age. A decade ago, he would have been violently opposed. And people go his way just to shut him up, otherwise he'll keep on until he wears them down. They tend to surrender early to avoid the angst."

"How does he have so much power?" Max asked.

"He was an original politician on Septimus. He was on a tour of the fleet when the Malibor attacked. They ran to protect him. They never fired a shot until they dropped him on New Septimus. He made them fly the ship into the sun so the Malibor wouldn't learn that a Borwyn warship had escaped."

Max gasped. "That's probably the most cowardly thing I've ever heard. I'm glad I didn't know that when I met him."

"He and my dad don't get along, for obvious reasons. Dad made it to New Septimus in a lifeboat since his ship was shot up. He fought to the end."

"Thanks, Hammer. Join Danny Johns and get yourself settled in. You can trust Danny. He saved my life."

"I know. Dad trusts him. Makes it easy." Hammer crouched and moved slowly across the sixty meters to where Danny and Zurig were digging in.

Max finished his tour and returned to the center, where Deena and the others had dug out their Malibor food bags.

"Try to only eat half of what you have. Today wasn't as strenuous as tomorrow will be. It's the same thing I told the troops."

"I thought today was strenuous," Kelvis said. "I'm not sure I can do more tomorrow than I did today, so *more* strenuous has no meaning. I'll do what I can, and then I won't. I guarantee that I'm going to be stiff and sore in the morning, even if I do get a good night's sleep."

Max and Crip shared a look.

"Kelvis, you can't stay with the ship, no matter how much your whining makes our lives miserable. Look up at the stars!" Crip pointed toward the blue sky.

"It's still light out," Kelvis countered.

"Of course it is, because it's daytime. We stopped early because we care about your personal comfort and enjoyment of a pleasure stroll on your home planet." Crip nodded vigorously to show the sincerity of his sarcasm.

"This sucks." Kelvis shifted where he was sitting on the ground until he faced away from Crip. The vegetation covered most of the ground, but the moss-covered spaces in between represented a softness they were unused to.

"At a steady one gee. That won't change. We'll find some fresh water, maybe kill us some wildlife to roast over an open fire. I've read about the majesty of such things and the nature of bonding."

"You want to kill a defenseless animal?" Kelvis scoffed.

Crip replied, "Because we're going to run out of food sooner or later. Sooner if we eat like we're starved. Then we *will* be starving. You'll eat whatever we catch or find, just like the rest of us, unless we find our fellow Borwyn and they help us."

"Assuming they don't kill us first. I can't believe you didn't have a plan." He snorted before digging into his bag of

Malibor pasta and sauce. The scent wafted past Crip's nose, instantly making his mouth water.

"We have goals and steps we need to take. That's better than a plan."

"I don't think it is. A plan is better than no plan."

"Goals and strategy, my friend. Eat your dinner and try to relax. Even though you're right about being sore and tomorrow being a replay of today, we're going to do what we have to do. We're going to ignore how much it sucks because we can change none of it. Find the Borwyn. That is the entirety of our plan."

"They're out here," Deena said with a smile. "My mother came from out here. Maybe not this far out, but they live here, away from the Malibor. They're good people, or so I've heard from others like me."

"I didn't know there were others like you. Did your mother get captured? Was she a slave?"

Deena nodded. "The Malibor are the masters of this planet, but the Borwyn still fight them and make them afraid of the wilderness. The Malibor have technology that the Borwyn don't."

Max hugged her. "We'll find them, and then we'll figure out what's next. Maybe someone will know your mother's family. You might have aunts, uncles, cousins, or even grandparents you've never met."

"I'm half-Malibor. No one will accept me."

"That's nonsense." Max pushed her to arm's length. "I accept you, and so does everyone else here. Don't give up on the Borwyn you've never met. You're fighting for their freedom. That's worth more than blood, far more."

"You're a pushover for big blue eyes." She batted her eyelashes at him.

"What can I say? I accept people for who they are." He smiled. "We're going to need your help when we find the Borwyn."

"If," Crip corrected from behind him.

"We're trying to have a private conversation here." Max looked over his shoulder, attempting a hard glare.

Crip laughed. "In the middle of nowhere, surrounded by woods, you're trying to have a private conversation. Like you just said. That's nonsense. Now rest up. We'll take our turns manning the perimeter."

Max reclined onto the moss.

"Aren't you going to eat?" Deena asked.

"I'll hold off. I don't want to run out of rations. It would pain me greatly to see you hungry."

"Eat." She thrust the bag at him.

He turned to Crip for support. "Is this what married life is like?"

"Why are you asking me?" Crip started to laugh and kept laughing even after Max begged him to stop.

The night passed as a night should with the sounds of wildlife waking to a new dawn. The chill of the night deepened before Armanor made its appearance on the eastern skyline, later than what it would have elsewhere because it came in behind the mountains. To the west and north, the city waited.

They'd heard no artificial sounds, like those from a jet or rocket engine that would tear at the sky. Nothing except the buzz of the insect life.

"There are things that crawl," Larson complained. "They want to enjoy a little man-flesh, which I am obliged to deny them."

"How does one go to the bathroom?" Kelvis interrupted.

Tram's ears perked up. He'd been unusually silent throughout. He used to be the battle commander, but this was different. This was a ground operation and despite his training with the weapons, he had absolutely no idea what it meant to live off the land.

He looked as miserable as Kelvis sounded.

"You dig a hole, drop your personal delight in there, and cover it up again. That's why you have a folding shovel as part of your kit," Max explained.

"Really? I pick it up with my hand?"

"No. You hit the target on the initial drop." Max clenched his jaw to keep from making an untoward comment.

"This is unconscionable." Kelvis sighed with his eyes closed. He finally stood, psyched himself up, and headed away.

"Don't go too far. We don't know if there are any animals who might eat you," Crip said.

"There aren't any man-eaters out here," Deena added.

"He doesn't know that." Crip smiled.

Deena made a face. "I know what this is. I'm among toddlers."

Max turned serious. "The combat team has always had a

reputation for inappropriately juvenile humor but never to the level of toddlers. I think I should be offended."

Crip slapped Max on the shoulder and gestured for the team to take a knee. He pointed to his eyes and back at Danzig. Thirty meters ahead, Danzig held a fist in the air.

The soldiers were instantly all business. Tram opened his mouth, and Crip cut him off with a zip-it gesture. Max dropped to the ground and low-crawled forward, slowly to avoid making noise.

"Hey!" Kelvis called from behind the group.

Crip crouched and ran toward him.

"Shut up," Crip whispered harshly.

"They know we're here," Kelvis replied in a normal tone of voice. "Crip? Can you help me up?"

Crip stood and walked slowly to where Kelvis was squatting against a tree. In front of him stood a rough-looking man wearing a light tan jerkin held in place by leather ties. Crip raised his hands, keeping them away from his pulse rifle because the man was armed, aiming an old-fashioned shotgun at their energy engineer.

Crip waved, turning his back on the newcomer after he reached Kelvis. "My, isn't this unbecoming."

"Caught as I was born."

"Why did you take off your jumpsuit?" Crip glanced at the newcomer. He had light hair with brown eyes and a full beard. He didn't say anything while Crip continued talking about anything and everything to show the man that they spoke his language if he was Borwyn and that they weren't a threat.

Crip pulled Kelvis to his feet.

"I didn't want any accidents. It's not like we'll be able to clean our clothing. For the record, I'm never going to the bathroom again," Kelvis vowed. He turned around and climbed into his clothes.

Crip stepped between him and the man holding the shotgun. "My name is Crip Castle, and we're from the Borwyn cruiser *Chrysalis*. We've come to liberate Septimus from the Malibor. We've destroyed half of the Malibor fleet already with more to follow since *Chrysalis* is the most powerful warship in the system."

"The war has been over for fifty years, longer than I've been alive," the man said.

"The war is ongoing. In the intervening time, the Malibor have fought five civil wars, too. They are perpetually at war, and we've come to take control from them, return Septimus to the Borwyn."

"We don't want what they have," the man replied.

"What?" Crip eased forward, but the man pulled his shotgun into his shoulder and aimed at Crip's chest.

"I'll join the others." Kelvis strolled away, making a point not to look at the bearded man.

"We are free," the man said.

"What's your name?" Crip asked.

"Being free, I don't need to tell you that or anything. I suggest you leave."

"We're here to talk with the Borwyn, because whether you want it or not, war is here. We've been on the outskirts of the system for the past fifty years, dreaming of returning to Septimus, and it's every bit as beautiful as we thought it would be. There are other survivors, too, in a place called

New Septimus. They have come, too. We've been gone too long, and it appears that we've been forgotten."

"You have a Malibor with you. You want me to believe that you're Borwyn?"

"Deena and Max, could you join us, please?"

Max stood and walked toward the rear of the formation while the rest of the soldiers remained in their places with weapons ready. Someone was out front, too, but the combat team wasn't giving them a target.

Deena joined him and hand in hand, they walked to Crip's side.

"Collaborating with the enemy," the bearded man grumbled.

"I thought you weren't at war," Crip countered. "And she's one of us. We found her aboard the ship the Malibor called *Hornet*. She was little more than a captive, but now she's much more. We trust her with our lives."

"Give her to us." The man continued to aim his shotgun.

"You can kiss my ass." Max held Deena behind him. Her diminutive stature helped her to hide completely in his shadow.

"That's enough," Crip growled. "Playtime is over. Your shotgun and whatever else you have for weapons are no match for our pulse rifles. The last thing we want to do is kill fellow Borwyn, but we will not stand by and let you kill any of us, and make no mistake, Deena is one of us."

Crip moved to the side and in a movement almost too quick for the eye to follow, he raised his rifle and centered his aim on the man's chest.

"Lower your shotgun and tell me your name so we can talk like long-lost family and not enemies."

The man looked at Crip while holding steady aim.

Max held Deena behind him.

Tram stepped in from the brush behind the man and whispered, "The nice soldier said to put your shotgun down. I'd listen to him before you get punched in the side of your head."

The bearded man complied, but he wasn't happy about it.

"Isn't that better? We don't need to point guns. Here, take a look at this." Tram unzipped his jumpsuit and showed the purple scars on his sides. "Compliments of a Malibor saboteur. Danny Johns up front there—" Tram nodded toward him. "—killed him before he hurt anyone else. Help us start a dialogue with you and your people. Let's find what we have in common to avoid any more misunderstandings that result in someone getting sewn up."

The man cradled the shotgun in the crook of his arm. "You look like you've a rough go of it. When did that happen?"

"A couple weeks ago? I'm not really sure, but it's not fully healed yet. The trip from orbit to landing wasn't very friendly."

"We saw you come down. We've been following you ever since. Your people aren't very good at woodcraft."

"We were born on a starship and lived our whole lives on it. This is the only planet most of us have ever been on. Max and Crip have been on Farslor. Deena was born right here to a Borwyn mom, kidnapped by the Malibor. You shouldn't consider her an enemy. There are enemies out there—" Tram pointed in the general direction of the city. "—and they are who we have to fight. Even if you don't want to move into the city, wouldn't it be nice if you had the choice? You say you're free. Would you be free if you showed up at the city gates, or would you be dead?"

The man nodded. "We're free out here, unless the Malibor show up as they do on occasion. Then we hide until they go away."

"That's a strange definition of freedom. My name is Tram Stamper. What's yours?"

"I'm Paulus, Paulus Hunter."

Tram turned to Max and Crip.

"She said her dad came from a big family," Crip said. "I don't know any names beside our captain, Jaq Hunter."

"Interesting. They call me hunter because that's what I am. I hunt deer to deliver meat to our village."

Crip slung his rifle. "I don't want to point that at any of my fellow Borwyn ever again, please and thank you. Paulus, nice to meet you. I'm the deputy on board *Chrysalis*. I speak for all of us when I say it is great to make contact with our fellow Borwyn while standing on the home of our ancestors. Septimus. Understand that we don't take any breath for granted of this hallowed air." He breathed deeply. His smile turned to a frown. "Kelvis, did you cover your hole?"

A voice from the other side of a tree replied, "No, because someone was pointing their weapon at me."

Crip smiled and told Paulus, "You know what I meant."

He whistled facing the team and then turned toward where they'd come from and whistled again. The brush rustled as Borwyn materialized from within spitting distance.

"Impressive." Crip glanced from face to face. They'd been surrounded by at least thirty, double the number on the combat team.

"Like I said, your woodcraft has room for improvement," Paulus said. "There's no way you're Malibor, because they have no sense of humor. You don't seem to take anything seriously and say whatever comes into your head."

"Life is hard enough without making it harder on ourselves. Kelvis! Take care of that." Crip gestured toward the tree.

Some of the Borwyn natives chuckled. "Welcome to Free Septimus."

"May Septiman grant us the wisdom to clear a path to complete freedom," Tram intoned.

"You still believe in that nonsense? Where was Septiman when the Malibor were driving us from our homes? Where was he when we were starving during the lean years? Bah! Septiman is a myth meant to control an unwitting population. You'll not find your prayer warriors here." He shook his shotgun. "This is what will deliver. Not prayers."

Crip looked at Tram and nodded for him to continue. "We have a shepherd on board *Chrysalis*. Our parents thanked our shepherd and Septiman for delivering them when they should have all died. The ship was nearly destroyed. They kept it operational and saved the lives of the crew. Maybe that's where Septiman was looking and not at His people on this planet."

Crip stepped in. "Maybe we can continue this conversation in a more congenial atmosphere. Where we can put down our weapons and enjoy a bit of deer, maybe?"

"Venison is what the meat is called," Paulus replied. "And we haven't made a kill yet. You distracted us."

"We have provisions in our ship. We can throw a feast for you if we go back, if there's no threat of Malibor showing up and ruining our party," Crip replied.

"No. Your ship was loud and obvious. The Malibor could show up at any time. You should never go back there if you want to avoid bringing more of them here."

"That's not our goal. This is our goal—to meet with you and let you know that you're not alone and that the Malibor's days are numbered."

"How many ships do you have?"

"One. No, wait. We have four now, eight if you include scout ships."

"How many warships?" Paulus pressed. Crip noted that he was familiar with terms he shouldn't have while living in the wilderness his whole life. The oldsters had talked about the war in a way that the new generation remembered.

"Two, but since we won't return to *Matador* unless we find a power source, that leaves us with just one."

"One ship against the Malibor fleet and all their people? Are you insane?" Paulus shook his head while the edges of his mouth twitched upward like a patient parent might do with a wayward child who meant well but came up short.

Crip wanted to argue, but this wasn't the time. There would be more conversations. "We have about nine days remaining of our rations, but it looks like we're going to be here much longer. How can we help ourselves to live off the land?"

"You're on our land. We don't need you diminishing our herds. Do you know how to clean a deer?"

Crip laughed. "Not a clue. I don't even know that that means, but I suspect it's not washing his body and dabbing wax from his ears."

Paulus joined in Crip's mirth, wrapping an arm around Crip's shoulders. "You have a lot to learn. Come." He steered Crip ninety degrees from the way they'd been going. They headed deeper into the woods.

CHAPTER 20

The enemy will stop being the enemy when they lay down their arms of their own volition.

Five days until the combat team would attempt communication with the scout ship that Brad had ordered to move closer, even though they argued hard against it. They would assume a position between the station and the planet.

They were afraid, and Brad was afraid for them, but he understood why Jaq wanted them there.

"The Malibor are spun up, buzzing like the hornets they think they are," Brad said in a hushed tone. He didn't always speak his mind on the bridge, as if he'd been conditioned to not share his thoughts with the crew.

In the old Borwyn hierarchy, he would have been trained to remain above the others. The officers stood apart, and senior officers stood even farther away. He was still getting used to everyone using first names. He was used to being called 'Captain.'

"I pray that they are able to extricate themselves should they be discovered," Jaq replied.

A voice from nearby droned, "May Septiman guide the hands of His servants to deliver unto Him the greatness of freedom."

"Shepherd, give it a rest!" Jaq snapped. With a new deputy who was always nearby, she was unable to get the time alone that she needed. Then again, she had a deputy. "Keep us on track. I'll be in my quarters."

Jaq clapped him on the arm and clumped past. In her quarters, she strapped herself into her chair and kicked off her boots.

Her challenges weren't the next five days. They started once *Chrysalis* raced past Septimus a second time. After that, they wouldn't be able to use the high-speed flyby maneuver because the Malibor would figure out how to defeat it. What was their military-industrial complex capable of? With an imminent threat, they'd be able to do a lot more than just refit ships.

They could unite against the common enemy. The hated Borwyn had returned!

"You had to send a message, didn't you?" she berated herself until she thought better of it. "They set up an ambush and lost all their ships but one. How does that make you feel?"

She smiled. The Malibor were ill equipped to deal with the power of *Chrysalis*. Once they were out of cruisers, their gunships would be easily destroyed. Maybe she could get one or more to stand down instead of allowing their ships to be turned into space debris. She could hope.

Otherwise, *Chrysalis* would blast them out of existence.

She only needed to keep the Malibor from getting a lucky shot that hit the engines or the ion drives or one of the missiles.

"We don't need the missiles. They are useless because the Malibor can defend against them. Same with us. The Malibor missiles are large and unwieldy. If we only had more of our design. I'll have to ask Brad when New Septimus will have our missiles ready. We can return when necessary."

She looked around her quarters. They were stark, without color, the same as nearly every other berth throughout the ship. She didn't care. If she did, they would look different. They served her needs as they were. She didn't care about anything but the ship and the crew.

Because they were critical to achieving her goal of liberating Septimus. But they were more than tools. They were her family. "What am I without you?" she wondered aloud.

Jaq pulled up the most-recent image they had taken of Septimus. It looked innocent from space. Nothing more than a blue marble with splashes of white and green. It appeared to be welcoming, which took her mind back to Crip. Would he ever return to *Chrysalis*? Taurus was here. Would it bring him home or would it send her to a liberated planet surface?

Would it ever get liberated?

The lucky railgun strike. They were only one second from dying in the vacuum of space. *Chrysalis* would remain vulnerable as long as the Malibor retained the ability to shoot.

Being alone wasn't helping. Her mind was wandering and thinking of too many distractions. She could use sleep but wasn't tired enough. She closed her eyes, hoping for a respite from worrying about events she couldn't change. The only steps she could take related to putting *Chrysalis* into harm's way or not. "Maybe we don't return to Septimus. Reduce the risk to near zero."

She shook her head and began to argue.

"Then we leave Crip and Tram to the mercy of the Septimus wilds or the Malibor if they get themselves caught. Nah, they won't get captured. They'll fight and kill a lot of the locals. They'll create the distraction we need while the Malibor wonder if there is a full-on invasion underway. Not an invasion, since it's our home!"

Jaq wanted to be angry. She'd worked herself up to it, but it was all in her mind. Her alone time was serving to accomplish nothing.

"Chow solves all problems," Max would have said. She was beginning to agree.

She put her boots on and went to the galley, where she found Chef on a tirade. The mandatory rotation of personnel through the kitchen had been reimplemented since Deena's departure. No one was happy about that, least of all Chef.

Jaq tapped on the counter to get everyone's attention. "I would like everyone to stop yelling please and make believe like there's peace in the chow hall."

"See?" Chef pointed at the captain. "Chow. Like that is a sensible word describing everything I do. Chow. It's the last sound you make before you puke!"

Jaq watched Chef in disbelief. "If our people had any of the food from New Septimus, they would be far more grateful. Like me. I've put that in my mouth, and I can still taste it. I need some of that good Malibor food."

"They have access to ingredients I can't get." Chef tossed her hands in the air and turned away.

The assistant, a young engineer, showed her frustration by trying to slam a bundle of packets. One opened and spurted microgreens on her uniform.

"I have to go change," she said.

"No, you don't. Just wipe off the big chunks and wear it with pride." The captain pointed at the deck and held the young woman's gaze with a look that suggested the conversation was over. "It's perfectly fine. All is well. Peace is restored. Chef's dignity remains intact, as does yours. And the chow hall remains open for the finest dining in the system. We wouldn't be the happy and joyous crew we are without you, Chef."

"There's no doubt about that." Chef smirked. "I know we sent bundles of food to New Septimus. Is it really that bad?"

"Like eating right out of the black water tank. It was the most disgusting food and water I've ever smelled or tasted."

"Maybe everyone can get a serving of that."

"They'd go hungry first." Jaq pointed at a rack toward the rear of the kitchen where the Malibor food packs were stored.

"No microgreens or algae shakes?" Chef pressed.

"Definitely! But not today. I need my fix, and their stuff is addicting. I think the best we can do is eat it all, which will leave us with no choice but to eat our own food for a while." When no one moved, Jaq pointed again.

"What else is going on?" Chef asked. "You're usually not like this. You tend to take whatever we give you."

"We lost the entire crew of the cargo ship with one of the Malibor strikes. They had no purpose being here, and that makes it my fault."

"Nope. They'd be fine if the Malibor hadn't started this war. We could have lived in peace with them, but no. They're the enemy. Look what they did to Tram. They started this war, and they're the ones responsible for every single person who dies because of it. The sooner you can destroy their fleet, the sooner people will stop dying." Chef crossed her arms and assumed a smug expression, like she'd just delivered the winning argument.

Maybe she had, but the war was over. The Borwyn had lost, and it was the Borwyn who restarted it. In the old days, if the Malibor had found out *Chrysalis* was still alive, they would have done everything they could to destroy it. They would have deployed their fleet against a defenseless, drifting hulk with power enough for life support and not much else.

"The Malibor are the enemy, and we will destroy them. But first, we're going to eat their food." Jaq stabbed her finger at the Malibor food packs.

She happily accepted a meal called saucy meatballs. Even though the crew had been vegetarian out of necessity, most of them took to eating the so-called meat without any problems, ethical or physical. Very few believed the meat came from animals, thinking it was lab grown in some way.

And tasty, like nothing they produced themselves.

It took the edge off the hardest days and the losses they continued to have, albeit fewer than in the opening salvos of the new war.

When Jaq was able to dictate the terms of the engagement, *Chrysalis* took less damage.

Brad eased in next to the seat Jaq had taken.

"Aren't you supposed to be on the bridge?" she asked.

"Alby has it under control. We're in the watch-and-wait phase of the flight."

"How are the repairs going?"

"We're going outside the ship to complete them," he stated.

That went against what Jaq had wanted.

"How does that comply with my orders?"

"It needs to be done and you know it. We have to catch the window while we're ballistic, less chance of someone stepping off and not being able to get back. We can't have that spot with missing armor. We need to put the patch in place, which means two trips. One to get measurements and one to install the fabricated replacement. We have plenty of metal from the dismantled station. We'll get it done quickly. We plan on two tethers and a mobility pack to provide a triple redundancy."

He was correct, and he was doing his job as deputy. Not asking inane questions but doing what had to be done in the best interest of the ship.

"I agree. Please don't lose anyone out there." Jaq nodded and took another bite of her meal. The meatballs tingled on her tongue while the texture delivered a different experience for her teeth as they crushed and ground, something the Borwyn weren't accustomed to.

"We're sending the most expendable member of the crew."

Jaq stopped chewing and straightened. "How in Septiman's glory did you determine who is the most expendable member of the crew? Because there's no way I could answer that question, and I'd like to think I know them all."

Brad smiled. "I'll try not to get lost in space." He pushed off and backstroked toward the hatch, promptly slamming into the wall. He waved and turned around to help himself into the corridor.

"That instills confidence," she called after him, face twisted in dismay. She wasn't hungry all of a sudden, despite the draw of the fantastic scent.

"Eat!" Chef chided, arms crossed and giving her best matriarchal glare.

The captain conceded and continued working on the Malibor main course. Any debris or even space dust that hit an exposed body at two million KPH would vaporize said body. Brad was counting on luck to carry him through the repair. If they waited until they were under the centripetal acceleration speed, then debris would still destroy any body it contacted.

Might as well risk it now. Give themselves more time to finish the job and ensure the integrity of the welds before they reentered the combat zone.

Jaq chuckled to herself while shaking her head. Anywhere in the system could be a combat zone, as they'd already learned, unless the fleet had pulled back to Septimus entirely and waited for *Chrysalis* there.

She hurried through the rest of her food, even though it had lost its earlier appeal.

Chef was less than amused by the rapid ingestion.

"Sorry, Chef, gotta run." She returned the empty bags to the scullery and left.

"Next time, you're getting hydroponics food," Chef said.

Jaq waved over her shoulder. She found her way to the upper maintenance airlock, the one closest to the damage on the first deck. No one was there, so Jaq hooked her personal tether to the mid-rail and floated in peace.

Having something to think about helped her focus. The ship and all that needed to be done to keep it operational, to keep it in peak performance. That took a committed and well-rested crew. She'd decrease work shifts until the slingshot maneuver around the star and then on the return trip to Septimus.

Eventually, Brad showed up with a two-person entourage that consisted of Teo and the thirteen-year-old welder. They carried a plate that was already shaped.

"Did someone already go out there?" Jaq asked.

"We brought a three-dimensional imaging camera with us from New Septimus. The hole was big enough that Teo could stick it out the opening and capture the scope of damage. It takes precise measurements as part of the images."

Jaq looked at Brad.

"I didn't know that when I talked to you ten minutes ago. I do now. One trip outside is all. That makes it far more palatable. The deputy approves. And since I'm in charge of repairs, I made the call."

Jaq nodded. There was nothing to dispute. He was right. She didn't need to stomp on him to prove she was in charge. "Do not get yourself killed, because then who would I argue with?"

"Bec?" Teo offered. "Kidding. You can argue with Bec anytime, even when you agree."

"Send this miscreant out the airlock!" Jaq declared, waving her fist.

The young welder gave a couple last-minute instructions while Brad checked through the equipment. He was traveling heavy, but zero-gee made most of those issues irrelevant. All except for the bulk. He couldn't carry it all in his arms, so he tied the equipment together and staged it in the airlock. He squeezed past it to the far side, waved, and secured the inner hatch. The air was pulled back into the ship, and the outer hatch opened.

Brad latched his first tether to an eyebolt inside the airlock. He stepped outside, pushing the metal patch while the equipment bounced along behind him, hooked to his belt. Once outside, he connected another tether while keeping his boots magnetized. He had thirty meters to walk to the damaged section of the hull.

The speed they were traveling at was incredible, yet he could feel none of it. Nothing was rushing past. The stars were stable, including Armanor with all its brightness.

He stepped carefully, one foot after another, holding the metal plate in two gloved hands in front of him. That lasted a few steps until he was fed up with not seeing where to put his feet. He rolled the plate sideways and tucked it under his arm. Brad increased his speed commensurate with the increased visibility.

He remembered Jaq's warning to minimize his time outside and that focused him on the task ahead. He looked for the tear in the ship's outer hull. It wasn't as easy to see from the outside. With Armanor in his face, Brad had to shield his eyes to stop the glare from impacting his ability to see.

Brad stopped and scanned back and forth across the hull. He wasn't as familiar with the ship as those who had spent their lives aboard. He knew he was close to the forward section, but how close, he couldn't be certain. Step after slow step. It was taking too long.

He activated his comm. "Jaq?"

"Teo here. Handing the comm unit to your girlfriend."

There was a brief scuffle and then Jaq spoke. "Are you lost?"

"I'm having a hard time finding the breach. Besides the tear in the hull itself, are there any vertical monuments that will help me zero in?"

"There should be a chain gun about five meters from the damage, and it'll be around the hull to the right, if you're looking toward the nosecone."

Brad searched. "There's a lot of damage out here." The hull was peppered but had been repaired, more than once. Asteroid impacts, shrapnel, and even railgun penetrations. The ship had been through two wars and was still flying.

He finally found the chain gun installation behind him. He walked to it and looked to his right. The breach wasn't obvious because of the internal repairs that had been stacked to nearly fill the gap.

"Got it. Installing the patch. It's a good fit, Teo. Well done." He kneeled on it while bringing his bag of equipment in front of him. Two magnetic clamps held the custom-cut metal in place. He removed the welding machine and activated its magnetic feet to fix it to the hull. He torched a half-meter length to pre-heat the metal.

With his face shield down, he touched the rod to the gap. It puckered and beaded, not settling into the void as easily as it should have.

Pre-heating the metal had minimal effect since it was the cold vacuum of space. He should have remembered. With the torch in one hand and the welder in the other, he fought to maintain his balance. The ship vibrated with the energy that coursed through its soul.

Brad took a moment to appreciate the monumental effort it took to keep the ship flying. He was adding a small contribution by delivering a patch that would do its part when the ship was attacked. He continued torching and welding, following the gap around the metal plate until it was firmly in place.

He put the clamps in the bag. He unclamped the first foot on the welding machine. It exploded in his face, spraying him with shrapnel. The shell of the casing drifted away, leaving three magnetic feet attached to the hull.

His suit lights started to blink. The material had been torn and air was leaking out.

Brad checked his tethers to find both still attached. He released his boots and pulled himself hand over hand to the airlock. He ducked in without looking toward the front of the ship, sealing the hatch as soon as he was inside, but it wouldn't seal because the strap holding the bag was in the way. The bag was still outside. The air bled quickly through the multiple rents in the fabric. Brad started to gasp for air. The airlock wouldn't cut the tether.

He released the hatch, pushed and pulled to help it open, and dragged the bag inside. The hatch shut, and the small space pressurized. He ripped his helmet free and hauled in great, heaving breaths.

When he opened his eyes, he found a hole in the bag attached to his tether. More than a hole, the bag was ruined. One clamp was all that remained within the tatters.

Brad opened the inside hatch and smiled weakly at the group waiting.

He presented the remains of the bag and one clamp to Teo. He turned to Jaq. "You were right. There's stuff flying around out there. The hole is sealed, but none of the gear survived."

"I'm glad you're all right. We can replace the equipment because this is the modern Borwyn fleet and not that ragtag mob of two months ago. Prayers to Septiman for a new welding machine will be answered when we return to the ERS."

Teo held up the destroyed bag and the clamp. "Dad!" She dove in and hugged him fiercely.

He smiled at Jaq over Teo's shoulder. "The thing with death is most of the time, we never know how close we are to it. That wake-up call tells me, no outside work at speed, and you don't have to tell me that you told me so. It needed to be repaired, but not at the cost of anyone's life. I see the struggles you've had."

Teo let go.

Brad continued, "There's nothing more precious than the

lives of the crew. We are the only ones left. Without us, this ship is nothing. With us, this ship is the master of the sky."

Jaq nodded once and walked away.

She didn't want the others to see how the incident had scared her.

CHAPTER 21

Traditions could be overrated.

Crip and Paulus walked toward the back. The hunters were out front, away from the main group because they couldn't return to their settlement empty-handed.

They had gone out to bring home meat, something they did a couple times a week. Most of the time, they returned the next day with multiple deer carried on poles, ready to be processed.

The group traveled perpendicular to where they were going, getting no closer with each step but no farther away. The signal to halt rippled down the line. Everyone crouched and silently waited for new instructions from those who had issued the signal.

"Good to see the hand and arm signals have not changed," Crip whispered to Paulus.

The local nodded while holding a finger to his lips.

That hadn't changed, either. Crip had been born and

raised on a ship. Paulus had been born and raised on Septimus, where he'd lived his whole life. The two could not have been further apart in their upbringing, yet they had their ancestry in common.

The children had come home.

There would be only one home for the Borwyn. Not New Septimus. Not *Chrysalis*. Over the course of fifty years, they had never abandoned the idea of a home on Septimus, even though the local survivors considered home to be the wilds away from the city, away from the Malibor, where they lived in an uneasy balance.

The enemy mostly stayed away from the forests and mountains, while the Borwyn avoided anywhere the Malibor lived. The Malibor hadn't expanded beyond the city and the walls they'd built to keep the Borwyn out.

Maybe the walls were to hold the Malibor in. Five civil wars would keep the Malibor population from growing and expanding beyond their current settlements. The local Borwyn never asked why the Malibor fought among themselves. It saved them from having to fight.

The signal arrived for the group to rally.

"How many Borwyn are still alive on Septimus?"

Paulus shrugged. "As many as the land can support," he replied nebulously. "We have five hundred. We know of other villages and even towns. Some are closer, but most are farther away. The Borwyn are scattered to the four winds. We stay that way because we aren't a threat to the Malibor. They mostly leave us alone."

"That's not freedom," Crip replied. "You exist with their approval. Has anyone established trade with the Malibor?"

Paulus shifted uncomfortably and looked away.

Max and Deena walked nearby, where both were paying attention. They shared a knowing look with Crip.

"We have found the herd," Paulus said. A wave holding four fingers in the air passed back to them. "And we have killed four of them!"

Deena winced, and Max smiled.

Crip asked, "Can you teach us how to clean one?"

"Why?" Paulus replied.

"In case we have to live off the land. We'll need to pull our own weight. I don't want any of us to be a burden." Crip continued his efforts to build a bridge. They had much in common, but a concerning chasm existed between the interests of the two groups.

Doing what Crip would eventually ask of them would result in deaths, though not participating would probably make their lives harder when the Malibor retaliated. The fragile truce between the races would end, and explosively so.

Five days remained before they'd attempt to send a message to a waiting scout ship. Maybe the scout would have a message for them. Crip could only hope. He wanted to know how the attack went. Jaq might have an idea of how long it would be before *Chrysalis* would return.

Crip embraced the hope of victory.

There was no normal anymore. They'd have to create their own. Crip couldn't wait to set eyes on the city to personally see the monumental challenge before him. He had fifteen people on his team and not all of them carried weapons. A dozen pulse rifles against the entirety of Malibor ground forces.

"Do you know what kind of ground forces the Malibor are able to employ?"

It was a different question before. This one wanted specifics. Paulus snapped, "Why would you want to know that?"

"I always think like the soldier that I am. I'm sorry. No need to answer that question. It was simple curiosity on my part."

Paulus nodded while frowning. He lifted his chin toward the front of the group. "They're working on the deer now. Hurry up to watch. Feel free to ask questions, but keep it down. We might get another shot. We can handle carrying a lot more thanks to your bunch. We can never have too many."

Crip worked his way to where the kills had been made. Deena stayed where she couldn't see, along with Tram, Kelvis, and Larson.

"Cool!" Hammer declared. He took a knee and offered to help.

"Got a knife?" the man working the carcass asked.

Hammer pulled his blade and was shown what to do. Anvil leaned close and watched.

Max and Crip stayed at a discreet distance where they could see without being in the way. The other members of the team stood in a semicircle around those working the kills.

"That turns my stomach," Kelvis said too loudly. He was immediately shushed.

Paulus eased up to stand between Crip and Max. "Your people might have a hard time out here."

Crip glanced at the foliage above him. He was used to seeing an overhead with lights and a railing to use when in zero-gee. Birdsong returned after the violence of the kill. They scattered through the branches overhead where they twittered and chirped. Through the leaves, the blue sky continued to amaze.

"Our people will learn," Crip replied. "With your help, we'll learn more quickly. Thank you."

"Finding wayward Borwyn is our purpose in life," Paulus said. "I'm joking. We're happy to learn that our people made it and are returning. That changes things. I'm trying to get my head wrapped around it, trying to think what our role will be. You want us as more than teachers."

"I think that's a conversation for a different time. Right now, we should celebrate your success in the hunt. Enjoy the fact that we are alive. For us, we will revel every moment we stand under the blue skies of Septimus."

"As you wish." Paulus tipped his head and turned his attention to the short work his people had made of the deer. Three bucks and an old doe.

"Let us carry one, please?" Hammer pleaded.

The locals laughed. "We really don't want to, but since you insist."

Hammer and Anvil high-fived each other.

Crip and Max sighed. "We're not all like that. Actually, only those two are like that. Brothers, if that comes as a surprise."

"It doesn't. Maybe they were dropped as children, but on your ship, there would have been zero gravity. They would not have fallen." Paulus looked skeptically at the two young men.

"They were born and raised on New Septimus, a hidden

enclave. Where? It doesn't really matter, but not on a ship and not here. They're new to the team. We only found them after we returned. By our count, there are some thirteen hundred Borwyn not on Septimus. That's it. And that number is nearly one hundred percent their children, although there are a few originals who have defied aging and are still with us. Like Danny Johns over there. He was born on Septimus over seventy years ago."

Paulus snorted. "How could that be?"

"They found the secret to long life while hiding. I won't try it because it tastes horrible. Worse than that. It smells horrible, too."

"Anyone who wants an extended version of this life is a deviant. Life gets hard and stays hard. We can only hope to survive."

"I'd like to think we can do better than that. Life is to be enjoyed. I left my wife on the ship. I would love for her to see the sky, touch the trees. I will fight to see that come to pass. We'll talk about what we have in mind and what we're doing upstairs to realize that. Understand that the Malibor have been made to suffer. Their fleet is half what it used to be. We'll reduce it to zero if the Malibor keep fighting. We'll end their ability to resist and then we'll dictate terms of their surrender. That is closer than it has ever been."

"I don't like the Malibor, but they've done little wrong by me, so I'm not as hostile toward them as you seem to be. But you're right. We can talk later when there are no distractions. We're almost ready to head home. We are a half-day's walk away."

"We're up for it. Can we walk beside your people, ask

questions, talk, get to know you? And Hammer and Anvil weren't wrong. We'll carry the deer for you."

"How can I turn down a deal like that?" He waved his arm in the air. Crip did the same thing. Seeing forty-five people assembled in one small area was refreshing. It was like the rally on New Septimus that ended with people raising their hands and saying, "I'll go."

"Thank you, Paulus." Crip nodded to Max, who delivered the orders for four others to pick up one of the carrying poles.

Crip knew what that meant. "You and me?" he asked but already knew the answer. "Join us," Crip said. "We'll carry and you talk. Tell us what makes your group happy?"

They walked and talked in hushed tones, not because of fear of the Malibor but for respect of the forest and the wildlife within. *Disturb them as little as possible,* Paulus had said, *and they'll abide your presence.*

Not that the Borwyn needed their permission, but it was nice to have it.

The carrying crew switched at the halfway point, all except Hammer and Anvil. Despite rubbing their shoulders and showing the trial of their efforts, they wanted to complete the journey. The locals told them that they never carried more than two hours at a time, but Hammer and Anvil had to show how hard they were.

The locals shrugged their indifference while both laughing at them and respecting their desire to prove their mettle.

Once free of their burden, Crip was able to talk again.

Paulus hadn't burdened him with a great number of questions, but now was the time.

"What do you want from us? And don't tell me it's to learn woodcraft."

"We want to create a diversion. We want to distract the Malibor from the attacks in space, sow confusion, and disrupt their operations until they think they are in a war they can't win."

"They always think they can win," Paulus countered. "I'm not going to sacrifice my people."

Deena stepped close. "They think that," she said softly, "because they've never been punched in the mouth. The younger Malibor haven't earned their arrogance. When they learn of their fleet losses, they'll realize they're going to die. They haven't faced that before. Even the civil wars had less destruction than the fleet is currently experiencing. The younger generation only needs to see the truth and they will step back from the fight."

"Too bad it's the older generation that lives in the city and makes the decisions."

"You trade with them. I know you do." Deena wouldn't let Paulus off the hook. She stared at him until he nodded.

"It helps us keep the peace. We trade and they don't attack us."

"I believe your agreement has come to an end. *Chrysalis* announced to the Malibor that the Borwyn had returned and were going to destroy the fleet and any Malibor who stood against them."

Paulus nodded. "I suspected your arrival announced a significant change. We aren't to meet with the Malibor for another week. They'll be looking for hides and certain herbs they can't grow in the city."

"We'd like to join you," Crip offered.

"I don't think that's a good idea, but I doubt we'll be able to stop you. If things have changed, it may come down to your weapons protecting us. We'll have to get into place earlier than them. Dammit!" Paulus turned angry, but only for a moment. He deflated. "It was inevitable."

"I'm sorry. I think the end result will be worth it. We will reclaim what is ours."

"We already have what is ours," Paulus replied.

Crip could only nod and apologize once more. "I'm sorry. We'll do the majority of the heavy lifting if your people show us where the pressure points are, those places where a small team can make a huge impact."

CHAPTER 22

The only constant is change.

"Seven hundred and eighty thousand KPH," Ferd announced.

One maneuver was finished, and another would start soon. "Turn us around and vector us for the slingshot around Armanor to put us on course for Septimus. Begin acceleration once we're around the star. Two million KPH at one-point-two gees."

"Roger," the flight team confirmed.

Mary added, "Rotating the ship, nose first to Armanor."

"All hands," Jaq started over the intercom, "into your seats and prepare for a rough ride. Seven-gee centripetal acceleration. You'll get bounced about. Once we're around Armanor, less than twenty minutes, we'll accelerate at one-point-two gees for eight hours to bring us back over two million kilometers per hour. You have five minutes to take care of your personal business, and then we start the slingshot maneuver."

Jaq leaned against her seat. She would be the last in before the maneuver and the first one out of it once they were around the star.

Brad moved into his seat and settled in. He ran through the department readiness screens. They were one-hundred-percent functional. The damage from the last battle had been repaired. The crew was fed and rested. They were ready for the next engagement.

"Alby?" Jaq called.

"Targeting systems are online. Offensive and defensive weapons are idled and secured." The barrels were locked into place during lateral maneuvers to keep them from losing their alignment. Increases and decreases in speed had lower risk. Seven-gee lateral acceleration created a shearing force that the cannons didn't respond well to.

It would be the harshest maneuver they had taken since their return.

"It'll all be just fine. We've been flying this ship our whole lives. There's nothing to worry about."

Brad roared with laughter. "If you want to make someone worry about something that's coming up, tell them there's nothing to worry about. That's pretty funny." He wiped tears from his eyes.

Jaq reactivated the intercom. "Stay in your seats and enjoy the ride. As soon as we assume normal gravity, you'll be able to get up and back to your jobs. Jaq out." She looked at Brad. "Better?"

"The seed is already planted and starting to grow."

"It isn't." Jaq huffed and crossed her arms. The clock counted down.

"Ten seconds," Mary reported.

Jaq finally climbed into her seat and secured herself.

A low droning began, and the ship started to vibrate. The droning grew in volume until it drowned out other ambient noises.

"Harmonic vibration," Slade shouted. "The ship is leaning into the shear."

"Are we going to come apart?" Jaq asked with more fervor than intended. The stress pressed them into their gel, which responded as designed.

"Not as far as I know. The ship is solid. We've hit the right frequency for *Chrysalis* to sing to us."

"Sing?" Jaq would have shaken her head if it hadn't been held tightly in place. The pressure on their bodies was severe, pushing them in a different direction than acceleration stress.

The main screen showed the course as green, then red, then back to green. It flashed back and forth as the centripetal acceleration threatened to throw the ship away from Armanor.

"Attempting to compensate using thrusters," Ferd called out.

They were coasting, but the energy gauge ticked down to ninety-four percent. Nothing to worry about.

Jaq called Engineering. "Bec, get ready to kick the ion drives into gear. We might lose the battle completing the slingshot maneuver. We'll have to accelerate to bring us back on course."

"Engines are five by five, Jaq," Bec replied. "Nothing to worry about."

Bec closed the channel.

Brad laughed. "See what I mean? You're worried now, aren't you?"

Jaq wanted to tell him he was wrong, but he wasn't. Why was Bec being nice?

Chrysalis continued around the star, right on the edge of breaking free and flying off before they were ready. Ferd was nearly maniacal in his efforts.

When the ship finally cleared the star's most-intense gravity, Ferd became nothing more than a puddle in his seat. Ten seconds later, he was asleep.

Mary took over. "On course to Septimus. Acceleration is now one-point-two gees."

On course meant they were heading toward the point in space where Septimus would be in five days.

Jaq had to force her way out of her seat because the gel had not yet decompressed. She stretched as she always did after high-energy maneuvers. She stood on the deck, happy to have apparent gravity return.

Brad joined her. "Nicely done, Captain. Request permission to contact the scouts for an update."

"Of course." She nodded toward the comm station. Amie was trying to get her feet under her but failed and collapsed back into her seat.

"Stay there, Amie. I need to send a message to *Starbound* and *Starstruck*."

Amie took deep breaths, slowing with each new inhale.

She glanced at Brad and then to her screen. She tapped the keys and pointed.

"This is Brad, Captain Yelchin. Request status update." He didn't expound like he wanted to, asking them if they'd complied with his orders or were shirking their duty. He expected the latter. They were risk-averse. Asking them to dive close was probably one step too far. There would be no punishment. He couldn't do that to his people, who lived in the most-austere conditions for months at a time. Anyone working in the scout program had already given enough.

"It'll be at least six and a half minutes before we get an answer." Amie started a countdown clock on her terminal.

"Take a break. I'll wait here." Brad helped her from her seat.

"These old muscles aren't what they used to be. Still, I'm happy to be on board this wonderful ship. Thank you for having me." She touched her eyebrow with a finger in way of saluting while looking past Brad to Jaq.

"It's hard on everyone, but we have a few days of pleasant joy and happiness before we're back into the grind," Jaq told her. "Get yourself sorted and finish out your shift."

Amie walked slowly off the bridge. She had grown used to point-seven gees on New Septimus. One-point-two was a challenge for the volunteers since it was close to double what they were used to.

They would acclimate. They had been on board for more than three weeks, but much of that time was at zero-gee.

It was the way it worked in space. They couldn't always accelerate, but they would as much as possible, using longer duration acceleration at lower gees rather than spinning up quickly and winding down just as fast. They needed to save that for combat operations.

"What will the Malibor learn from our last attack that they can implement this time?" Jaq wondered aloud.

Brad answered from where he leaned against the comm position. "That getting in front of us is a death sentence. They'll try to throw things at us, but unlike our resident geniuses and two weeks' worth of calculations, they won't be able to adjust their targeting software before we return. Give them enough time and they'll refine how they shoot, but you're not giving them enough time."

"Plan for the same thing, and this time, take a look at what an end-shot would look like. Can we send a barrage down the inside of the station, down its length from north to south, without hitting the station?"

"We've already hit the station," Brad replied. "We only hope that it wasn't catastrophic. It should have been obvious that we weren't trying to hit the station, at least to military minds, since we destroyed the two cruisers who were targetable."

Alby chimed in. "I agree with Brad, but I'm not sure we can get the shot we want. Although the center of the station is fairly large, the rounds will have a forward momentum commensurate with the ship's. They'll go sideways, just not as fast as they'll go forward. We'll have a microscopic window through which we're trying to shoot."

"What about coming around the other side of the planet, where we last saw that mini armada? I'd be good with killing only a cruiser and two gunships on this next pass. Leave the station alone, because I don't want there to be any doubt that we're not trying to kill civilians. Terrify and subjugate, maybe, but not kill."

Alby snorted. "We don't want responsibility for Malibor civilians. They're probably as mean as their military. I would settle for getting the civilians to demand suing for peace."

"They probably won't surrender, because that would make the last fifty years of their hatred look misplaced," Jaq said. "Their people won't forgive them for misleading them. They won't forgive them for being wrong. If we come to an agreement that ends the war, does it matter if they surrender or not?"

"Only insofar as we won't accept Malibor rule. They'll have to move if they don't want to be under a Borwyn-led Septimus." Brad smacked his hand with his fist to emphasize his point.

"I'm sure they feel the same way."

The radio crackled, and Brad waved his arms for silence.

"This is *Starbound*. We watch, all by ourselves, farther away than before because the Malibor have been driven into a level of activity that we've never seen before. It can be considered as nothing less than frenetic. They caught *Starstruck* as she attempted to get inside their perimeter and was immediately destroyed, caught in the crossfire from their surviving cruiser and a gunship. They are towing weapons platforms into place around the space station. I wish I had better news, but we, too, will come under fire eventually as their patrols reach this far out. Where are you?"

Brad replayed the message while staring at the bulkhead. When it ended, he hung his head and stared at the deck.

Jaq had given the order, strong-armed them into obeying it. They gathered no intelligence from their effort. They died as they suspected they would.

"I'm sorry, Brad. I wish there had been another way."

Brad nodded. He spoke in a voice barely above a whisper. "We all knew the risk to them and to us. Look what happened to *Chrysalis* after the attack. We have all suffered, but no one more than the captain of *Starstruck*."

"Add her to the list of those lost in this war. Remember her name. Remember her sacrifice. She tried to get us the information we needed to do the job we must do. It was all about saving lives. Her loss could be our loss. We will stand up and face it."

"Drop me off beyond Septimus. I'll take *Starstrider* and execute the mission that *Starstruck* was supposed to complete."

"No. The risk is for this pass, not something in the future. You would be throwing your life away to collect intelligence that we couldn't act on. Send *Starbound* home, and you can follow in *Starstrider*."

"Is that it? You're going to kick me off the ship?"

"If you're going to be mired in the misery of loss, then yes. You are of no use in this war if you can't separate yourself from the people who are taking risks on our behalf. You think I don't lament my lost crew? Every single day! But it doesn't mean we stop fighting. Every decision is made with the risk versus the reward calculated. What is the greatest chance of the best result? That's what we do."

Brad lifted his head. "There's no need for me to take *Starstrider*, then. I won't let *Starstruck's* sacrifice be in vain."

Jaq's face turned red, and she waved her hands passionately. "We're all in this together, and it sucks a whole lot. We didn't even volunteer for this war. We were handed the war by our parents and in some cases, grandparents. And that's it. Fight the war or die in the cold of space accomplishing nothing with your lives. It's not enough to just exist. We have to live for something. Even if it's not for us. I intend to hand our children and grandchildren their freedom, something we never had. It's worth risking our lives for."

Jaq strode off the bridge. She didn't want to argue. She only wanted to feel their loss, but not in front of the others.

"Captain!" a voice called after her. She continued to her quarters but left her door open. She flopped into her chair and waited.

The shepherd stopped in the doorway. "Captain... Oh, there you are. How are you feeling today, a day that Septiman has blessed us with?"

Jaq stared at him without answering. She didn't want to say something to placate him and didn't want to belittle him for asking a question, showing that he cared about the spiritual well-being of the crew.

"Septiman suggests that our lives are wasted when they are not in His service, which I interpret to mean not in service to His people. No one has sacrificed more of their life to our freedom than you. We recognize this and appreciate you for it. May Septiman grant you peace in the turbulence of your soul." The shepherd touched his fingers to his lips, nodded, and walked away.

Jaq watched the empty doorway, waiting for him to return with more wisdom, although he was showing himself to be far more astute than she had given him credit for before they embarked on their crusade to liberate Septimus.

The rush of emotions threatened to overwhelm her. Her eyes filled with tears, but she wouldn't let them stream down her face. She blinked them away while gritting her teeth.

Her soul darkened with each loss. Only the liberation of Septimus could free it from the anguish she inflicted upon herself and her crew. With each victory, they continued to drive forward. With each loss, they stutter-stepped and still moved forward.

Nothing could stop them except the Malibor.

Jaq continued to blink. Her vision cleared to find Brad standing in the doorway.

"I don't like getting chewed on in front of the crew."

"I'm sorry. You deserve better than that," Jaq replied.

"I deserved exactly what you gave me. Threatening to leave. All risk for no reward. Suicide. What you showed is that every life is valuable, and none should be given so cheaply. The loss of the Malibor crew bothered you. The loss of *Starstruck* bothered you, too, but you didn't show it."

"We don't have that luxury. The crew looks to us to be steady in the face of strife. We have to give that to them, no matter how we feel. We can't lead with emotions."

"But we can hide in our quarters and feel what needs to be felt."

A tear escaped Jaq's eye and crawled down her face to fall into her lap. It was better than a zero-gee tear that floated until it splashed itself away. She wished she didn't know that truth.

"We care, and the crew knows we care. That's what matters. How we show we care is something completely different." Jaq wiped her face. "Yes, Brad. The loss of one of your scouts hurts me greatly. Even more in that we learned nothing for the loss, except that the Malibor are spun up, thanks to our attack. Will that make them more vulnerable, and if so, how? Those are the questions that need answers."

"We will answer them, Jaq," Brad promised. "I'll leave you to it." He bowed his head and backed out. Unlike the shepherd, he closed the door behind him.

Jaq opened her computer and checked the status reports, which she always did. It was a habit she'd developed, learned from the previous captain who said logistics was the key to a successful battle. The one with the functioning ship would forever be victorious.

Even if they had to run away to fight at a different time.

A battle favored the one choosing its time and place, even in space.

Jaq leaned back and closed her eyes. She was suddenly bone-weary. There was nothing that needed her attention until she could get some rest. She called the bridge. "Alby, you have it unless Brad is there. I need to sleep. I'll be back as soon as I get some rest. And thank you."

Jaq laid down. Her breathing slowed as she headed toward slumber's darkness.

A pounding on the door roused her. Her brain twisted into a knot. She didn't know if she had slept or not. She didn't feel refreshed, only more tired than when she laid down. She groaned and stood. The ship was still under acceleration, so she hadn't slept for longer than eight hours.

"Yes, come in," she grunted, sitting on the edge of the cubicle that passed for a bed when there was gravity or a restraint during zero-gee.

Alby entered. "Captain, we've received a disturbing message. You need to listen to it."

CHAPTER 23

The only thing more valuable than life is freedom.

The Borwyn village created a fantastic setting. Before the war, the Borwyn dominated Septimus, leveling it to build the structures that served as monuments to mankind, but now, they were one with nature. Large trees with man-made wings that were homes, blended in with trunks and branches. People were sparse, either inside or obscured by the foliage. They worked together with nature, not in spite of it.

"I'm not in favor of your war," Paulus started, "but I understand the need to fight it and that whether we want to or not, we are involved."

"I'm sorry," Crip apologized. "We'll try not to expose ourselves during your trade."

"If they show up…" Paulus groused.

Crip had no idea. All he could do was prepare for them to appear. If they didn't, it wouldn't hurt anything. If they did come and tried to cause trouble for Paulus and his group, then the combat team would deal with them.

"What do you get from the Malibor?"

Paulus hesitated. When he looked up, he wasn't wearing an expression of pride. "We get a promise that they won't attack us."

"Do the ones you trade with have the authority to make that guarantee?"

Paulus shook his head. He knew the truth.

Crip continued, "They take from you, and you allow it because it's the path of least resistance." He smiled and rested his hand on Paulus's shoulder. "I would do it, too, for my people, to keep them safe. You don't have the means to resist a Malibor attack. If we hit this location with the gunship, most of your people would die. It would take us ten seconds and no effort. We left two Malibor gunships in orbit who could make short work of your settlement. Maybe your deal is healthy for both parties. They get what they want, and you get left alone. We'll see if they remain congenial."

"We've dealt with the same individuals for a long time. They are more friends than enemies," Paulus admitted.

"Yet they trade you nothing besides their promise of status quo. They don't ever bring you samples of what they made from what you provided?"

"No."

"I suggest you be more demanding of those who would be your friend."

"Are you our friends?" Paulus raised his eyebrows in expectation.

"Not yet. I suggest we are family, distant relatives who

happen to be in the same place at the same time, each with goals that are diametrically opposed. But we can have a discussion without being violent."

A flock of birds winged through the opening between the biggest trees in the settlement. They screeched and squawked while turning in an instant and flocking into the upper branches.

"So much noise," Crip said.

"It's a nice price to pay to live here. Singing and crying birds tell us that we are safe. They are the first to leave if a storm approaches."

"They haven't left. We're getting great signs from the universe." Crip checked his chronometer. "Time to call *Chrysalis*."

Like the good leader he was, Crip had delegated the setup and preparation of the comm system. It was high power, and the expanded wires of the dish created a virtual twenty-meter parabola for optimal transmission.

Max handed over the microphone. "Everything is operational from this end."

"Armanor One, this is Beta Actual, come in." Armanor One was the callsign for any scout ship close enough to receive the transmission. Crip repeated himself twice, waiting a minute in between. He checked the time to confirm that if anyone was there, they would be listening right then.

"*Chrysalis*, this is Beta Actual, can you hear me?"

A crackle came in response. "This is Armanor One. I didn't think we'd hear you this far out. Not safe to get closer. Will be leaving soon."

Crip delivered his report, even though he knew the transmission was delayed a lengthy amount of time. "We have positive contact and are entering phase two of the operation. All hands on deck, even our pilot and engineer. Beta out."

They waited for the confirmation, and it came after nine seconds. "Message received. Will forward to *Chrysalis*. Armanor One out."

"Nine seconds. That's two-point-seven million kilometers, give or take." Max frowned. "At least we were able to talk with them, but they're nowhere near where they're supposed to be."

"A man's voice. Where's *Starstruck*? She should have been closer."

"Something happened. At least *Chrysalis* is flying, and the mission is still a go."

"We're going whether we heard something or not," Crip replied. "The Malibor won't stop being our enemy."

"No vendettas," Max interjected. "We only want peace, and not the kind where the Malibor are in charge."

"We'll need to get going if we want to get there well ahead of the Malibor. We can continue this conversation when we stop."

The combat team formed up. Kelvis and Tram showed up without their gear. "We're not going," Tram stated unequivocally.

Crip shrugged one shoulder. "As you wish, princess."

"What?"

"Learn something useful that we can take back to the ship."

"Soldiers are mean." Tram pointed at Crip's face. "Mean just to be mean."

"Soldiers have a warped and unevolved sense of humor that transcends time and space to be forever misunderstood by lesser beings."

"Off with you, ground pounder. May your blisters get blisters." Tram bowed at the waist. When he stood up, he waved on his way toward two female members of the settlement.

"More women than men here?" Crip asked.

"A lot more. An oddity of the environment. They are born two to every man."

"We cannot ever allow our crew to come down here."

"Exotic strangers beware," Deena said ominously. "Look at me." She waggled her eyebrows at the two men and joined Max in getting ready to leave. The locals were already moving.

Paulus glanced back and forth. "Freedom is a wonderful thing, don't you think?"

Crip smiled. "That's the point I've been trying to make. Freedom for all Borwyn, unfettered." He motioned for Paulus to lead the way.

The local stepped off. Since they weren't hunting, they didn't limit their noise. Their goal was speed, not silence. They walked fast. Despite being in good shape, the combat team members were soon huffing and puffing. Deena struggled to keep up.

Paulus called for a short break. He told the others to stay while he hurried to the front of the loose formation to talk with those setting the pace.

Deena flopped to the mossy ground in the shade of a heavy tree limb. She laid there with her mouth open and focused solely on breathing. Her chest heaved with the effort.

"Are they trying to leave us behind?" Max wondered aloud. He was breathing hard, but it hadn't been beyond his abilities. He would make it to the meeting point at the locals' pace.

They carried packs with the trade items, but they weren't as heavy as the combat team's packs. They carried everything with them, from spare ammo to spare power packs. Each soldier carried four because they weren't sure they'd be able to recharge them. The Borwyn village had no power. The solar chargers were time consuming since the team had to chase the sun's rays through the woods without a close area that was wide open to the sky.

Things were lining up as Crip had hoped while at the same time manifesting issues that he had not foreseen. Malibor as friends? And trading partners?

The one thing he had a surplus of was time. It was unlike the space battles that Jaq was fighting without him. They were conducted over tens of seconds. They had to be planned and programmed into the computers well ahead of the engagement with limited opportunity and no time to adjust during the battle.

It was the same with a ground engagement, as the team had learned on Farslor. Once the shooting started, there was little time to think. It would end quickly, depending on which side delivered precision violence upon the other. Hit the target where they were weakest.

With the trading party, where would that be?

Crip waited for Paulus to return. He told the group to get ready to go.

"Where is the weakest point of the Malibor traders? How many show up? Do they have a vehicle?"

"Of course they have a vehicle. They're not condemned to a life in the forest like we are."

Crip chuckled and looked away. "*Condemned*. I thought the forest was freedom."

"It would be nice to have some amenities, at least every once in a while. Not all the time. We don't want to become lazy or entitled," Paulus replied. "I may have embellished our embrace of life in the forest."

"I figured." Crip wrapped his arm around Paulus's pack. "It's okay. I would have done the same thing. Don't trust strangers or their motives. How many traders are coming to the meet?"

"Maybe five. They have no fear of us. We've been trading for twenty years, maybe more."

"Have any of your women been kidnapped as part of the trade?"

"Kidnapped? No. Voluntarily went home with the Malibor? Yes. They weren't welcome back when they changed their minds, and they all changed their minds."

"Deena came from such a collaboration, but the mother died shortly after Deena's birth."

Paulus nodded. "She's probably from our village, but she doesn't look familiar. She looks more Malibor than Borwyn to me."

Deena tried not to listen in but couldn't help herself.

"You think my mother was from your village?"

"Why not? We have more women than men, and some went over to the Malibor. The draw of the city. Who knows? I find it disappointing. It's like volunteering for jail because you're tired of living."

Deena bristled. Max wrapped an arm around her waist. "I hope we can bring this to an end, it's what we're here for, but I think our timeline has to change. We need to learn what motivates the Malibor. We have to find their weakness. With our limited resources, if we are to attack, it needs to be with surgical precision."

Paulus accepted the conversation without further comment. He often glanced at Deena to find that she continued to glare at him. He couldn't place her mother, if he had known her at all. Dozens had gone over to the Malibor, but not all volunteered for the exchange. It had been a long time since the Malibor had made demands for women, and Paulus tried to forget the darker days.

Deena's presence brought it all back. She had every right to hate him. He hadn't made the decisions two decades earlier, but he hadn't opposed them, either.

The freedom he extolled hadn't been free. It came at a steep price, one that he or his fellows living in their village hadn't paid.

"What does this trade point look like? Is it in the woods where we have cover?" Crip asked to break the silence.

"It does. It's protection for both groups as neither wants to be in the open."

"We need to pick up the pace, then. We'll need time to

get ourselves into a position where we can hit them hard should they bring more than the desire to take your goods."

"I don't want you to kill them," Paulus pleaded. "These aren't the same ones from that time long ago."

"I know. These are almost friends, and that's what I'm counting on. That they'll be willing to talk, maybe even help a couple of us get into the city. We can't accomplish any of that if we kill them."

"You want to go into the city?"

"Hang on, Crip. No one ever talked about going into the city. We can't expose our team like that." Max shook his head, adamant about his rejection of the proposal.

"Team? It would be me and Larson only."

"Why me?" Larson perked up. "Go into a Malibor stronghold? I'm not good with torture, Crip. I'll fight bad guys all day long, but if they do the Malibor thing where they start peeling my skin off, I'm going to tell them everything."

Crip knew he would. Larson wasn't posturing.

"I think your technical expertise would come in handy, otherwise I'd go alone because this isn't even a volunteer mission. I think it's critical to our success. Imagine if we could get inside their command structure and show them a picture that wasn't reality. Ghost ships and invasion fleets. Terror. We could win without a fight."

"But when they learned the truth, they'd rise up and strike at any Borwyn they could find," Paulus countered. "They are vindictive. The only war they'll lose is one in which they are physically defeated. We won't beat them with fake news."

"No, but with the right misinformation planted, we could

make them vulnerable where we can hurt them the most. We don't want to go toe-to-toe with them down here. We want *Chrysalis* to take care of that from space. They have the firepower to destroy all power projection capabilities. They'll surrender to maintain some of their lifestyle. That's what I'm betting on. And it'll take us getting inside."

Paulus raised his fist in the air and pumped it up and down. With shifting of gear and creaking of packs, the combat team jogged to keep up.

Deena ran but started to fall back. Max relieved her of her pack and carried it in front of him. He panted hard but maintained his pace.

Paulus nodded in appreciation of the man's efforts.

It only took an hour more to get where they wanted to go. The combat team tried to stay upright but ended up with their hands on their knees, ready to spew their breakfasts.

Crip walked through them. "Drop your packs and take a seat. You've got five minutes to get yourselves in order."

Max had already placed Deena's pack on the ground. She helped him out of his and put it next to hers.

"Good effort, Max. You'll make somebody a good husband one day," Crip joked.

"If I could lift my arms, I'd punch you."

Crip one-arm hugged his friend. "Take care of him. Five minutes."

Deena nodded, but she wasn't in much better shape. She hadn't worked out with the team. She wasn't in shape, not for what they just went through.

A signal from up front passed down the locals.

"Our contacts are coming early, it seems. We need to set

up in the clearing. If you're going to move into the trees, now would be the time." Paulus gestured toward the forest surrounding the clearing that opened in front of them.

Crip looked to the sky where clouds drifted lazily. He noticed that the birds weren't singing.

CHAPTER 24

There are roads which must not be followed, armies which must not be attacked, towns which must not be besieged, positions which must not be contested, commands of the sovereign which must not be obeyed.

Jaq leaned over the console and listened closely. "The troopship is on its way here. ETA four days. Request assistance." Godbolt's message repeated.

"The troopship is going to the ERS? They have a thousand personnel on board. We'd lose everyone and everything."

Brad hovered nearby. "We've already calculated the course and speed to get to the ERS as soon as possible. Recommend seven-gee acceleration for one hour followed by zero-gee to recharge the energy storage. Then back to seven gees.

They could cut a nine-day trip to less than five days, but they'd arrive with little energy. Against the troopship? As long as they could fire one missile or one E-mag battery, it would be sufficient.

They only needed to get there first.

"Incoming message from the ground team, relayed by *Starbound*," Amie reported.

Jaq impatiently rolled her finger.

The message played with Crip's voice making a succinct, cryptic report.

Jaq looked at Brad. "At least one thing is going right."

"Here's to Crip and the combat team. May they deliver the diversion we need."

"Send a message to the ERS. On our way. Be there in five days. Use all means at your disposal to delay the enemy. We're coming." Jaq waited for the acknowledgement. "Send a message to *Starbound*. Diverting to ERS. Increase standoff distance by five million. Protect yourself at all cost."

"What about comm with the combat team?" Brad asked.

"They'll get the message from the planet surface. It'll take a while longer, that's all. I don't want to put your scouts at any more risk. Your people have already sacrificed enough."

"We'll go all the way if we have to, but I agree. Now is not the time to commit our forces. When the time is right, we'll be where we have to be."

"I know." Jaq took his hand and held it for a few seconds before gesturing for the crew to get into their seats. She accessed ship-wide from her seat. "All hands, prepare for an extended seven-gee burn. We have to run to the ERS. It'll soon be under attack by the Malibor troopship that I left in orbit over Sairvor. We're going to deal with it as I should have done before."

"Don't be so hard on yourself, Jaq. We'll get there in time. We'll let it know that it made a poor decision following us to Farslor." Brad climbed into his seat.

"Five days minus four days means we'll arrive one day too late."

"You don't give the ERS credit for developing a defensive strategy that will buy them a day. They'll buy us the time."

Jaq moved into her seat and checked the status board. The instant every light turned green, she gave the order. "All ahead, flank. Seven gees, Ferd and Mary, on the shortest and quickest course to the ERS."

———

Godbolt stared at the cargo ship's screen. There it was, lumbering toward them. The troopship.

"Why would they come here instead of returning to Septimus?"

"Strike a blow at the Borwyn, plus it was a lot closer coming here. At their speed, it would have taken another month to get home. So they followed the cargo ship, their meal ticket," replied Romar, an original who specialized in biology but had experience in warehousing. She was trying to get the inventory under control, but the sheer volume of what was on the cargo ship caused most of the problems.

"Are there any weapons on this ship?" Godbolt wondered aloud.

"A single crate of projectile launchers. I'm not sure how useful they would be shooting at something like a ship."

Godbolt waved erratically. "Get them out and bring them

up here. We'll repel boarders! We'll make them pay for messing with us."

"They haven't done anything of that. And they may not. I think they'll probably want food. They were left on Sairvor with enough to get them to Septimus, but then they took twice as long to get here. Their engines must be in bad shape."

"Does that mean they might not be able to stop?" Godbolt raised an eyebrow. "What do we do if they fly by and keep going?"

"Throw a few pallets of food in front of them?" Romar replied.

Godbolt snort-laughed. "That's not right. It's downright morbid. They might be in trouble."

"If we blasted their ship over Sairvor, then they would have been in trouble. Their ship is flying. Things could be worse." Romar made a face.

"What if they're all dead and the ship is on a ballistic trajectory toward interstellar space? And nothing will stop them?"

"Then we don't have to worry about coming up with weapons to fight them, but I think we'll probably need the weapons."

"And we don't have any beside some handheld projectile launchers, according to the inventory, but we don't have a single person who knows how to use them." Godbolt shook her head. "We have four days to figure it out. I'm pulling the team together. Putting our heads together, we'll come up with something."

Godbolt released her boots and pulled herself toward the

airlock. Romar announced an all-hands meeting in their makeshift mess deck on board the remains of *Butterfly*.

Godbolt stopped by the bridge to make the announcement to the crew. Bring everyone in from outside. She strapped herself into the captain's chair and scrolled through the screens. They'd done a great deal of work to make *Butterfly* a functional workspace. They'd removed a great mass of equipment and had a lot more to go. They'd removed the chain guns and transferred those to *Chrysalis*. There weren't any left. Same thing with the missiles.

They had a lander they could fill with something to make it go boom.

She didn't want to lose the lander. Could they build an E-mag to throw debris at the inbound ship?

She contemplated the engineering and construction needed to make it happen. Could they make landing too dangerous for the troopship? Did the Malibor have spacesuits? They could weld the airlocks shut, remove access. What kind of weapons did they have?

Godbolt talked herself in a circle. Worry lines creased her face.

"We have everyone," Romar said, shaking Godbolt from her thoughts.

They joined the group on the mess deck. Twenty eager faces watched their leader, an engineer put into the position because she knew what it entailed.

"We have a situation. The Malibor troopship that was left in orbit over Sairvor is coming this way. It'll be here in four days. According to those who know, there are some thousand Malibor soldiers on board. Needless to say, if they get on either *Butterfly* or *Cornucopia*, we're finished. I need ideas of how to fight them. I'm drawing a blank."

"Why do we have to fight them?" a voice asked. "We have a ship. Let's load up on the cargo ship and leave."

Godbolt contemplated the beautiful simplicity of it and laughed, slowly at first, building as she thought.

"And that is exactly what we'll do," Godbolt said, tipping her brow to the voice in the crowd. "If we're going to leave, it's best we not leave anything the Malibor can use, which means we have a lot of work to do to move everything useful from here to there. The troopship does not have ship-to-ship weapons, as far as I know, so as long as we're flying, they won't be able to hurt us. Who suggested that? I want to shake your hand."

An original raised his hand. "Smith. I've lived most of my life in New Septimus. I could never leave. Having a ship available is something I've waited fifty years for. Let's fly, my fellow Borwyn. *Chrysalis* is counting on us to resupply them, and we had best be ready when they need us."

"I couldn't have said it better." Godbolt contemplated the older gentleman. "Why didn't I think of that?"

"Because you've been on this hulk since it was captured. Giving it up isn't in your psyche. I don't care about this hulk, but I do care about that ship filled with supplies. Nothing personal, Captain."

"I'm not a captain," Godbolt corrected.

"You are to me."

"And me, too!" The group pounded on the tables. It wasn't as impressive in zero-gee as it would have been with gravity.

"We'll organize into capture and move parties with a receipt team on board the cargo ship to document and organize the loads. We're taking the lander, too. We need to be done in three days and underway at least twelve hours before the troopship arrives."

Godbolt selected the groups, put one person in charge of each, and turned them loose.

"Romar, it's all you on board *Cornucopia*."

"I don't get any help?"

"Snag one person from a transfer crew."

"Or you," Romar countered.

"I need to make sure we're clearing everything out here." Godbolt pointed helplessly in one direction, then another.

"You know I'm right. You only need to check after spaces have been cleared or on one last walk-through before we push off. You're helping me, *Captain*. Consider yourself snagged."

Jaq sulked. She couldn't call Bec and beg him for more speed without increasing the energy drain. They'd burn forty percent with a one-hour, seven-gee burn and then recover all of that in less than ten hours. The math wasn't cutting it for her.

One hour would bring the ship to a speed of nearly one million, six hundred thousand KPH. Another ninety minutes of seven gees would put the ship at nearly three million kilometers per hour, but the ship would need three and a half hours at seven gees to come to a full stop. If they were at one-hundred-percent energy, they'd have one hundred and fifty minutes at seven-gee deceleration before they'd be out of power.

That left them an hour short. Ten hours of coasting to restore forty percent. They could decelerate for twenty hours at one-point-two gees and maintain a neutral energy generation-usage state. They would shave six hours off their trip because they would never run the energy down to zero. Fifteen percent was as low as Jaq was willing to go before needing to idle the ion drives.

"Math suggests it'll take less than five days to get there if we redline our energy use," Jaq grunted in Brad's direction. They were able to talk while at seven gees, but it was a chore.

"The intercept arc is longer than a straight line," Brad said needlessly. The entirety of the bridge understood movement within the orbital planes. "It's not getting there that will be the problem. Slowing down is going to be the hard part."

"That's where my math gets gerfunkled," Jaq admitted.

"Hard-burn slowdown leaves us with no energy. The troopship isn't going to be a threat once we arrive. We could destroy it using nothing but chain guns. I'd prefer we send a Malibor missile to them. It's about the only thing the missile will hit since the troopship doesn't have defensive systems."

"My thoughts exactly. Do we have to slow to a full stop to fire a missile?" Like the question about orbital astrophysics, everyone knew the answer to this question, too. Jaq continued, "Maybe we slow just enough to hit that ship. That saves us a lot of time. A seven-gee inverted burn for two hours brings us down to one-point-two million KPH. Alby, can you hit just the troopship at that speed? There can be no collateral damage."

"Even with a Borwyn guidance system, I can't guarantee what the missiles will do. Even the E-mag cannons will depend upon the angle. The Malibor could take away our angles by moving behind *Butterfly*. I think we need to near a full stop, line them up, and take them out with a precision delivery from point-blank range."

"Four plus days it is. We'll need our people to hold out. The biggest risk is that they get troops aboard our ships. We lose the ships if they board us. We don't have a single pulse rifle aboard *Chrysalis*. We'd have to fight them with axes and fire extinguishers."

"Burst transmission from *Cornucopia*," Amie announced. "They are going to evacuate the ERS, putting everything aboard the cargo ship, and fly away."

Brad chuckled. "That makes more sense. They should do that."

"They are doing that," Amie clarified. "Oh, you're being sarcastic."

Jaq's reverie over the loss of the Malibor crew was short-lived. She was surrounded by good people who were doing the right things to support the mission. *Cornucopia* was more important than staying aboard the remains of *Butterfly*.

"Alby, what do you think?" Jaq asked, since he had established the expeditionary resupply base.

"I think its time has come and gone. That hulk and the bits and pieces on it are not worth dying for. It'll be there when we return, if the cargo ship has departed. The troopship will find little of value there, depending on how much Godbolt and her crew will be able to remove. They need to take the power generator. We can't hand that to the Malibor."

"I'll send that as part of a response," Jaq said, "once we end this acceleration leg."

"Begs the question," Brad started, "do we need to go there?"

"The troopship needs to be destroyed," Jaq replied.

"Vengeance?" Brad pressed.

"Correcting an error from my past. We never should have pulled them out of the atmosphere. They've been downright unappreciative of the risk we took to save their miserable lives. Since you begged the question, do we need to slow down to a full stop to engage if there's no risk of hitting our people since they won't be there?"

The shepherd droned from the rear of the bridge, "Vengeance will not lead to Septiman's good graces. Mercy will lead to peace."

"Got it, Shepherd. We're going to destroy that ship because good military tactics suggest you don't leave the enemy in your rear areas." A draft of cool air passed through the command deck.

"Your grasp of military history is impressive." Brad grunted and coughed. "I've talked too much. You young people can handle these high-gee maneuvers much better than your elders. Someone called me an ancient. Come to think of it, I think that was you. We prefer originals, but I'm feeling ancient right now. Teo laughed at me pursuing a younger woman. She said I needed to find someone who not only knew CPR but could perform it, maybe recognize the signs of a stroke, too."

Jaq couldn't reply. She wanted to be angry enough to torch the troopship, but the emergency had passed. Her people and a wealth of spare parts and supplies were going to be out of harm's way. Did she still want to destroy the ship?

Yes. By chasing after the cargo ship, they learned the location of *Butterfly* and made it unsafe for *Chrysalis* to return there, except on this one pass. Maybe Jaq needed to destroy *Butterfly*, too. Leave nothing behind for the Malibor.

Where had the rest of the enemy fleet gone? What if they were on their way to Farslor?

"We need to have plenty of power on hand when we reach Farslor. I think we're going to run into the missing Malibor ships. It's a setup."

"How did you come up with that?" Brad asked.

"A hunch. And it's the only thing that makes sense. Why would the troopship attack another ship when it doesn't have weapons? I think its whole purpose was to make us do exactly what we're doing, but we're not going to do it as they expect. When we transition to zero-gee, we'll decide on how we'll approach the area, including directing *Cornucopia* where to go to draw them into a counter-ambush. How about that?"

"I like how you think, Jaq."

The main board showed forty minutes left of seven-gee acceleration.

CHAPTER 25

The whole secret lies in confusing the enemy, so that he cannot fathom our real intent.

They shoved their packs into the bushes and bent living foliage over the top. The locals wouldn't let them uproot the plants because they would die and change color almost immediately, giving away their hiding place.

Crip, Max, and Deena waited on the ground while the others scrambled into and behind trees, keeping at least two trees between them and the clearing. It hampered their visibility, but it was necessary. Crip didn't want a fight if he could avoid it.

The local Borwyn stepped into the clearing and waited. They put their packs on the ground in an orderly fashion as if on a military inspection. On the far side of the clearing, a wide trail had been tamped down, leading directly to the open plain beyond the woods. Crip, Max, and Deena waited in the clearing behind the locals. They carried only combat knives after they hid their body armor, pulse rifles, stunners, packs, and combat harnesses.

"I feel naked," Max whispered.

A wheeled vehicle came toward them from the open plain. The racket its engine made suggested stealth wasn't necessary.

"You are naked, you sexy beast," Crip whispered back.

"We could die, and you're making jokes?" Max tried to keep a straight face.

Crip nodded. "That's the best time for them. What do you think, Deena?"

"I think you two deserve each other. You're both crazy." She stiffened at the sight of the Malibor behind the vehicle's front screen.

"Nah. You can have him. I miss Taurus."

"We know," Max said. He tried to look nonchalant, but that only made him appear more alert, like a predator ready to pounce.

The vehicle ground to a halt, and the engine wound down. Silence returned to the clearing, but the birds were long gone. The trees rustled with the rush of a gentle breeze.

"Benjamin," Paulus said, stepping in front of the packs with his hand out to greet the visitors.

The Malibor looked skeptically at the new faces. He shook Paulus's hand. "I recognize the others, but who are those three? And a Maliborwyn? Where did she come from?"

"They are visitors from another village. They want to start trading." Paulus left the explanation open.

"What village? You know we're at war with the Borwyn."

"War? That ended fifty years ago. We've been trading for twenty years. There is no war."

"Not here, but then again, you are cutoff from your fellow Borwyn and don't know."

"Don't know what?" Paulus pressed.

Crip, Max, and Deena stood as rigid as statues.

"The Borwyn on the far side of the city have never surrendered to the inevitability of their lives. They continue to fight us and with our *own* weapons. How they got them is a mystery, but I assure you, the war is very much ongoing. These three probably knew that. They are here to infiltrate the city, probably even try to kill me. Isn't that right?" He glared at Deena.

She composed herself and walked forward. "My name is Deena, and I assure you, we aren't here to kill you. The war must be a closely guarded secret, since our village in the mountains hasn't heard of it. We are here to find out what trade items we can deliver, although we'll need something more tangible than a promise."

The Malibor threw his head back and laughed. "You told them the terms of our agreement!" He slapped Paulus on the shoulder. "I shouldn't be surprised. But these three want more? I'm sure I can't deliver more because then you'll want more, and I have nothing to give." He tossed the back of his hand against his forehead. "Alas, I am but a poor merchant with a mess of kids trying to put them through private school. We're lucky to eat something more than scraps."

Crip laughed. "I like you, Malibor. You're entertaining. But if your word is good, then what influence do you wield that can enforce such a guarantee?"

"The skeptic. Of course, it would be the one with the age wrinkles and permanent frown. Never happy with anything, I suppose."

Crip smiled. "I have a wife. I'm happy with her. *Very* happy." He waggled his eyebrows suggestively.

"Is she happy with you?"

"It took me a decade to wear her down. She settled for me, probably not her finest moment." Crip offered his hand. "Call me Crip."

"Is that your name?"

"You sound like me," Crip blurted. "Crip *is* my name."

The Malibor shook with a strong grip. Crip didn't try to outdo him, but he demonstrated that he wouldn't be intimidated.

Max reached out. "I'm Max, and you've already met my wife, Deena."

Establish the hierarchy.

"A Borwyn marrying a Maliborwyn. How droll."

Deena bristled but kept quiet.

Max smiled. "We're happy. Can you say the same with your mess of kids and private school? Whatever that means." He had no idea what it meant. Every child on board *Chrysalis* was brought up in the same way with the same lessons. It was a one-room school, no matter the age.

"Private school. As opposed to public school. Don't you know anything?"

"About polite Malibor society? No. I'm not a throbbing member of it."

Benjamin's mirth ended with the verbal jockeying.

Crip jumped in. "We didn't know about the war. Does that change our opportunity?"

"Yes. I won't trade with you because you have no samples, and I won't share that you're looking to work with anyone else. I have what we call a monopoly on Borwyn-produced, all-natural products. I'm going to keep it that way because I think your price would be too high."

"I understand, and I appreciate the explanation. For the record, there's no need for us to fight. We're all here doing the best we can. I can't wait to get back to my wife. At least we won't have to make this trip again."

"Where are you from?" Benjamin asked, pointing one way and then another, looking for some indication from the three newcomers.

No one flinched. Crip tapped his nose with his index finger.

"Not telling, eh? Probably wise. Not that I'd tell anyone. The less they know the better. I provide the products, and they don't ask questions."

"Like you never answered the question about how you can guarantee the safety of the Borwyn who trade with you. We each have our secrets, but ignorance is bliss. Maybe it's faith in Septiman that carries the day."

"That hokey Borwyn religion? Say a prayer for me. I could use a blessing. Don't forget, mess of kids and private school." He pointed at Paulus. "Let's see what you have. Although I'd love to debate the finer points of Malibor civilization with our Borwyn hosts, we should get going. It's a long drive from the city."

Paulus showed Benjamin what was within each pack. He

took it all—packs, skins, and dried leaves full with a variety of herbs.

He shook Paulus's hand. "It was nice doing business with you. Please don't bring them next time. No strangers."

Paulus nodded.

A Malibor woman who had not been introduced threw their newly acquired treasures into the back seat of the vehicle. After a final wave, Benjamin entered the vehicle and started it. The engine barked and snarled like an angry beast, shattering the calm of the forest.

Benjamin backed up, turned around, and pointed the nose of the ground car down the road. After two minutes, they could no longer hear the vehicle's noise.

Paulus finally breathed normally. He looked at Crip. "What were you trying to do?"

"Plant a seed that he might want to side with the Borwyn if he wants to live."

"I didn't get that from you," Paulus replied.

"Me neither." Max strolled toward their stashed gear.

"It was subtle. He'll rethink our conversation, playing it over and over in his mind. He'll figure it out." Crip met Deena's gaze. "You didn't know there was a war still going on?"

She recoiled. Max's nostrils flared. "What's your point, Crip?"

He held up his hands as if surrendering. "It was a statement. It means that if you didn't know, then your average Borwyn doesn't know. If we join the fight, the leadership will be reluctant to tell people because the population will find out that the all-powerful Malibor are getting their butts kicked and can't pacify a population living in the woods like barbarians, not even after fifty years. This is what we're looking for. A ready-made diversion. We only have to ratchet up the intensity of the war."

"We're not going to fight your war," Paulus stated clearly.

"No need. It appears we have Borwyn who already engaged."

"That's on the far side of the city. It would take months to get there." Paulus waved for his people to start walking.

Max smiled. He knew the answer Crip was heading toward. "We have a ship."

"Exactly that, Max. Time to return to the ship with our new and improved woodcraft."

The combat team rallied to reload and follow the locals to the village.

"Goodie," Danny grumbled. "More walking."

"If they ain't complaining, they ain't happy," Max said. "By the time we're done with this, you'll embrace the walk as a joyously enjoyable retreat to joyland. Or we'll work out until you do."

"Nice," Crip said. He didn't mean it was nice at all.

"We're going to the other side?" Deena asked.

Crip replied, "We're going to join the fight. And all things being equal, we're going to make a difference for the Borwyn, those down here and our friends up there." He looked skyward, already composing the message he was going to send.

CHAPTER 26

Slow is smooth and smooth is fast.

Chrysalis raced through space on the final leg of decelerating from two million KPH. Their plans had changed. They were no longer in a hurry to get to the ERS. Expeditiously, yes, but in a rush, no. They were going to arrive ten hours later than their original plan.

And that wasn't the only thing that had changed. They were coming in on the short side of Farslor, not passing in front of its orbital trajectory but behind it after one final gravitic assist, skipping off the upper atmosphere to come in below and behind the enemy ships—if they were where Jaq thought they would be. The question was whether they'd activated the remaining weapons platform. At least there wasn't a gunship available to bring back to life.

Jaq smiled. Taken from the Malibor before they could use it against *Chrysalis* or the ERS. She wished she still had it nearby, but it was on a different mission. It would be a couple more days before they heard from the combat team. Jaq wished it would be sooner. A week was a long time for those on Septimus, but if they communicated too often, they risked being discovered by the Malibor.

She had to be patient, which always increased her anxiety because waiting was the last thing she wanted to do.

Jaq lifted out of her seat the instant the engines cut out. They would coast for an hour to add four percent to their energy reserves, which were at fifty-two percent. She wanted more but wasn't going to get it. There was a limit to how long they could expect the Malibor to wait before they grew suspicious.

"Are we ready?" Jaq asked the command team.

"Orbital maneuver in fifty-eight minutes," Mary reported.

"Targeting is ready. We'll bring offensive and defensive weapons online in fifty-five minutes." Alby gave two thumbs up.

Brad checked the status throughout the ship. "Board is green."

"Missiles?" Jaq asked.

"Three in the tubes with no plan to launch them. E-mags are sixteen for sixteen."

"Target priority is the cruiser first. We take it out and then hit the gunships as fast as we can adjust aim."

"We'll get it done," Alby replied confidently. "They won't know what hit them. It'll be another step toward their surrender when we destroy another cruiser and two gunships. What if there are more than that?"

"Then we better adjust aim more quickly or we're going

to have problems." Jaq didn't want to contemplate an enemy force that consisted of more than their usual flight of one cruiser and two gunships. She needed it to be the standard formation.

Brad eased close to her. "They don't have more than that available. I'm sure you're correct."

"Was it that obvious?"

"Real fear. It was that obvious to anyone who was watching. Way to play it cool."

"Thank you." She rested her hand on Brad's arm while staring at the screen. "We have to be right, and we have to win this fight."

"I'll be surprised if there's no one on the other side. If we can't find Malibor, we know there's a troopship flying around that we can take out our frustrations on."

Jaq laughed. "There is that. Maybe we'll send them one of their Malibor missiles. Open up and say ahh."

"That's an evil streak that I like to see. Mercy until they prove they don't deserve it. Then, no mercy."

"It bit me, but I have to live with my conscience. I'm glad we saved them. And I'll be just as glad to be rid of them."

Brad excused himself and left the bridge. Jaq didn't bother asking where he was going. He spent a great deal of time getting to know the crew, doing what Jaq had done for years. Encouraging them while showing appreciation. He'd probably stop by Engineering, too, say a few words to his daughter while checking in on Bec.

The former chief engineer was best managed in bite-sized pieces. Jaq was happy to have help with her brother.

She floated around the bridge until she bumped into

Chief Ping. "We need location and targeting data on the enemy as soon as we come around the planet."

"How are you so sure they're hiding back there?" Slade asked.

"Because they're nowhere else." She made sure Brad wasn't within hearing. "And the scouts are under a great deal of pressure. We pushed them toward looking at Septimus and not elsewhere in the system. We know they missed ships leaving. I think every ship that was capable of flying got underway. And that troopship must have transmitted information about the ERS, while they saw us coming too fast to slow down, so they sent an ambush team to hit us after we passed."

"Do you want active scans?"

"I think we better. We can't have any surprises. As soon as we have a course and speed on the enemy ships, we can hit them. Dolly did a great job with Donal in refining the software. It's nice to destroy the enemy."

"I agree. We're better integrated with offensive weapons. We needed combat to understand what we needed and then to test it. We learned, Jaq. Every time we fired the cannons, we learned. We're better than the Malibor and will always be as long as we stay alive. The Malibor have to get lucky. We have to be good, and we are."

"Well done, Slade. You and your people. Be ready to engage before we enter Farslor's shadow." Jaq pushed off and assumed a lounging pose as she drifted across the bridge. She caught the mid-rail by her seat and pulled herself to a stop.

Fifty-three percent. She knew the energy burn from the E-mags firing at the cyclic rate as well as the ion drives. One minute per barrel at the cyclic rate burned one percent. Or sixteen percent firing all of them for that time. A nine-gee burn was another percent over a minute. Seven gees used a percent over a minute and a half. That meant two minutes of cyclic firing and no more than fifteen minutes of maneuvering at high gees.

Space battles generally didn't take that long. If this one did, *Chrysalis* was going to be in big trouble.

"Surprise is our secret weapon. Speed out of the slingshot?" Jaq asked.

"Thirty-five thousand KPH," Ferd answered.

"Relax, Jaq. We're ready, and the Malibor will be sorry they tried to fight us."

"They will," Jaq promised. She moved into her seat to scowl at the board. Time was her enemy as well as her friend. Fifty-six percent. It had to be enough. At thirty minutes of coasting, the gauge moved to fifty-four percent. Thirty minutes to go-time.

Jaq left the bridge. "Alby, you have it," she called over her shoulder. "Be back in fifteen."

She headed for the mess deck to find she wasn't the only one with that idea. In fifteen minutes, Chef would close the mess and keep it closed until after the fight, after the damage control teams went to work, if they were needed.

Jaq moved to the end of the line. She ushered late arrivals in front of her.

"You'll want to get something," Vantraub said, trying to keep the captain in front of her.

"Not going to risk you missing out. You work for a living and need your energy."

"I'd like to think you work, too, Jaq."

"How's your job working out in Engineering?"

"First, it's great that I don't have to deal with blood and broken limbs. Second, with Teo being chief engineer, Bec isn't a pain in everyone's side, only Teo's, but she's armored against it like radiation shielding. I've never seen anything like it. As abrasive as he can be, she just smiles and redirects him toward something productive. He doesn't even realize how he's been played."

"We could all use that kind of quality leadership. Not the getting played part, but doing what needs to get done. I'll talk with her and see what secrets she can share."

"Be prepared for a long conversation," Vantraub warned.

The line moved quickly. Jaq pushed two more in front of her before she reached the front. She checked the time. She had five minutes to eat.

Chef handed her a bag of microgreens with algae and salt.

"I know," Jaq said. "I promised."

Everyone else was enjoying Malibor rations.

Jaq inhaled the meal and returned the bag to the scullery. She wouldn't have tasted the good food, so she was okay with a meal that didn't taste as good. She hurried back to the bridge.

Brad had returned. The board showed green. Their trajectory toward Farslor's upper atmosphere was solid.

Jaq stretched and flexed, getting herself ready in case of high-gee maneuvers. She leaned against her seat while looking from face to face. The command crew looked to her for a speech. She always said something right when they needed it. She wanted to avoid transferring her anxiety to them, but it was too late. She'd been too on edge since they learned the troopship discovered the secret location of *Butterfly*.

"We go once more into the field of fire and fury. We have succeeded each time and will again, because we have Septiman on our side. As important, we have each other. He is strongest who watches his brother's back."

The shepherd piped up from his seat, "Septiman grants the prayers of those He deems worthy. Be true. Be worthy."

"We fight to restore freedom for all Borwyn!" Jaq nearly shouted.

"It's good to have a cause," Brad replied. "In your seats and make ready. You know the drill. Everything happens fast in the middle of a battle. Keep your eyes open. No surprises. Sensors?"

"We are ready," Slade confirmed. "Going hot when we approach the shadow."

"Jaq?" Brad climbed into his seat.

Jaq ignored the chronometer and stayed out of her seat until she felt the first bump. She slid into the gel and strapped in as the buffeting increased. The ship slammed back and forth, slowing with the friction, but not too much. They wanted velocity to maneuver. Slow targets flying in a straight line were easier to hit.

Chrysalis raced around Farslor, not going too deep in the atmosphere so they didn't become a giant fireball signaling their approach around the far side.

The ship hit the midway point and started to rise toward space. The sensors radiated, ready to populate the board with whatever signals returned to their receivers.

Jaq strained against her straps, as if leaning closer to the main screen would help her see the enemy faster.

Devious Two, the second moon, came into view. The crescent edge became more as they continued around the planet.

Still nothing.

"On course past the moon, please," Jaq said. "Straight on to *Butterfly*, and let's find that troopship."

Zero-gee returned to the ship.

Jaq sighed. She didn't like being wrong, while also being pleased that they hadn't been attacked.

But she wasn't wrong.

A red icon appeared on the main screen, followed by two more. A cruiser and two gunships. Sometimes she hated being right.

The E-mags kicked in, all sixteen batteries simultaneously. The ship rolled fifteen degrees to achieve an optimal shooting angle. The droning vibrated to their very souls.

"Swirl pattern one zero," Taurus called. The tactical view appeared angry with so much red on the board. Three enemy ships, expected but still a surprise.

Red lines originating from the cruiser and gunships appeared on the screen. "Vector one-five star angle minus ten, all ahead flank, seven gees," Jaq ordered.

Thrusters changed the orientation, and the ion drives kicked up to one hundred percent.

The crew pressed into their seats as the ship struggled to change course. The inbound lines changed to green, which meant *Chrysalis* was out of the line of fire. The enemy changed direction, the three ships maneuvering independently.

The E-mag batteries hammered the cruiser. Three hundred and twenty obdurium projectiles per second raced across the void and slammed into the enemy ship. The impact was visible as a section of the hull was blasted free. Emergency lighting backlit venting atmosphere.

It started to tumble. The ship executed a final fire, launching two missiles and firing all railguns until the power slipped away. The ship darkened and became nothing more than a hazard to maneuvering spaceships.

"Target the gunships!" Jaq shouted.

The cruiser flashed from a massive internal explosion that turned it into a sphere of expanding debris that appeared like a pink cloud on the tactical board.

The gunships leveled their maximum fire at *Chrysalis*.

The ship strained to clear the final firing pattern of the Malibor cruiser, but it had been too close to the intense fire of its final breath.

Chrysalis screamed from a long series of impacts that stitched it from bow to stern. Two rounds tore through the command deck, blasting the navigator's station. Mary jumped in her seat. She clutched her leg, fighting the heavy gees to put pressure on her wound.

"Nav is under my control," Ferd announced. He wasn't able to check on Mary. They were still maneuvering.

"Batteries one and six are down," Taurus reported. "Firing the remainder."

The E-mags continued to cycle, streaming high-energy projectiles across the short space.

The targeting program performed perfectly. The rounds drove home at the center of their aimpoints.

The gunships came apart quickly, one after the other. More rounds impacted *Chrysalis*, but the ship held strong. Red lights appeared on the board, then more.

"Acceleration one-point-two gees. Damage control teams report to your stations," Jaq ordered.

Slade screamed, "Inbound!"

It was too late. Malibor railgun rounds pounded the aft end of the ship. Lights flashed and went out before coming back online. The energy gauge went from forty-eight to eighteen percent.

"Firing!" Taurus hammered at her screen. A new red icon disappeared as quickly as it had arrived.

Chrysalis stopped accelerating. Zero-gee returned.

"Where'd it go?" Jaq asked. "Where'd it come from?"

"Came from behind the moon, an ambush within an ambush," Brad said. He studied the screen, but there were no answers there.

"Gunship is destroyed," Slade confirmed. "If they're close enough to hit us, we're close enough to hit them. The gunship was vaporized."

"Status?" Jaq climbed out of her seat and fixed Brad with a hard stare.

"We're hurt. Ion drives are down, engines are offline, and we're bleeding energy."

As if on command, the lights flickered and went to their emergency state. Ship systems—everything but life support—went offline.

Without thrusters, the ship started to tumble end over

end, creating some acceleration toward the bow as well as the stern.

"I'm going to the engine room. Brad, find that power leak and seal it! Alby, you have the conn. Mary to Medical. The rest of you to damage control. Get us operational enough so we can figure out what needs fixing."

The crew rushed out right behind Jaq. She was on a mission and pulled herself at a high speed into and then down the central shaft. The rest of the command crew turned toward the bow.

At least they had atmosphere. Whatever atmosphere they vented had stopped. They'd generate more oxygen from the excess water they'd loaded, and they knew where more was.

Jaq understood that the ship was out of action. They were hurt, and badly, but how badly? That remained to be seen. If the power gauge reached zero, they would die. Nothing would work, not even life support. There were no emergency batteries. There was only one energy storage.

Lights flickered on each deck where the DC teams worked, fixing systems that had been damaged or destroyed. They'd patch holes later. First, they needed to get the power on and motors running. She flailed as she accelerated downward, the tumbling ship throwing her toward the stern as if she was in a centrifuge.

Her fingers touched on the ladder and rail, but she couldn't get a grip. She tucked to lessen the impact. The instant she hit, her world went dark.

CHAPTER 27

The tragedy of winning a fight is the price your people have paid.

"An emergency message?" Godbolt wondered aloud. "*Chrysalis* is here already?"

"So was the enemy. Ambushed by the Malibor. The message was cut off," an original named Nokes said. "I'll try to raise them."

He tried valiantly, but there was no response.

"What's it mean?" Godbolt's voice rose with the alarm inside her. "Is *Chrysalis* in trouble?"

"As are we," Nokes replied. "That troopship is still coming."

Godbolt knew that only too well. They'd been running in front of the troopship. It was one day behind them in the slow-speed chase away from Farslor.

"Time to turn around and see what assistance we can provide." Godbolt set her jaw and crossed her arms. "Rotate the ship and decelerate. We're going to the last-known location of our people."

Nokes tapped the control screens. "This thing is a pile of junk," he mumbled.

"But it's our pile of junk and it saved us to fight another day. Now is our time to shine."

"I agree." Thrusters slowly spun the ship until the nose faced Farslor. Nokes ran the engines to two and then three gees. The crew grumbled and complained. There weren't enough compression seats, and many were reduced to lying in their bunks or on the deck.

Hastily strapped cargo broke free and crashed down the cargo bay.

"Time to return course, eleven minutes," Nokes announced. That was how long it would take for the ship to stop flying away from Farslor.

The ship rocked and shook with the acceleration. "Slow it down, Nokes. We're no good to anyone if the ship comes apart."

Nokes dialed acceleration to two gees. "Nineteen minutes to zero."

The buffeting stopped. The ship groaned as if lamenting the change. A loud pop reverberated throughout, and the engines went offline.

"I'll be in the engine room," Godbolt said, taking advantage of their return to zero-gee to fly off the bridge and down the corridor.

A pair of hands pulled Jaq to her feet. She couldn't focus enough to see who it was.

"Jaq?" Brad's voice.

"Shouldn't you be forward?" she muttered, her tongue feeling thick and unresponsive behind her teeth. "What happened?"

"I saw you rushing downward and thought I better check. You've been out a few seconds, but you hit pretty hard. Is anything broken?"

"My pride," she said. She tried to take a step, but her eyes rolled back in her head. She passed out.

When she came to, Brad was still holding her.

"This sucks," she whispered.

"You have at least a concussion. I need to get you to the doc."

"No. Engineering. We're going to die if we don't get the power on. Medical is the last place I need to be."

"It's the first place you need to be, but I'll take you to Engineering for my peace of mind."

Her legs were rubbery under what felt like a third of a gee of acceleration. The ship had to be tumbling fairly fast. Her mind drifted away from the centripetal force calculations. Jaq felt like she was going to pass out again.

Brad picked her up and carried her. She laced her fingers behind his neck to hang on, surrendering to her injury and the help Brad provided. Brad climbed the ladder slowly, holding her before him. Engineering was one deck up. He climbed out, still holding her.

The hatch wasn't sealed, and Brad used Jaq's feet to push it open. He eased through to avoid hitting her head.

Bec and Teo worked on wall panels and not the drives.

"Status?" Brad asked.

Bec snarled a retort without looking up.

Teo glanced at him, doing a double-take when she saw her father carrying the captain. "What happened?"

"Hit the bottom of the shaft on a freefall. She'll be okay but insisted on checking in with you."

"We need to replace these switch panels. We took a whole lot of damage." Teo turned her attention to the work in front of her.

"The ion drives?" Brad pressed.

"They were spared any impacts. My emergency shutdown program saved them from overloading."

"We're at ten-percent power. When will the engines come back online?"

"Never? Soon? We don't know," Bec snapped.

"We can't run the ion drives without the engines, otherwise we could generate power. We need to get these control panels repaired or bypassed to bring at least one engine up. The second might be unrecoverable."

"One engine."

"That's a *maybe* on one engine, but we have to get this repaired first. The more time we waste talking..." Teo implied the catastrophic result.

"I'll take Jaq to see Doc Teller. Do you need anything from me?"

"Engineers. Vantraub. Donal. Those who can do equipment swaps."

"We'll take care of it," Bec said, waving violently for Brad to go away.

"We can't. Not in time, Bec. Now get back to work. They're leaving." Teo tipped her chin to her father.

Brad headed out. Jaq was light enough. She wouldn't be a burden in a third of a gee or two gees. She'd predicted the attack but missed one small piece. She would curse herself for it when she was already two moves ahead of everyone else.

"I should have taken the scout ship out and led the way in so you had a complete picture."

"Easy to say that now," Jaq mumbled. "We slowed down in a way that would have destroyed your scout."

"I could have sped past the moon. It would have been better."

"If we survive this, then yes, we'll do that next time, even though they could have destroyed you more easily than they hit us."

"We caught them facing the wrong way," Brad explained while accessing the manual override for the elevator. "You're a genius, Jaq."

"They hurt us. How many casualties?"

Brad shook his head. "I don't know. The systems went offline before any section had time to report."

The elevator was offline, Brad realized. The only functioning system was life support, and that was limited to air handling. Heating was out, which meant it was going to get cold inside the ship. How long would they have? Not long. There were a great number of hull penetrations.

Brad shifted Jaq to his back. "Hold on to me."

"What are you going to do?"

"Climb the ladder and take you to see the doc."

"He'll tell me I need rest and to not bounce my head around, limit sensory input. Just leave me down here."

"Nope. Your quarters. Now hang on tightly so you don't get bounced around. Did you break anything besides your head?"

"Just bruised. Neck hurts."

"I'll get you some pain reliever. I'm taking you to bed." She held on, and he started to climb. "I imagined it a little differently, but I'll take what I can get."

"You don't get to see me naked," Jaq said.

Brad snorted. Climbing the ladder became easier quickly. He was soon pulling himself upward hand over hand until he reached the command level. He floated into the corridor, where no one was working. Once in Jaq's quarters, he stuffed her into her sleeping cubicle.

"Rest. I'll be right back." He hurried out and headed to Medical, only one deck away. The corridor was filled with damaged and broken bodies. Doc Teller hurried from one to another. Vantraub was assisting.

"They need you in Engineering," Brad told her.

"They need me here." She gestured to take in the mass of injuries, at least twenty moaning and groaning casualties.

Brad leaned close to her ear. "If we don't get an engine online soon, we're all going to die."

Vantraub blinked quickly.

"Hang on to the ladder on your way down so you don't faceplant into the deck like Jaq did. I need a painkiller for her."

She pointed. "Bottom shelf in the cabinet on the right."

She touched the arm of the person she was standing beside. "Someone will see you soon."

Brad moved into her place after Vantraub launched herself toward the central shaft.

"What's got you down?" Brad asked.

The woman winced and grunted. She pointed to her leg. Once Brad looked at it, it was clear that she had an open fracture. The bleeding had stopped, but the bone needed to be set and the wound stitched.

"Where's Vantraub?" Doc Teller demanded.

"She's off to fix the engine."

"What? Who ordered that?" The doc glared in between glancing up and down the corridor at the overwhelming number of patients.

"I did, because we need power. Broken bones won't matter if we don't have air or heat."

Doc Teller sighed. "If it's not one thing, it's another."

"I'll help, as soon as I get back from dropping off pain meds with Jaq."

"What happened?"

"Mashed her head on the deck. Concussion."

"Keep an eye on her in case it's something worse. Anti-inflammatories. Hang on." The doc entered the medical room, where three patients waited in a space designed for one. He handed Brad a packet of six misshapen pills. "Should be enough for the next twenty-four hours."

"I hope we have that long," Brad replied. He took the bag and disappeared into the growing crowd.

Vantraub joined Teo and Bec. Teo directed her next door to start working on a bypass. Vantraub returned in five seconds. "Area is hot. Need a rad suit."

"Fix that before the bypass," Teo directed needlessly.

Vantraub was already in the cabinet pulling out the lead-lined suit. She zipped as she walked back to the engine space and passed through, securing the hatch behind her.

Teo checked the energy gauge. Seven percent. The heavy bleed had been stopped with the shutdown of everything but life support. It told her which system was not the problem but gave no insight beyond that.

She continued to work feverishly and almost haphazardly on the panels.

Bec was doing the same thing.

Teo knew that he was quicker when it came to emergency repairs. He was hyper-focused and worked through the tasks in a non-sequential order but completed them quicker overall. She knew his mind was different, but it never failed to amaze her how different.

No wonder he had a hard time getting along with people.

Teo stepped away from her panel and wiped her forehead with her arm. She shivered. Why was she sweating?

Bec had completed two panels in the same amount of time.

Teo checked a temperature gauge on the bulkhead. "It's dropped three degrees."

"It'll drop a lot more. We're going to freeze to death before we run out of air." He continued to work despite the defeatist tone.

"We won't," Teo replied, confident that they would get something running before the power gauge hit zero.

She started on the next panel, then stopped.

"We need to get the bypass in place."

"We're going to hotwire the ship? We'll electrocute everyone if we can't distribute the energy in a way the systems can tolerate."

Bec didn't usually say 'we' when he meant the person he was talking to. He was more direct about fault—as in, it would never be his.

Teo nodded. "No choice. We're not going to get the distribution systems working before we run out of power. After that, it'll be moot. Hotwire it is."

Six percent.

She grabbed a radiation suit and headed for the engine room. She hurried through the double entry and secured the hatches behind her.

Vantraub was plastering lead tape on the casing where a railgun round had impacted it. A glancing blow that exposed the radioactive core and could have blown the entire engine.

Like the other one next to it. One round had ripped through the middle of it, destroying the conversion element and turning the heat of radiation directly into electricity. In the old days, they superheated water for steam to turn a turbine. This system skipped two steps, but it had a single point of failure.

"I think we can rebuild the converter, with parts and time" Teo said, and that was the extent of the time she could allocate to non-productive work. The remaining engine needed to come online. "We'll cannibalize the down engine."

"My thoughts exactly." Vantraub finished sealing the casing. A temporary fix only but good enough. "Tear that apart. Shrapnel got in there."

Teo accessed the system where Vantraub pointed. "Yeah. It's in bad shape. We need the circuit board and two capacitors." Teo moved to the second engine and located the identical parts, but they'd also been impacted by shrapnel. She carefully removed each and took a third capacitor in case one of the others wouldn't work.

"We need them all to work," Teo said, more to herself than Vantraub.

With the gloves on, the detail work was difficult. Finally, Teo gave up and pulled them off.

"We can't vent the space without power," Vantraub warned.

"And we're not going to get the power on if I can't get this done!" Teo was losing patience. She wanted to know how much power remained, but she didn't want to know in case it had dropped to two or even one percent. The pressure weighed on her. She started to slow down.

The hatch opened, and Bec came through. He looked for a grand total of five seconds and then tapped Teo's shoulder to move.

"I'll do it," he said.

"I've got it. No sense in both of us getting exposed. Where's your suit?"

"We'll bring this up and vent the space. I took a massive dose of potassium iodide. I'll be fine. Go on. Wait for my word to engage the startup sequence."

Teo stood with her gloves in her hand. She nodded to

Vantraub, who pointed at Bec while he was elbow-deep in the engine working on what only he could see.

Teo returned to the main engineering room, where she pulled off her suit and dumped it on the deck. She used a manual pump with gel to scrub her hands. She wiped them clean on a rag that she tossed on her suit.

She stood at the control panel and waited.

The energy gauge was like a lighthouse beacon shining to the core of her being. One percent.

"Come on, Bec. Make us proud once again. It's your gift!"

The gauge flashed zero and then turned off. The silence of a ship where not a single motor ran, not a single circuit transmitted power, and not a single soul moved was quiet as the tomb it had become. Emergency lights ran on batteries. They would probably last as long as the crew without fresh air.

A lump formed in Teo's throat. "Is this it?"

She latched her tether to the control board and waited. She expected the miracle of Bec, but it didn't come. Her mind drifted as she slowed her breathing in the hopes of extending her life for as long as possible.

CHAPTER 28

It'll all work out in the end. If it's not working out, then it's not the end.

A gentle tapping brought Teo to her senses. She'd fallen asleep.

The screen before her was flashing once again. It showed one percent. "Was I dreaming the waking nightmare?" she asked.

"No," Bec replied. "The engine is running, but at fifty percent. I'm not sure it can handle more. Without a backup, I'm not willing to stress it."

"Good call. And, Bec, good job. You saved us."

He smiled. "Not yet. We have a long way to go before we're saved."

"But at least we can work on it. What do we need to do?"

Vantraub cleared her protective gear and piled it on Teo's. "We need to let the captain know."

"I'll take care of it," Teo said. "I'll let my dad know, since the captain is out of it."

She unhooked herself from the control panel and kicked off. Her muscles were stiff. She didn't know how long she'd been out, but it felt like it had been too long. She wasn't sure she had ever been oxygen deprived, but the carbon dioxide levels could have risen too far. Her headache suggested the CO_2 was oppressive, but the scrubbers were operational, and air was flowing.

Like Bec said, they had a long way to go before they were saved. One percent was better than zero. At one percent an hour, it would be nine hours before other systems could be reenergized. They still had a leak unless someone found it and repaired it.

She pulled herself up the ladder until she reached zero-gee. She pushed off to fly the rest of the way up the shaft.

The ship was still spinning. It would keep spinning until they had enough power to activate the thrusters.

Teo made it to the bridge, but the only person there was Alby. "One engine is up but at fifty percent. Second engine is hard down and will need to be replaced."

"I can't thank you enough. Even with just me, it was getting stuffy in here." Alby tried to smile. "We're in a world of hurt."

"You got that right. Do you know where my dad is?"

"I don't. They left the bridge over an hour ago as far as I can tell."

Teo nodded. "I'll start on Deck One and work my way down. Keep your head up, Alby. We're only mostly dead, which means we're still alive and getting better with each moment. Wait a minute. The scout ship."

"It's in the cargo bay. Can't get it out because the doors have no power. It would take forever and a team of strong people to crank that thing open manually."

"It has an engine, not big enough to bring *Chrysalis* online but big enough to take some pressure off our remaining power plant. Tell my dad I'm looking for him and to meet me aft, either cargo bay or Engineering."

"Will do, and good luck." Alby wasn't sure the systems were compatible, but if anyone knew, it would be Teo. She had helped to upgrade the scout ship's engines.

She pulled herself down the corridor and dove into the shaft. She kicked off the other side to bounce to the ladder, following it down until she needed to use it to finish the climb.

Teo jumped the last few rungs to the bottom, then climbed out to get to the aft cargo bay, the one-time home to a Malibor weapons platform and new home to *Starstrider*.

The cargo bay had an auxiliary power feed. With alternating current, energy could go both ways as long as energy wasn't being fed in the direction of the scout.

Teo found that the ship was already plugged in to the bulkhead. She only needed to adjust the circuit. She moved into the corridor where the panel was located to find significant damage all around it. Multiple penetrations scarred the bulkheads and decks, but the circuitry was untouched. She shined her penlight down the cabling to see that the casing was intact.

"It can't be this easy," Teo told herself. She returned to

the ship and ran it through the startup sequence. The engine came up to ten percent and quickly rose to fifty percent. She tapped the controls to bleed excess energy through the cable. She left the ship running with the drives disengaged. By bleeding the energy, it could idle all day long without an issue.

She hovered her hand over the cable. It was already warm. She'd need someone to monitor it. Teo strolled the corridor looking for anyone, but this section of the ship appeared to be abandoned.

Teo found blood on the deck near a railgun penetration. Someone had been hit. A little farther, she found the lower part of a leg and a lot more blood. In the next space, she found a body covered with an emergency blanket. She didn't lift it to see who died, not that or the body next to it. Two people died in this corridor. No wonder no one was down there.

It had been a deathtrap.

Teo moved to the central shaft. "Is anyone up there?" she called.

"What do you need?" a familiar voice replied.

Benjy, the lander operator. During combat, he would have been in the center of the ship with the children.

"I need someone to watch a power cable and let me know if it gets too hot. Simple. Got any kids that could use a job?"

"I have a few. I'll send them right down."

In a few moments, the patter of small feet preceded the group down the ladder. The oldest wasn't very old and the youngest was young.

"How old are you?" Teo asked.

The tallest of the bunch answered, "Nine."

In a crisis, everyone had to carry the load.

"Follow me." She led them to the cargo bay. "Don't touch any of the controls. If you activate the drives, you destroy the ship and kill everyone. I would prefer not to be killed. So, put your hand over this cable but don't touch it. Feel that?"

"It's warm," the boy replied.

"If it gets hot, come and get me. I'll be in Engineering. Do you know where that is?"

He nodded.

"You guys can play or just relax and wait, but I need someone sitting by this cable at all times. You'll know if it gets hot because it'll hurt to put your hand too close. And then I'll need to power down the ship. This is helping us, so we need to keep the scout ship running, but we also can't destroy *Chrysalis*."

She was over-explaining. The children were losing interest.

"Just let me know if it gets hot."

She hurried out with no other choice than to trust the children, just until she could send Vantraub to provide oversight, or someone else. "Benjy?" she called up the shaft. "I need you down here."

"On my way."

It took him longer than Teo had patience for, but that was because he was ushering four more children, all younger than five.

"It's okay, Benjy. Cargo bay. Let me know if the cable gets hot. It's a job anyone can do, but I can't have the kids playing with the ship's controls."

"I understand." He herded the small group down the corridor and to the cargo bay.

Teo returned to Engineering.

"Four percent!" Vantraub cheered. "What did you do?"

"Scout ship plugged in to the main line."

"When it hits ten percent, systems are automatically going to come online," Vantraub warned.

"And that's what we can't have. We have between now and ten percent to change the reactivation sequence to manual, so we don't overload the feed. We have to isolate the circuit coming from the cargo bay so it only feeds power storage."

"Three percent." Vantraub pointed to the gauge.

"No! We're generating power." She looked at the board, but nothing registered.

"Two percent."

It was going down way too fast. Something was pulling juice. Teo took off running for the cargo bay. She covered half the engineering section with her first step. She pulled back to keep from slamming into the hatch. She landed with her hands in front of her to stop her breakneck forward speed. She eased out the hatch, leaving it open because the spinning motion would slowly close it.

She slid down the ladder with her feet braced outside the railing and her hands sliding along. Teo hit the deck and ran to the circuit panel.

It had fused where shrapnel had damaged two cables. She rushed into the cargo bay and to the ship, where she chased one of the children out of the captain's seat. She shut the system down. Took a moment to smile at the children filling the scout ship with Benjy watching them from outside.

"I need to put an insulator between the feed trunk and secondary line," she said casually. She dug through the scout ship's storage bin for bits and pieces necessary for underway repairs. A piece of hard rubber, non-conducting. With a small prybar, Teo went to work.

She was gone for two minutes. She chased a child from the captain's seat once more and restarted the engine. She brought it up to seventy-five percent since she had competent authority watching it.

"Not too hot, Benjy."

He waved and returned to a place on the deck where he could rest while watching the cable.

When Teo got back to Engineering, she found the energy gauge holding at two percent.

"We went to one and I thought we were going offline again," Vantraub said softly.

"Is this what we're going to do now? Fight to stay alive?"

"It's what we do every day," Teo replied. "We reset the clock of our death every time we take a breath. Then we do it again and again. We keep resetting the clock, Van. We're going to be okay if we can find the energy leak and fix it."

"Will we?"

"We have to keep the engine running to keep the lights on. And the air. Heat would be nice, too."

"It's dropped another five degrees," Vantraub noted.

"That's eight centigrade from the start. Our food is going to freeze pretty soon. We should probably eat before that happens," Teo replied, "and advise everyone else to do the same."

"I'll let Chef know," Vantraub said.

Teo watched her go. There wasn't much they could do without power. She could head into the ship but didn't feel up to it.

Bec held out two potassium iodide tabs. "Take these and choke them down."

She took them without argument.

"You'll feel better soon enough, once Van brings food and water."

Teo hung her chin to her chest and stared down. She was running out of energy to do anything. The highs and lows of imminent death were trying. "How do you do it, Bec, act like nothing is going on?"

"Everyone else is living in my world now. I always feel like there's a crisis. This is business as usual for me. It only looks like I'm not anxious because I'm better practiced at this. You are not, so you see me as a bastion of serenity."

Teo chuckled. "That's not what I'd say, but I'll give it the relativity that applies. Good one, Bec."

The hatch opened, and Brad walked through. "Good job on the power. I see we're up to three percent, but it's going to take nine hours?"

"Not anymore. We're hardwiring *Starstrider* into the grid."

"Is that safe?"

"We're not dead," Teo replied. "It'll be once we get safeties in place."

"Can you do that from here?" Brad looked toward the corridor.

"Always a dad." Teo shook her head. "No, we can't do it from here, but we're catching our breath while waiting for a little food and water. Power up before it freezes."

"You won't have the power online before it gets below freezing in here?"

"Probably not."

"Does anyone know what trajectory we're on? I would've thought we'd have crashed into the moon had we been going that way." Brad eased toward the corridor. "I'll get the info from *Starstrider*."

Teo pointed at Brad. "Don't use too much power. That's one thing that is at a premium right now. There's a difference between nice-to-know and need-to-know."

"Roger." Brad waved over his shoulder and left, calling on his way out, "The battle is joined!"

CHAPTER 29

When will we be out of the woods?

Brad found his ship filled with children. He chased the smallest out of the captain's seat, but then caught her when she tried to scurry away. He put her in his lap and activated the sensor systems. They didn't work inside the cargo bay. He shut them down.

He activated the radio. "*Cornucopia*, this is *Starstrider*, status please."

"*Starstrider*, *Cornucopia*. We've been trying to reach *Chrysalis*. It's been hours. What is going on?"

"*Starstrider* is on board *Chrysalis*. We've taken heavy damage and are on emergency power with barely enough for life support. If you're available, we could use a tactical assist."

"We'll be there in twenty minutes," the voice replied. "But there's one problem. The troopship is right behind us. They're slowing down with us. Do you have any weapons?"

"Negative, *Cornucopia*. We are lucky to be breathing. We are capable of nothing else."

"We will dock with you, *Chrysalis*, port-side roller airlock, but be prepared to repel boarders because they're coming in behind us."

"Roger. We'll take your assistance, and we'll pay your price," Brad replied. "Brad out."

He leaned back for a moment and then decided what he needed to do. He plopped the child down in the captain's seat and ran from the cargo bay straight to Engineering.

"Teo," he interrupted her mid-bite, "I need power to one missile tube for a manual launch."

Teo shook her head but capped her food bag and stuffed it into a thigh pocket.

"Bec, I'm going to need you for this, and you, too." She pointed at Vantraub. The three left Engineering.

"I'll be at the manual launch station, Deck Three."

Teo waved before she disappeared into the central shaft.

Brad headed up the ladder until there was no gravity and kept going until it pulled him the other way. He found it odd to stand on the ceiling of Deck Three, but that was what it came to.

He activated his magnetic boots and got into position. The station had no power whatsoever. He had to wait. He verified that the cables and couplings were intact before returning to find that there was still no power.

Brad could do nothing but wait. He had twenty minutes from when he contacted the cargo ship.

He clumped to the ladder and headed downward. He pulled himself out of the shaft when he reached the command deck. He knocked gently on Jaq's door. She didn't answer. He went in and found her asleep.

The second-last thing he wanted to do was wake her. The last thing he wanted was to die.

But Jaq didn't have to be the one. He left the captain's quarters and flew to the bridge, where he found Alby doodling around. "Come with me. We have a troopship to kill."

"With what?" Alby asked.

"From the Malibor we receive, to the Malibor we send. We're going to return one of their missiles."

"How?" Alby followed but was still surprised that they could do anything, not until they reached the magic ten percent.

"Teo is going to bypass everything to feed *Starstrider's* power to the launch tube."

"How do we know where it is?"

"*Cornucopia* is going to tell us. They'll be here any minute."

"We have help?"

"We have help," Brad confirmed. They reached Deck Three and walked down the ceiling until they arrived at the manual launch station.

The power had not yet come on.

The time suggested *Cornucopia* should have arrived. "You have it," Brad said. "I'll be right back."

Without the relays active, the portable comm units were nearly useless. Brad had tried his once and stuffed it back into his pocket when no one answered.

Brad had to descend seven decks, but after the first

couple, it was zero-gee. He flew down the corridor to the airlock, where he found the space beyond the window had turned dark. Brad opened the inner hatch and used the manual lever to crank the outer hatch open. A quick rush of air showed the pressure in *Cornucopia* was higher than what was in *Chrysalis*.

"Am I happy to see you," Brad told Godbolt and Nokes. "But I need targeting data on that troopship. We are trying to fire a missile."

Godbolt grinned and headed inside the cargo hauler. "Gangway!" she shouted on her way down the corridor with Brad close behind.

The tactical screen was active. The troopship was less than thirty minutes away. Brad repeated the coordinates three times to make sure he'd remember them.

"Gangway," Godbolt repeated. "We got us a troopship to destroy!"

Brad led the way to the manual station where Alby waited. He brightened immeasurably with Godbolt's arrival. The two hugged like more than old friends.

The power appeared on the panel. "Alby?"

Brad didn't know how the system worked. Alby dove in with great zeal and asked for rough coordinates. Brad stated them, and Godbolt confirmed that was what she had seen.

The missile tube powered up, and the outer hatch opened. The tube capacitors energized to send the missile out on an electromagnetic launch-rail. "Go forth and conquer!" Alby pressed the button the second it turned green.

The sound of the capacitors discharge signaled the missile's launch. The panel exploded beneath Alby's hands, spraying him with tiny shards. He stumbled, and his boots disconnected from the floor. He fell to the ceiling. Godbolt joined him.

A thousand cuts on his arms and face. "Take him to Medical." Brad took one arm and Godbolt took the other. They walked him toward the central shaft.

"Nokes, check on my missile. See where it went," Brad directed.

Nokes was off like a shot.

Going down the ladder was tough with the injuries to his hands, but Alby made it, leaving bloody handprints nearly the whole way.

"Take him to Medical. If we didn't kill that ship, I'm going to be real busy, real soon."

Brad bounded into the shaft and hurried down until he grabbed the ladder for the last three decks. He found himself alone in Engineering. He turned to run to the cargo bay, but Bec, Teo, and Vantraub staggered in, looking defeated.

"What happened?"

"We couldn't do it. We ended up shorting the whole system. I'm sorry, Dad."

"But it worked. The missile is on its way."

"It did?" Bec was the first to be skeptical.

"You said you shorted the system." Brad looked to his daughter for an answer.

"We have to run cabling and bypass everything. The system inside the bulkhead is destroyed. We can't open the cargo bay doors at present, so we might as well use *Starstrider* for power production. Only we can't until we run a direct line from there to here."

"I'll help you carry the spool of wire," Brad offered. "But let's wait until after we find out where my missile went. I don't want to work harder than I have to. I'll be right back."

He headed up the ladder and to the port-side airlock. The crew from *Butterfly* carried spare parts to a growing line of damage control personnel.

"That's how you do it. In the old days, we called this an unrep for underway replenishment. Coming through." He squeezed past those working and found his way to the bridge. "Please tell me good news."

"See for yourself, Captain." Nokes pointed at the screen.

A pink cloud was heading toward them. "Looks like we might get some debris impacts."

"No doubt. I wonder if their power plant is intact."

"I wouldn't risk it. Does this tub have any extra power plants around?"

"Now that you mention it, the one Bec had running on *Butterfly* is in the hold and looking for a new home."

Brad smiled. "It's hard not to love you guys. I seem to be surrounded by the best people. I need to check on my girlfriend, and don't you tell her I called her that or she'll be pretty mad."

"I hear you, Captain. I'll work with Teo. We'll get that plant installed right quick and in a hurry. As soon as we can help you stop spinning, that is. It'll be much easier to move that thing in zero-gee."

―――――

"Shouldn't we have heard from Crip by now?" Jaq groused.

Brad nodded. She was still in her quarters under Doc Teller's orders. The energy gauge on her monitor showed eighty-one percent and climbing.

"We're out of the woods, Jaq. We have time."

"We never have enough time," she scoffed. "Are you the only person left on my ship? Why does no one else visit me?"

"They think we're naked," Brad replied.

Jaq's mouth fell open. "They better not think that."

"I'm just a pawn in the game of life," Brad replied.

"What did you say?" Jaq nearly came out of her cubicle. Brad laughed. "I'm getting up."

"Doc Teller said later today. I guess this is late enough. And I said nothing to the crew besides your proclamation of enduring love while in your concussed delirium."

"I didn't. Did I?"

"No. I'll wait outside."

He left the room so she could dress. She bent over too quickly to pull her jumpsuit on, making her head swim. She stopped, grabbed the mid-rail, and forced herself to breathe slowly. She recovered enough to finish dressing. *Don't overdo it,* she warned herself.

Brad gestured for her to lead the way.

She returned to the bridge quietly, not as part of a triumphant procession. The command crew clapped softly and welcomed her back. It had only been two days.

"Message from the combat team?"

"Not yet. We have sent our message to *Starbound* for transmission to the combat team."

Jaq nodded. The board had an alarming number of red lights.

Alby held up a bandaged hand. "I have the enemy order of battle reduced to two cruisers and ten gunships. The Malibor fleet is almost finished."

"That's good news, Alby. Nothing against the old girl, but I'm not sure how much more *Chrysalis* can take."

Brad added, "Nothing against her at all. The finest ship and the greatest crew."

"Victory is ours," Jaq said softly. She found the louder the noise and the brighter the lights, the more her head ached. The lights on the bridge had been dimmed and the ambient sound kept to a low roar.

Jaq stopped to talk with Mary. Her leg was bandaged, but they were at zero-gee because they were on a ballistic trajectory away from Farslor, not actively engaging in anything other than repairs. She didn't need to be there, but she insisted.

"I'm fine. It was a flesh wound, as Doc Teller labeled it."

"How many stitches for a flesh wound?" Jaq asked.

"Fifteen. My lucky number."

"Fifteen is your lucky number?"

"It is now." Mary winked. Jaq gripped her shoulder for a moment before moving on.

Donal was off helping the damage control teams rebuild one of the primary junction boxes. Slade was working on a sensor receiver. Dolly was the only one present from that section on the bridge. Jaq eased over to her.

"Good work on the targeting interface. Without it, we wouldn't be here."

"It was important to get right."

"If we keep getting things right, then one day soon, we'll be standing on Septimus, celebrating life."

"I look forward to it. Donal talks of blue skies and green lands. I want to experience it myself."

"You will," Jaq promised.

"Message coming in," Amie reported.

Jaq pulled herself across the bridge and waited.

"Crip here. We've found the Borwyn who are actively fighting the Malibor. We are going to join them and open the gates of Septiman's wrath."

"That's it?" Jaq asked.

"There is no more. It was a short transmission. Your message regarding the delay in our return has been sent."

"Thanks." Jaq frowned deeply. It was a cryptic message but one that carried promise. "Let the Borwyn rise against the enemy."

"It's what we'll do until the Malibor stop fighting or we can rise no more," Brad said.

To be continued in Starship Lost Book #4 **Confrontation**

The Borwyn's fate could not be contained in a single volume. Please leave a review on this book, because all those stars look great and help others decide if they'll enjoy this book as much as you have. I appreciate the feedback and support. Reviews buoy my spirits and stoke the fires of creativity.

Don't stop now! Keep turning the pages as I talk about my thoughts on this book and the overall project called *Starship Lost*.

You can always join my newsletter at https://craigmartelle.com or follow me on Amazon https://www.amazon.com/Craig-Martelle/e/B01AQVF3ZY/ so you are informed when the next book comes out. You won't be disappointed.

AUTHOR NOTES - CRAIG MARTELLE

Written June 2023

Bring the Pain! Sorry, that's a different series. I wanted *Starship Lost* to be grittier and more focused on the military aspects of one ship fighting many. A generational crew. It's coming together quite nicely. When you bought this volume, you found that the first five books are ready, if not already up for pre-order.

We want to deliver this entire series quickly, so I started writing the first book a long time ago. As you read this, it's been over a year. We call that stockpiling to deliver the volumes in rapid succession to feed a hungry but time-challenged readership. It was the best we could do for you guys since there is no one more important in this business than you. If you aren't reading, there's no value in writing.

Names! I made a general call to the most excellent Kurtherian Gambit readers, who rose to the occasion. First up is Cryl Talan, suggested by Monika Holland Krisinski. We made him a Malibor saboteur.

Second up is Amie Jacobs, offered by Nancy Bolland McClellan. I was well into the third book before it was time to give the communications officer a name. We made her an original and put her on the radio.

Next is Barbara Lambock, who gave me Zurig, Finley, and Tomans. I needed to fill out the combat team for their time on Septimus—not just numbers but each individual. I have to do them justice since they are representing all Borwyn.

Lissa Sheppard gave me Paulus, and I changed the last name to Hunter.

This is what I do for a living, although it is my third retirement. I'm not very good at doing nothing. People say I can't relax. I cannot, not in the traditional sense of the word, but I can within my own definition.

I'd like to say that this book came without baggage, but alas, it was not to be. I had an umbilical hernia repaired while writing this volume. More pain. More scars. I'm proud to say that I took no pain medication whatsoever after the surgery. Not the heavy hitter stuff they gave me or even an ibuprofen. Nothing at all. You can take the man out of the Marines, but you'll never take the Marine out of the man. I can deal with pain. It's the not-breathing part that caused me a lot of grief.

As a reminder, https://www.omnicalculator.com/physics/acceleration —need to keep that acceleration calculator close at hand.

Peace, fellow humans.

If you liked this story, you might like some of my other books. You can join my mailing list by dropping by my website at craigmartelle.com, or if you have any comments, shoot me a note at craig@craigmartelle.com. I am always happy to hear from people who've read my work. I try to answer every email I receive.

If you liked the story, please write a short review for me on Amazon. I greatly appreciate any kind words; even one or two sentences go a long way. The number of reviews an ebook receives greatly improves how well it does on Amazon.

Amazon—www.amazon.com/author/craigmartelle
Facebook—www.facebook.com/authorcraigmartelle
BookBub—https://www.bookbub.com/authors/craig-martelle

My web page—https://craigmartelle.com

Thank you for joining me on this incredible journey.

OTHER SERIES BY CRAIG MARTELLE
#—AVAILABLE IN AUDIO, TOO

Terry Henry Walton Chronicles (#) (co-written with Michael Anderle)—a post-apocalyptic paranormal adventure

Gateway to the Universe (#) (co-written with Justin Sloan & Michael Anderle)—this book transitions the characters from the Terry Henry Walton Chronicles to the Bad Company

The Bad Company (#) (co-written with Michael Anderle)—a military science fiction space opera

Judge, Jury, & Executioner (#)—a space opera adventure legal thriller

Shadow Vanguard—a Tom Dublin space adventure series

Superdreadnought (#)—an AI military space opera

Metal Legion (#)—a military space opera

The Free Trader (#)—a young adult science fiction action-adventure

Cygnus Space Opera (#)—a young adult space opera (set in the Free Trader universe)

Darklanding (#) (co-written with Scott Moon)—a space Western

Mystically Engineered (co-written with Valerie Emerson)—mystics, dragons, & spaceships

Metamorphosis Alpha—stories from the world's first science fiction RPG

The Expanding Universe—science fiction anthologies

Zenophobia (#) (co-written with Brad Torgersen)—a space archaeological adventure

Battleship Leviathan (#)– a military sci-fi spectacle published by Aethon Books

Glory (co-written with Ira Heinichen)—hard-hitting military sci-fi

Black Heart of the Dragon God (co-written with Jean Rabe)—a sword & sorcery novel

Starship Lost – a hard-science, military sci-fi epic published by Aethon Books

End Times Alaska (#)—a post-apocalyptic survivalist adventure published by Permuted Press

Nightwalker (a Frank Roderus series)—A post-apocalyptic Western adventure

End Days (#) (co-written with E.E. Isherwood)—a post-apocalyptic adventure

Successful Indie Author (#)—a nonfiction series to help self-published authors

Monster Case Files (co-written with Kathryn Hearst)—A Warner twins mystery adventure

Rick Banik (#)—Spy & terrorism action-adventure

Ian Bragg Thrillers (#)—a hitman with a conscience

<u>Published exclusively by Craig Martelle, Inc</u>

The Dragon's Call by Angelique Anderson & Craig A. Price, Jr.—an epic fantasy quest

A Couples Travels—a nonfiction travel series

Love-Haight Case Files by Jean Rabe & Donald J. Bingle—the dead/undead have rights, too, a supernatural legal thriller

Mischief Maker by Bruce Nesmith—the creator of Elder Scrolls V: Skyrim brings you Loki in the modern day, staying true to Norse mythology (not a superhero version)

Mark of the Assassins by Landri Johnson—a coming-of-age fantasy.

For a complete list of Craig's books, stop by his website—https://craigmartelle.com

THANK YOU FOR READING PRIMACY

We hope you enjoyed it as much as we enjoyed bringing it to you. We just wanted to take a moment to encourage you to review the book. Follow this link: **Primacy** to be directed to the book's Amazon product page to leave your review.

Every review helps further the author's reach and, ultimately, helps them continue writing fantastic books for us all to enjoy.

You can also join our non-spam mailing list by visiting www.subscribepage.com/AethonReadersGroup and never miss out on future releases. You'll also receive three full books completely Free as our thanks to you.

Facebook | Instagram | Twitter | Website

Want to discuss our books with other readers and even the authors? Join our Discord server today and be a part of the Aethon community.

ALSO IN THE SERIES

Starship Lost
The Return
Primacy
Confrontation
Fallacy
Engagement

Looking for more great Science Fiction?

An elite unit. A dark secret. Can they stop interstellar war before it starts? Hex Thorn, a hard-bitten veteran of the elite Special Operations Unit of the Dominion Empire, was content with retirement. He'd seen his share of firefights and bloodshed in a bitter war that ripped the galaxy apart. But when an enigmatic stranger makes him an offer he can't refuse–a chance to own a legendary Lancer ship–Hex is thrust back into the fray. His mission? Hunt down the elusive Dr. Attica Tharand, a person whose secrets could shatter the galaxy's fragile balance of power. Hex must reassemble his old Special Ops team, a ragtag crew of soldiers as skilled as they are unpredictable. But they soon find out they aren't the only ones after the doctor. With galactic tension on the razor's edge, Hex will need all his grit, guile, and gunfire to uncover the truth about his target and those who wish him caught. **SHADOW WATCH is the start of a pulse-pounding interstellar adventure from the minds of Brandon Ellis and Max Wolfe. Buckle up for this high-stakes military sci-fi adventure where the line between friend and foe is as blurred as the starlines in hyperspace.** *Alliances will be tested, friendships will be forged, and through the darkest of trials, heroes will be born!*

Get Kethurg War Now!

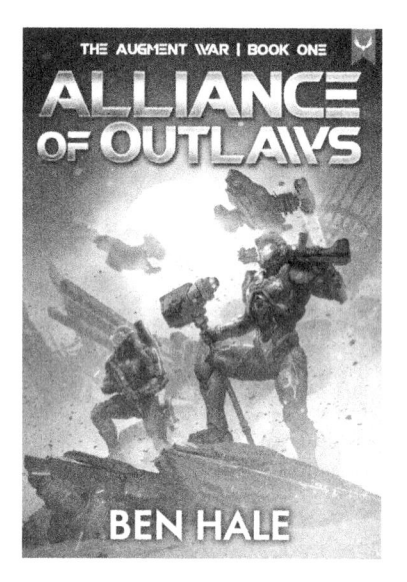

A lost weapon. A forgotten enemy. A new alliance will rise. An old enemy has returned. Militant zealots backed by a new leader who harbors a thirst for revenge. To face them Reklin, a retired soldier, must enter the Grand Hunt, a brutal contest where people are prey, and rival teams are culled from the best soldiers in the galaxy. On such a mission, not everyone is coming home. Ero Bright'Lor, an outcast krey noble, has a mad plan to form an alliance from the outlaw clans. If he can overcome centuries of enmity, their combined might would threaten the entire fleet of the Krey Empire. But the cause needs a leader. Fortunately for him, a distant scavenger vessel has discovered the wreck of a drifting starship. Beneath the twisted hull of the derelict, Siena has waited twelve years for rescue. As a youth she was augmented into a living weapon, and her power has only grown in captivity…

Get Alliance of Outlaws Now!

A ragtag crew stumbles upon the secret to preventing galactic war. When newly-unemployed dock worker Salome Jones inherits a near-derelict spaceship from an uncle she never heard of, she thinks she finally has the key to freedom. Joining forces with Skyler Rysen, a charming rogue with an urgent (if not exactly on the up-and-up) cargo, Salome and the crew of Luminous Void set out on their first mission. Unfortunately, some things are too good to be true. Unbeknownst to Salome and company, the ship has a bounty on it and a secret hidden in its databanks that could start a galactic war, and somebody wants that secret badly enough to capture the ship and kill all her crew. Salome has no intention of letting her faceless enemies get their hands on the secret, but what can one small ship and her ragtag crew do against all the forces arrayed against them? The answer is, whatever they have to!

Get Luminous Void now!

For all our Sci-Fi books, visit our website.

OTHER SERIES BY CRAIG MARTELLE

 # - available in audio, too

Battleship Leviathan (#)– a military sci-fi spectacle published by Aethon Books

Terry Henry Walton Chronicles (#) (co-written with Michael Anderle)—a post-apocalyptic paranormal adventure

Gateway to the Universe (#) (co-written with Justin Sloan & Michael Anderle)—this book transitions the characters from the Terry Henry Walton Chronicles to The Bad Company

The Bad Company (#) (co-written with Michael Anderle)—a military science fiction space opera

Judge, Jury, & Executioner (#)—a space opera adventure legal thriller

Shadow Vanguard—a Tom Dublin space adventure series

Superdreadnought (#)—an AI military space opera

Metal Legion (#)—a military space opera

The Free Trader (#)—a young adult science fiction action-adventure

Cygnus Space Opera (#)—a young adult space opera (set in the Free Trader universe)

Darklanding (#) (co-written with Scott Moon)—a space western

Mystically Engineered (co-written with Valerie Emerson)—mystics, dragons, & spaceships

Metamorphosis Alpha—stories from the world's first science fiction RPG
The Expanding Universe—science fiction anthologies

Krimson Empire (co-written with Julia Huni)—a galactic race for justice

Zenophobia (#) (co-written with Brad Torgersen)—a space archaeological adventure

Glory (co-written with Ira Heinichen)—hard-hitting military sci-fi

Black Heart of the Dragon God (co-written with Jean Rabe)—a sword & sorcery novel

End Times Alaska (#)—a post-apocalyptic survivalist adventure published by Permuted Press

Nightwalker (a Frank Roderus series)—A post-apocalyptic western adventure

End Days (#) (co-written with E.E. Isherwood)—a post-apocalyptic adventure

Successful Indie Author (#)—a non-fiction series to help self-published authors

Monster Case Files (co-written with Kathryn Hearst)—A Warner twins mystery adventure

Rick Banik (#)—Spy & terrorism action-adventure

Ian Bragg Thrillers (#)—a hitman with a conscience

Not Enough (co-written with Eden Wolfe)—A coming-of-age contemporary fantasy

<u>Published exclusively by Craig Martelle, Inc</u>
The Dragon's Call by Angelique Anderson & Craig A. Price, Jr.—an epic fantasy quest

A Couples Travels—a non-fiction travel series

Love-Haight Case Files by Jean Rabe & Donald J. Bingle—the dead/undead have rights, too, a supernatural legal thriller

Mischief Maker by Bruce Nesmith—the creator of Elder Scrolls V: Skyrim brings you Loki in the modern day, staying true to Norse Mythology (not a superhero version)

Mark of the Assassins by Landri Johnson—a coming-of-age fantasy.
For a complete list of Craig's books, stop by his website—
https://craigmartelle.com

Printed in Great Britain
by Amazon